The Cousins. Secrets. Everybody Has Them.

Copyright 2015 © Caron Allan

The author asserts the moral right to be identified as the owner of this work.

No part of this book may be reproduced or transmitted in any form or by any means, including but not limited to: graphic, electronic, or mechanical, including photocopying, recording, taping, or by any informational storage retrieval system without advanced prior permission in writing from the publisher.

No part of this book, including the cover, has been generated using AI.
No part of this publication is to be used to train AI technologies.

This is a work of fiction, and is not based on a true story or on real people.

ISBN: 9798277593073

The Cousins

SECRETS.
EVERYBODY HAS THEM.

Caron Allan

Dedication

To all my cousins. Love you, guys!

Contents

Chapter One 4
Chapter Two 18
Chapter Three 37
Chapter Four 47
Chapter Five 57
Chapter Six 74
Chapter Seven 89
Chapter Eight 106
Chapter Nine 117
Chapter Ten 138
Chapter Eleven 159
Chapter Twelve 181
Chapter Thirteen 195
Chapter Fourteen 212
Chapter Fifteen 225
Chapter Sixteen 240
Chapter Seventeen 257
Epilogue 265
About the author 272
Also by Caron Allan: 273

The Cousins

Chapter One

The hospital receptionist was efficient yet still conveyed sympathy. In the waiting area there was a potted palm and a table of smart magazines. If it wasn't for the overwhelming scent of antiseptic, the posters about infection control, and the squeaky floors, Caitlin could have been in any reception area of any business corporation. As soon as Caitlin said why she was there, the receptionist summoned an orderly to show her the way to the intensive care ward.

It was a long walk down a hectic, bewildering network of white corridors, sidestepping trolleys, wheelchairs and clusters of people with clipboards or sporting stethoscopes around their necks. Everywhere phones rang and people dashed in and out of lifts and wards or there was the flip-flap of doors opening and closing. They seemed to walk for miles. Caitlin wondered how she would find her way back. Would the orderly wait for her?

The orderly smiled a sad, grave smile and left her standing in the doorway beside the nurses' station, waiting for the duty nurse to look up from her computer screen. When she did, she immediately got up and came to the counter.

'Yes, love?'

Caitlin gave her name again.

'He's just along here, in Bay 7. Had a nasty fall at home, we believe; he was brought in a few hours ago. He's been asking for you, though I think he's asleep at the moment. He's as stable as you could hope for, but as you know, he's very weak, things are beginning to shut down,' the nurse said. Her rueful quirk of the lips told Caitlin everything she needed to know. Not long now, the end was near.

The nurse came out from behind her counter to lead Caitlin further along the corridor to the cramped side ward. She headed for the final bed at the end, and she pulled back the curtains just enough to allow Caitlin to slip through. 'I'll leave you to it. Any questions, come and find me.'

Caitlin nodded, biting her lip. She took the seat by the bed, and reached out to take the thin, cold hand that lay on top of the covers, taking care not to nudge the canula. Like another visitor looming over his frail body, the machine on the other side of the bed made this corner of the tiny ward seem crowded.

Her grandfather was sleeping. The tiny V of his taut, pale skin showed at the neck of the pyjama jacket. He seemed to have shrunk, even since yesterday. His face was greyish, hollowed, not at all like the man she had known all her life, and it seemed as if part of him was already somewhere else: he was a half-empty house waiting for a new tenant, although this body had finished playing host.

If she had been shown a photo of him as he looked

now, she wasn't sure she would have recognised him, and that made her feel even more guilty.

His hair, sparse and silvery grey, seemed glued to his forehead and cheek. It had grown long, but he hadn't been taking care of himself for a while. She hadn't visited him as often as she should have. His wrinkles seemed more deeply etched, the mobility gone from his cheeks and mouth. His hands were blue-veined, with liver spots all over the backs of them, and the fingernails were over-long and ragged, yellowed from long years of smoking, the knuckles knobbly and stiff.

She didn't know what to do with her own hands. Surely the next of kin of the dying were compelled by love to perform some last caring service, something to reassure and comfort, but she had no love for him, just a desire to do her duty. That didn't mean she wanted him to suffer. Quite the opposite. She wanted his suffering to end and for him to move on to that better place people always talked about. Then she could go home and forget him forever.

Her phone pinged in her pocket, but she'd better not pull it out just yet. Hopefully it wasn't urgent. Well, not as urgent as this, anyway.

She loosened her coat—it was too warm in the hospital—and pushed it back into the chair behind her. She set her bag down on the floor beside the chair. She leaned back and fixed her mind on the long night ahead. She would be here. Whatever time he awoke, if he woke, he would find her there, ready to hold his hand and act her part. And if he didn't wake... she'd still be here.

Half an hour later, the nurse popped in again, and in hushed tones gave Caitlin the run-down on the tests and observations that had been carried out since his admittance. There wasn't anything they could do, that much was clear. Apart from making him as comfortable as possible.

'Now you're here,' the nurse said, 'he may well want to just say goodbye to you and let go. Sometimes they don't wake, they just slip away quietly, other times it's as if they've been holding on until you got here, just for one last goodbye. They often do that. We did ask him if there was anyone else we ought to contact, but he said there was only his wife. So he must have been a bit confused as the records show she passed away some years ago. But you were down as his next of kin. Are your parents still around? Is it your father or your mother who... As I said, he's very weak. I don't think it'll be much longer.'

Caitlin nodded, lips pressed together, struggling to retain her composure. Then the moment passed, and she said, 'No, my mother's dead too. There's only me.'

There was a pause and the nurse nodded sympathetically. 'Okay, well I'll leave you in peace. If you need anything at all, just ring the bell.' She showed Caitlin where it was and then hesitated between the two flaps of the curtains. 'If you're worried, or if you feel upset, or if you just want someone to be with you, we can do that. Or if you want to speak to the chaplain, don't be afraid to ask, he's only down the corridor and he's ever so nice, he'll be glad to help. He popped in earlier and sat with your grandfather for a while.'

Caitlin smiled and nodded to each suggestion, murmuring at the end of the list, 'That's very kind, but I think I'll be fine.' The nurse's final offer, a cup of tea, Caitlin accepted gratefully and with more than a little surprise.

Five minutes later, a young student nurse pulled

the curtain back and tiptoed in with the tea in a dainty teacup, a couple of biscuits resting side by side in the saucer.

'There you are, my lovely. Is there anything else I can do for you?' she whispered.

Caitlin smiled and shook her head. 'No thanks, I'm fine. He's still asleep.'

The student nurse nodded, smiling, and turned to leave. 'I'll be back in forty minutes to do Mr Mitcheson's next set of observations. But if you need anything, or you're worried or upset, you can...'

'I know,' Caitlin said hastily, keen to stop her from repeating the entire list again. 'I can ring the bell. Thank you, you're very kind.'

'Okay then, I'll leave you to it.' She disappeared through the curtains, her shoes squeaking with every step as she went back to the nurses' station.

Relieved to be alone again, Caitlin turned back to look at her grandfather.

There was nothing to do except just wait. His hair remained smoothed back from his face. His covers were still wrinkle-free and straight. The student nurse had tucked his hands under the sheets, folded on his chest, and now they made a small mound beneath the covers. His eyes were still closed, and the lines on the screen of the monitor still meandered gently back and forth to indicate small breaths, small beats, a small life dwindling inexorably, but without hurry, to its unremarkable end.

Caitlin sat back in the chair and sipped her tea, nibbled her biscuits and felt another odd twinge of guilt. It felt wrong to be drinking her hot, strong tea and eating the jammy dodger and the shortbread finger when her grandfather was on the point of death a matter of three feet away. If it happens now, she thought, they will rush in to help him and see me sitting here like this and they will think how callous I am, sipping my tea whilst Gramps is right there dying. I'm like the Emperor Nero, fiddling while Rome burned.

So she drank her tea quickly, ate her biscuits, wiping her fingers on her jeans so that there was no trace of sugar, and this distraction from her duty was set aside.

She leaned forward again, watching him carefully for any signs of awareness. Of course, he may not wake at all, as the nurse had told her, he may just slip away. That would be best. But, Heaven forbid, he may be like this for days, even weeks. There was no way to be certain. And just because they don't appear to be awake, doesn't mean they're not aware of you, sometimes they can even understand what you say to them. She had read that somewhere quite recently.

She stayed leaning forward in spite of the aching in her back; she wanted to be in his field of vision the second he should open his eyes, wanted to be the first thing he'd see, didn't want him to become anxious or upset if he was disoriented. He had to know she was there.

The nurse and the student nurse came to take the next batch of observations, and Caitlin stepped back to give them room, standing between the curtains, where she could see them but not him. It was a relief to be on her feet for a short while. The student was doing all the measuring and recording, and the nurse was nodding her approval at a lesson well-learned, then asking the odd question designed to stimulate the student's memory of her classroom practices.

'No change, I'm afraid,' the nurse said as they prepared to depart a few minutes later. She patted Caitlin's arm and with a wave of the hand, indicated the student should remove the empty teacup and saucer. They left, and Caitlin went back to sit beside her grandfather's bed and wait.

She took a moment to check her phone, secure in the knowledge that no one would be coming in for a little while at least.

Two messages. Both from her besties.

Jen said, *Are you at the hospital now? What's happening?*

Caitlin quickly typed, *Yes, got here about an hour ago. He's not awake. I'm just sitting with him.*

Almost immediately she got a message back, which was just a heart emoji and *OK*.

The other message was from Sonia, and just read, *Jen said your grandad is in hospital. Is he okay?*

To Sonia she typed, *No, sadly think this could be the end. I'm sitting with him now. Everyone is being so kind.*

Again almost as soon as she'd pressed send, she got through: *OMG I'm so sorry. Thinking of you xx*

She put her phone away again.

There were so many sounds encroaching from the world beyond this curtained area. The neverending ringing of the phones on the desks, how on earth did the staff stand it? Now and again a patient would cry out or call for help. And then there were the hush-voiced conversations between members of staff. The squeaking of shoes on the polished floors that you could hear coming closer and closer, or veering off in another direction. It was a wonder anyone could sleep with all that noise.

Finally, when her watch showed ten o'clock, the ward lights dimmed, leaving just a few spots of light here and there. Caitlin sighed and stretched her arms above her head to unknot her spine and her shoulder muscles. She got up, stretched and yawned, took a couple of steps in each direction to loosen up her stiff knees and back muscles. Her stomach rumbled, she'd missed her dinner, leaving the library late then coming directly to the hospital when she saw the message.

It was going to be a long night. The dawn may as well be a year away. She sat back in the seat and stared up at the ceiling, at uniform grey tiles with the occasional brownish rust patch on a corner. The air-con had leaked a few times over the years by the look of it.

Over the next five hours his vital signs wavered and had Caitlin on the edge of her seat. A couple of times his breath seemed to hitch in his chest, and he gasped for breath before regaining an even rhythm. But once, it seemed that the fight for breath went on a few beats too long, and Caitlin, leaning forward, gazed at the restless figure in the bed. Was this it? She pressed the bell and heard a ding away down the corridor.

The nurse who came took one look then hurried away to the nurses' station to call for the duty doctor. But then Caitlin's grandfather seemed to settle again, so the call was cancelled. Caitlin tried to relax back on her chair, but there was a change in the room. Something felt different, something was imminent, and she didn't want to miss it.

As she looked at his face—looking a little greyer, a little more masked than it had been for the last five hours and forty minutes since her arrival—it occurred to Caitlin that she should turn off her phone. This was completely the wrong time to get a notification that someone had sent her the latest cat video, causing the phone to beep just as her grandfather was drawing his last breath. She could put it on silent, but that didn't feel quite solemn enough. She fished it out of her pocket again to turn it off completely. The girls would understand.

As she depressed the tiny button on the side to turn off the phone, she glanced up to find his eyes open and watching her. Shocked, and biting back an oath, she shoved her phone back into her pocket and scooched forward to take his hand.

'Gramps. It's me,' she said softly. She had been about to add her name, but he spoke.

'Isobel? Your hair looks l-lovely in the fire—firelight, my darling.'

His words, halting, hushed, made her sad, but she forced a smile, not about to correct him. Her grandmother had been dead for sixteen years.

He gripped her hand in a painful clasp of his cold bony fingers, and drew her closer to him, making a huge effort to say, 'You didn't—say—any—anything about the—the boy?'

Caitlin's brow furrowed. He must be wandering in his mind.

'Wh–what? The... the boy? Sorry, Gramps, but I don't...' She couldn't make sense of his words.

'Ah, I see we're awake again, Mr Mitcheson,' said a nurse from behind Caitlin's right shoulder, moving silently for the first time in almost six hours. She came around the bed and took a look at her charge. Caitlin wondered if she ought to move again, half getting to her feet, but the nurse patted her on the shoulder as if to tell her to stay put. She left with another of her sad smiles at Caitlin which seemed to speak volumes.

Caitlin was once more alone with her grandfather as he slept again. She was still puzzling over what he had said and made a mental note to ask him about it when he next woke. If he woke. He may have been muddled about who she was, but he hadn't seemed to be actually rambling, it had been a coherent sentence. Even if it had taken a lot of effort to speak it. She sat back in the chair and waited.

Just twenty minutes later he stirred again, attempting to move his stiff ankles into a more comfortable position. He turned his head and saw her sitting there, still alert for his barest movement. He smiled and moved his hand slightly in hers. His voice seemed almost its normal strength as he said perfectly clearly:

'You don't need to sit up all night, it's only a stomach-ache, Isobel. Get your rest, dear. The children will need you in the morning.'

Whilst she was still searching her mind for some small lie to tell him to set his mind at rest, she saw he had gone back to sleep again. She'd been on the point of telling him that her mother had come to take care of the children, but then she realised she didn't know if Isobel's mother had still been alive when their children—her mother and her aunt, who had lived in Canada for the last thirty years—had been small. She knew so little about her mother's family. He was her last contact with that side of her own past, and he was about to leave her forever. She didn't know why the tears began to flow just then, but she found a tissue in her pocket and wiped them away.

He spoke again, 'Don't cry, pet. I know you didn't tell anyone, just like you promised. No one knows. No need to fret, it'll be all right. You'll see. Told you I knew what I was doing. All done and dusted. Nothing more to worry about.'

Caitlin looked at Gramps but he was already drifting off again, his eyelids fluttering closed.

'Gramps?' she said softly, squeezing his hand with the lightest pressure, afraid of hurting him. The touch woke him, he turned towards her. Another beatific smile. He had his good teeth in, she noticed and was a bit surprised the nurses hadn't removed them in case of choking.

'I didn't see you there, my darling,' he said, but slowly. It took him a while to get the words out. Caitlin felt as though her brain was clutching at each word as it came out of his mouth and holding it to her breast, as if afraid it would escape. 'You get more beautiful every day. You're a stunner, you are, and I'm the luckiest man in the world.' It was an effort and it cost him a good deal. Caitlin noticed he was breathing harder, faster. The monitor noticed it too.

'Oh Gramps,' she whispered. 'You mustn't tire yourself,' she added, thinking that was what people always said, wasn't it? It was appropriate. 'You need to rest.' She put her tissue back in her pocket.

He managed a tiny chortle. 'Plenty of time for that when I'm dead,' he said.

Caitlin bit her lip. What a thing to say. She almost laughed.

He reached out his hand. She leaned forward and he stroked her cheek with his dry chilly fingers. And he touched her hair.

'Beautiful,' he said. His eyelids fluttered closed again, and Caitlin felt a surge of panic, but he opened his eyes again immediately and said in a pondering voice, 'Remember when we were young?'

'Yes, I do.'

He smiled again, patted her hand again, seeming stronger. 'There was a photo, all of us, that spring. It's still here somewhere.' He raised a trembling arm to point towards the corner. Caitlin followed the motion with her eyes, but in her mind she pictured the tall-boy in the corner of his bedroom. She knew that was what he was seeing, that he was thinking of.

His arm fell back to his chest, and for a few minutes he dozed before having another gasping fit.

The monitor showed some fluctuation, noticed by the nursing staff whilst popping in during their routine tours of the ward.

A nurse peeked through the curtains.

'Everything okay?' she whispered.

Caitlin nodded. 'He seems a little better,' she said. 'He's been talking. Quite lucidly, except that he thinks I'm my grandmother. But yes, he's definitely a bit better.'

The nurse nodded, biting her lip, and said nothing. She bustled away to see someone else.

A few minutes later, as Caitlin sat there, Gramps breathed in a great gasp of air. It seemed to leak slowly out at the corner of his mouth. Caitlin held her breath, watching, waiting. Then finally she realised it had happened, that thing she had been waiting for. Dreading. Almost without her noticing. He had not breathed in again. As the seconds stretched to minutes, she realised he wouldn't breathe again.

She sat a bit longer, uncertain what to do. It had been so ordinary she found she wasn't upset, after all, only vaguely surprised, and not quite sure if she was right about it, or if somehow she was imagining that he wasn't breathing. She was still holding his hand. It still felt warm. She patted it sadly, then stood to tuck it back under the covers and to straighten the sheet. She bent to kiss his cheek.

'Goodbye Gramps.'

It felt odd, like a betrayal, to just walk away. She went to find the sister, still in a bit of a daze. As she approached the nurses' station, it must have been there in her face, for the nurse she'd seen a little earlier took one look at her and coming round the counter, said, 'Tsk, he's gone, has he, poor love?'

Caitlin nodded, unable to speak. Putting an arm about her shoulders, the nurse guided her to a seat.

'I'm so sorry, love. Now, just you wait here for a minute while I call the doctor.'

She bustled away. After a moment, Caitlin seemed to surface and looked around her with interest. Papers, folders, bits and pieces of medical stuff, the computer screen flashing the hospital's blue logo in the semi-darkness. A photo of a bunch of people, one of them the nurse, clearly in a restaurant, all wearing Christmas party hats and raising glasses in a toast.

The nurse reappeared and sat down next to Caitlin.

'Now then, sweetheart,' she said, 'how are you doing?'

'I'm fine. Fine,' Caitlin said. 'He is really gone, isn't he?'

'Yes, my love, he is. I'm so sorry. The doctor's with him now and will sign the paperwork for you which you'll get in due course, I'll just need to check we've got your address. And is there anyone we can call to be with you?'

Caitlin shook her head. 'No. But there's no need, really, I'm...' She shrugged. What on earth was there to say?

'Okay, well if you're sure. Now, would you like to sit with your grandfather a bit longer? You can if you want to?'

'No, that's all right, thank you. I'd like to go home now, if that's okay. I've said my goodbyes.'

'Of course it is, lovey,' the nurse said. 'Now here's a wee brochure to help you with what needs to be done. And here's my card, in case there's anything you need to ask me later, sometimes you don't think of things right away. And here's the details for the registrar, it tells you when he's here, you'll need to pop back, I'm afraid. I'm very sorry for your loss, Mr Mitcheson was such a lovely gentleman. Doctor will be along shortly for a quick word, and then you'll be

able to get off home.'
Caitlin rose. 'Thank you for all your hard work and care. I really appreciate it. Thank you.'
Then someone rang the bell somewhere down the ward and the nurse excused herself. Almost the moment she had gone, the doctor was there, and it was some time before Caitlin could get away, a bulging envelope of papers in her hand.
It was such a relief to get outside and gulp in the fresh air. It was still dark, which she found somehow surprising, but it was cool and damp. The change in temperature revived her.
The lamps glared against the dark sky, hurting her eyes. She reached her car and got in. Moving automatically, all thought suspended. She turned the key in the ignition then paused for a moment to think about it. She had to rummage in her bag for a fresh tissue as the tears came.
He was dead.
Her last relation in the world. The last link with her own past and her only sense of who she was. Gramps. Gone.
Then another part of her, normally pushed so far back in her mind, broke free for just a moment and whispered in her head, 'Thank God the bastard's dead!'

*

Chapter Two

There was so much to do, more people to notify than Caitlin had imagined. For a man with a small circle of friends, and an even smaller one of relations, Gramps' passing had left her with plenty to do. She'd made an appointment to pop back to the hospital to register her grandfather's death the next day, before going to the funeral home to discuss arrangements.

The nurse offered her Gramps' few belongings. Caitlin didn't want back the pyjamas he had been wearing when he was admitted to hospital, or his slippers, bathrobe or toiletries, but there was his watch and his signet ring, and she was glad to have those back. Maybe she'd get something for them online.

At the funeral home, she promised to bring some clothes in for him to be buried in. A suit, a shirt and tie. Some smartly polished shoes. Did the deceased need underwear or socks? She just didn't know. It seemed irrelevant but the undertaker's assistant who talked Caitlin through the process said it was entirely her decision.

But she couldn't bear the thought of going back to Gramps' house just now, so it was easier to go and buy new clothes for him to be buried in. She promised herself that once the funeral was over, she would make herself go to the house. Regardless of how she felt, she would have to do that anyway, to clear the house and prepare it for sale. After she had spoken to the solicitor, of course.

She got the girls round to her place for movies and Prosecco. It helped a little. Jen had been through the same thing with her grandparents a couple of years earlier, and she had a ton of advice and useful suggestions.

It was a bright clear autumn day when Gramps was laid to rest beside his wife almost two weeks after he had passed away. Most people were cremated these days, but Gramps hadn't wanted that. He wanted to be with his wife once more. Caitlin felt it was important to honour his request, even if she felt sorry for her dead grandmother for having that man beside her once again. It seemed harsh that the dead couldn't be free.

She invited everyone who attended the funeral—just fourteen others—to a buffet lunch at a nearby hotel. There were several mourners Caitlin didn't recognise, and once the service was over, she went across to speak to them. In the end most of Gramps' friends, very elderly themselves, had made their excuses, said how sorry they were, and departed.

Jen and Sonia worked wonders there, getting Terry in conversation about his darts team at the pub on the corner of the street, and Bill to talk about his vintage vinyl record collection, and leaving Caitlin free to circulate.

In addition to these friends of Gramps' and her friends Jen and Sonia, Caitlin was joined by two distant cousins she had never met, together with their partners, and her grandfather's solicitor, a serious-looking young man by the name of Henry Jago.

Mr Jago seemed to sense that she was finding the day difficult, and he made a point of getting into conversation with the cousins and their partners, thus breaking the ice and setting everyone at ease. It gave Caitlin a few minutes' grace to collect her thoughts and find something to say.

Later, she realised how wonderful he had been throughout. An otherwise awful afternoon had gone off as smoothly and as pleasantly as such an occasion could possibly go. Although clearly not a chatty man, he had made conventional comments about the weather, asked the others about their travel arrangements and generally kept up the small talk.

'I'm so grateful to him,' she murmured to Jen and Sonia. 'He's been amazing, just getting everyone chatting, breaking the ice.'

'Maybe send him a bottle of decent brandy or Scotch as a thank you gift? You can get it delivered,' Sonia suggested.

'Or you could shag the poor bloke, he looks like he needs a bit of cheering up.'

'I'll treat that with the contempt it deserves, Jennifer,' Caitlin said with a snort. 'But the brandy's a good idea. I've got to go to his office tomorrow to sign some papers, so maybe I'll take it with me then.' Caitlin nodded, half to herself, hoping she'd remember. 'But what am I going to get you two as a 'thank you'? You've both been brilliant as well.'

'Idiot, we're just glad to be able to help, you don't

need to get us anything,' Sonia said with a laugh.

'Apart from the free booze, of course,' Jen laughed. She held up her glass, now empty.

'Of course!' Caitlin took it from her with a grin, bringing it back a few minutes later refilled.

A minute or two later, their table was ready in the restaurant and they filed in to take their places, Caitlin managing to secure herself an end of table seat, with her two pals on either side. Gradually they began to converse, the cousins telling her a little about themselves.

She had been surprised but pleased that her cousins had been able to come to the funeral. She couldn't remember having ever met them, although they assured her that they had met her once or twice when she was a baby. They were a little older than her, she thought, so that made sense. Had Gramps talked about them from time to time, or was she just imagining it?

Her thoughts were scattered and overwrought, with too much to remember. The cousins told her they had been in touch with her grandfather occasionally over the years, plus birthday cards, Christmas cards, holiday postcards, that sort of thing. As she watched and listened as they chatted with Jago, it sounded as though they had been in touch with her grandfather almost as much as she had. Yet she had never directly heard from them during her entire adult life, not even when her parents had died. It seemed odd, but with a mental shake, she reminded herself life was busy.

Laura and Michael were brother and sister, related to Caitlin through their mutual great-grandmother. Caitlin herself descended from one of her daughters, Isobel, her grandmother, and the cousins were descended from Isobel's younger sister Pamela. They were her only other family, so far as she knew, for although her mother had years ago heard of her younger sister's marriage in Vancouver, there had been no children. Caitlin didn't even know if her aunt was still alive, though it seemed likely, she'd only be in her early sixties.

Caitlin reckoned her cousins were about five, possibly as much as ten or twelve years older than her. Michael, the elder of the two, was a little jowly, his hair was greying and a little thin on top. Along with the middle-aged paunch, he easily looking around forty-six or forty-eight years old, whereas Laura looked about Caitlin's own age of thirty-six, or maybe a year or two older. Her clothes were expensive and up-to-the-minute, and her blonde hair was *very* blonde, her skin only slightly lined, her figure good and flexible. Yes, she's about my age, Caitlin though, so a bit younger than her husband who appeared to be a similar age to Michael.

Both cousins had brought their partners along with them to the funeral. As they talked over the buffet lunch, it became clear that Laura was married to her partner Gareth, whereas Michael and Becka had recently moved in together following their divorces, but were not married, and neither couple had any children.

'So, it's up to you to get married as quickly as you can and have a couple of kids to keep the old family tree sprouting new branches, or the whole lot of us will die out!' Laura said with a merry laugh, and her husband laughed loudly too, whilst Michael just smiled politely, and his girlfriend nodded, her expression a social mask.

Over her wine glass, Sonia smirked at Caitlin, knowing that she would find this uncomfortable, and not want to talk about her love-life with people she barely knew.

Caitlin smiled at this but said nothing, accidentally glancing up to meet Henry Jago's dark grey eyes that were fixed on her. She looked away hurriedly, saying, 'Oh I'm afraid it's a bit late for all that. I'll be thirty-seven next birthday, so I don't think there are going to be any more little buds coming along on our family tree.'

They demurred, and before they could ask even more awkward questions, Jen hastened to change the subject. As they tucked into the fruit and cream pastries that were the dessert, they began to talk about what they all did for a living.

Michael told her he was an estate agent—Caitlin hadn't been far off in her guess that he was in sales of some kind—and Becka was a mortgage advisor with the same firm. Laura was a part-time teaching assistant at a primary school near where she lived in Surrey, and her husband Gareth was something high-up in an auction house in London.

'What about you, Caitlin?'

'I'm a genealogist.' Usually, she didn't bother to tell anyone more than that, but they were looking at her with interest, so she expanded on it. 'You know, family trees and stuff? I work part-time for the local council, helping out with the running of their family and local studies institute which is part of the community library, and I do stuff like workshops and the occasional local history event. I also work with a number of law firms in my area to help them track down heirs to inheritances and that sort of thing. So I keep pretty busy. It's interesting and I meet a lot of nice people from all over the world.'

She stopped talking, suddenly self-conscious. They were looking politely interested and making encouraging noises.

Laura asked, 'Oh then I suppose you've already done a huge amount of research into our family? You probably know all our skeletons and scandals.' There was an odd frisson on the air, and Caitlin hurried to set their minds at rest.

'Not at all, no. I did a lot of investigation into my father's side as part of my training course years ago, because he was born into a military family, so it was a challenge, but that's all.'

Over the years, Caitlin had found people usually asked her either one of two questions, and it was only a matter of time before one of her cousins asked the inevitable.

'I expect people always hope they'll discover that they are descended from royal families? Or they hope you'll find them a forgotten inheritance?'

She grinned. 'Absolutely! Those are two of the most common things I get asked about.'

'But I should think you find out quite a bit that people wished you hadn't, as well?' Michael asked. He had chocolate sauce smeared on his chin. Becka nudged him and he wiped his chin on his sleeve. Caitlin tried to ignore the chocolate he was now smudging all over the table in front of him.

Bingo, she thought, returning to what he had said, which was most popular question number three.

'Yes,' she said ruefully. 'I do. People sometimes get quite upset. I'm afraid the past isn't always as long ago and far away as we'd like, and people can take things a bit personally on occasion. They can even get really angry as if they think I'm just making something up. But I always say at the outset, that if I undertake to do research on someone's behalf, they must understand that I occasionally discover sad or difficult things as well as good, interesting or exciting things. And, I always tell them, once you know something, you can't unknow it.'

'I imagine they usually dismiss such caution at the beginning?' Henry Jago asked, his tone soft.

Caitlin blushed under his steady gaze and was annoyed with herself for reacting to him like an infatuated teenager. She really needed to get out more. She could sense that beside her, her friends were grinning at one another. They knew her far too well. She answered him but found herself concentrating on his eyes rather than on stringing together coherent phrases. And anyway, he was probably happily married with six children.

'Hmm, er—yes, yes they do rather. They—er—they usually think I'm exaggerating or fantasising, and then if I do find out something,' she furiously told herself to stop gazing into his eyes, to break the stare, 'quite gorg—I mean—quite horrible, they can get angry and upset. Once someone refused to pay me, saying I was defaming his great-grandmother's good name.'

'And were you?' Henry Jago asked her gently, smiling behind his glass of sherry as if he was in on the joke.

'No, it was all true,' Caitlin said with a huge grin, suddenly relaxing and deciding to just go with the flow. 'She was genuinely a whore. It said so on the 1871 census under 'profession'.'

They all laughed. The waiter gave them an odd look and Caitlin remembered guiltily that this was supposed to be a funeral buffet.

She refilled her glass and raised it. 'A toast,' she said. They all raised their glasses to clink them against hers. 'To Richard Reginald Mitcheson, my Gramps. May he rest in peace.'

They repeated the toast and drank to it, everyone looking serious again now as they remembered the old man.

A few minutes later, Henry Jago got to his feet, looking at his watch.

'I'm afraid I have to be off, I have a meeting at four o'clock. So once again, Miss...'

'Caitlin,' prompted Caitlin, standing up.

'Caitlin, then. I'm so sorry about Richard. But I do look forward to seeing you tomorrow, and we will take a look at his will then get everything done and dusted. Goodbye for now.'

She'd half-hoped he would lean forward and kiss her cheek or give her a hug, but he held out his hand, business-like, and so she had to shake it. His clasp was firm and warm.

When he had gone, she turned back to her cousins. They too were making noises about the time, and saying they had to leave, a long drive ahead, that sort of thing.

She said, 'I do hope we will be able to keep in touch, now we've finally found each other. After meeting today, it would be a shame not to.'

'Oh, we will,' Laura said earnestly. 'And you must come and visit us, we're not so very far away from you. Far enough, you know, but it's not the end of the earth.'

They swapped phone numbers and email addresses. Michael asked, 'So you're seeing that solicitor chappie tomorrow about the will?'

'Yes. I'm not quite sure what to expect.' Caitlin replied.

Laura said, 'He's rather dishy.' Behind her, Sonia gave an unladylike snort and Jen murmured something Caitlin mercifully couldn't hear. Not that Laura noticed.

But Becka agreed with Laura, and Caitlin found herself blushing again. She tried to say she hadn't noticed but along with her so-called friends, they all just laughed at that. Conscious once again of being a bit too noisy and merry for a funeral party, Caitlin hurried to say,

'And then I've got to go to the house to start clearing everything out, ready to get it on the market.'

'Let me know if you need any help or advice with that, as someone in the business I might be useful,' Michael said, and Caitlin promised she would.

'What a shame he didn't go into an old people's home while he still could,' Becka said. 'I mean, I know old people can be stubborn and fiercely independent but if he'd already had a couple of falls, you'd think he would be glad to move to somewhere he could be properly looked after.'

'Hmm. I know,' Caitlin said. 'We did discuss it, but he kept putting it off. He'd had some improvements done to the house, rails to help him get in and out of the bath more safely, and handrails up the steps to the front door and so on. But I don't think he was quite ready to let go of his independence. Such a shame. We'd been to see a lovely place not far from where I live, but then he said he'd think about it until after Christmas. So sad. I suppose he didn't want to admit he had become so frail. We never want to accept it, I suppose.'

'I hope he didn't lay there for hours waiting for help. You know, conscious the whole time but not able to move, and in pain,' Laura said.

There was a long silence. They were watching her closely, she felt. Being kind, no doubt, but even so, she was uncomfortable with the close scrutiny.

Finally, glancing away briefly, she said, with a catch in her voice, 'I don't think so. I phoned him that evening for a chat, and the social worker found him early the next morning. The thinking is that he got up to go to the loo in the night. They think he'd been lying there about four or five hours. I mean, I know that *is* a long time,' she hastily added, 'but the doctor said he'd probably been unconscious for most of that time. He wouldn't have been lying there for a whole day, calling out for help and getting upset or frightened.' She thought that sounded fairly convincing, they wouldn't be likely to question that version of things.

'That's something, at least,' said Gareth. Everyone nodded. The mood was sombre now. After a few seconds more they took their leave, promising once more to keep in touch and call one another soon.

Caitlin was the last to leave. She was exhausted but more than that, she felt relieved it was all over, at last. One more item crossed off her list of things to somehow get through, leaving just the legal stuff then the epic hurdle of the house clearance and sale. She and her friends got a taxi back to her flat, glad the ordeal was over.

As soon as they got in the door, Sonia said, 'Prosecco?'

And at the same time, Jen said, 'How about pizza for dinner? I'll order it. You go and have a soak in the bath, try to relax a bit after that ordeal.'

'Ugh,' Caitlin said. 'You read my mind!'

The next morning, she took more care over her appearance than she probably would have done in the usual run of things. Not that there's any reason, it doesn't mean anything, she told herself crossly in the bathroom mirror. *But he is rather nice*, her mirror-image seemed to say. *He might be single. Hint, hint.* Which was exactly what the girls had said last night.

'Or,' she retorted out loud, to her mirror-self, as

she had also told Jen and Sonia as she topped up her glass, ignoring the rolling of their eyes, 'he might be gay, or happily married with six kids, or in a relationship with a perfectly wonderful tall, slim, blonde woman of twenty-five, or he might be a wife-beater or have a million pound cocaine habit. In any case, it doesn't matter. All that's happening here is that I'm going to my grandfather's solicitor's office to sort out some boring legal stuff and to find out the contents of Gramps' will. Not because the solicitor is tall, slim but broad-shouldered and has amazing eyes, but because being a grown-up means doing boring stuff like that.'

'Okay, we believe you!' they had laughed.

And, *Liar*, said her mirror-image now as she put on her best earrings and had a final fuss with her hair. To silence the voice, she added a defiant swipe of lipstick.

All this was still in her mind as a smiling motherly woman showed Caitlin into Henry Jago's office which proved to be very modern and minimalist.

Henry, she was thinking. Not my favourite name, rather old-fashioned, a bit stuffy and posh, very 1930s. Very *Downton Abbey* or even *Pride and Prejudice*. She blushed like a pre-teen as he came forward to take her hand. Was he going to kiss her hand, Darcy-style? Not that she'd want him to do that, of course. Did she imagine that he held her hand a teeny bit longer than strictly necessary?

She felt flustered. This was made worse by the difficulty she had getting out of her jacket–she'd missed a button–and by the time she finally took her seat, she was hot, embarrassed and her hair was no longer smooth and glossy. Her face had to be bright red. It was one of those Bridget Jones moments, she thought, annoyed with herself yet again. Her phone pinged in her bag. She didn't need to look at it to know it was either Jen or Sonia asking how it was going.

Jago appeared to have noticed nothing. He offered her tea or coffee, and when she declined either—not trusting herself with hot liquids when she was still hoping against hope to impress him—he resumed his seat on the other side of the desk and began to shuffle papers and ahemmed a couple of times.

'I'm so sorry for your loss. I didn't really know your grandfather personally, I'm afraid, I'd only met him twice, I believe. He was a friend and client of my father, who is retired now. He's out of the country at the moment, or he'd have wanted to speak with you himself. Um... Had your grandfather been ill, or...?'

'Er, thank you. And no, he fell down the stairs, unfortunately.'

'My goodness, how awful.' That seemed to shock him more than she'd have expected. He was biting his lip as if wondering how to proceed from there.

She felt was up to her to reassure him now. 'They said he didn't suffer, he would have been unconscious for most of the time before he was found. So that's a comfort.'

'Well thank goodness for small mercies.' Then he leaned forward on his elbows, hands clasped in front of him, and said, 'And how old was he?'

'Eighty-four last birthday. Not so very old by today's standards, I suppose.'

'No indeed. Apparently there have never been so many nonagenarians and centenarians. What a shame your grandfather couldn't have been with you a little longer.'

'Hmm,' was Caitlin's only response. That wouldn't have been ideal, from her point of view.

When she said nothing further, he asked, 'And

have you been to your grandfather's house recently?'

'No,' Caitlin said. 'I will probably leave that until tomorrow. I was thinking of popping over there and starting to clear it ready for sale, or—or whatever. Oh, although I suppose that depends whose property it is now?'

For only now did it occur to her that the house might have been left to someone else. She might not even be allowed to do anything further. Doubt nibbled at her.

She hurried on, 'There's still all his stuff—his furniture, his clothes, and you know—well—just all his belongings.' Then she added, 'I'd like to go through them if I may. Some of it belonged to my grandmother too. If there are any personal items, photos, that sort of thing, I'd like to keep them. If that's allowed. But of course,' she hurried on seeing he was about to speak, 'I quite understand that might not be possible. I have the door key with me, if you need me to hand it over.'

Jago smiled. He was holding in his hand a very large piece of thick paper: her grandfather's will.

'I don't think you need to worry too much about that. But I think you may have misunderstood me. When I asked if you'd been to the house, I was referring to the cottage in the village of Southdean, in Sussex.'

Caitlin gaped at him. She opened her mouth to deny she'd ever heard of a cottage in Sussex. Then shut it again as something clicked into place in the recesses of her mind, like a child's kaleidoscope turning and turning until an indiscernible pattern suddenly formed a whole picture.

'Oh.' That was all she said. Then, 'Was it near a windmill?'

Jago nodded. 'Yes, it's a replica of the famous one

in Rottingdean itself just a few miles away. The Southdean one was never actually used as a mill, perhaps it could be called more of a folly, or a place of interest. As for the cottage, possibly you visited it as a child? A lovely, chocolate-box style thatched cottage.'

'Not sure... I think perhaps I remember.' She was quiet for a moment, frowning as she thought back. Then, aware he was still waiting for an answer, she shook her head. 'Erm, no, to answer your question. I haven't been there for, well, decades. I'd forgotten it even existed.'

'Then I'm delighted to be in a position to tell you that both Mr Mitcheson's residence here in London, and Brook Cottage in Windmill Lane, Southdean, East Sussex, have become your sole property, together with a nice little nest egg of a little over four hundred thousand pounds, and of course, all the furnishings and property contained within those two residences. His entire estate, in fact, has been left to you as main beneficiary.'

She was silent for a moment. He seemed very pleased for her. She realised he was watching her and waiting for her reaction, expecting a smile or some expression of joy.

'That's—that's a lot,' she said, sitting back in her chair. 'Wow. Thank you.' She just said that without thinking, it had felt appropriate but as soon as she'd said it, she felt absurd. 'Sorry, I know you're just...'

He leaned back in his seat with a broad grin on his face for the first time since she'd met him. He looked suddenly much younger and almost boyish. Her heart did a little skip.

'The bearer of the good news? Well yes I am. I have the privilege of being one of the executors of your grandfather's estate, and my father is the other. We have already discussed the er—the—er—situation, and are in complete agreement as to the—er—situation.'

He dropped the pen he was twirling and winced a little at his sudden loss of language skills, causing Caitlin to look down at her hands to hide a smirk. He recovered his composure, and sitting forward once again, all stern legal practitioner, he went on:

'I have already deducted all the various fees and payments, plus sundry disbursements from the sum I mentioned, so that really is a net sum, a conservative estimate, and I will, of course, give you a full list of all of the disbursements for your approval. I've made a preliminary allowance for inheritance tax—the amount was exorbitant, of course, but nothing we can do about that. The funds are in escrow, so you may get a little back some months down the line, but I doubt it'll be much.

'You will see from the list that there is a sum of ten thousand pounds to each of your two cousins whom you met yesterday. But they weren't actually Mr Mitcheson's own flesh and blood, which is why he left them a relatively small amount. Confidentially I can tell you that they each inherited a more—er—*useful*—sum when their maternal grandmother passed away, let me see, what was it? Almost six years ago, now?'

'My great-aunt Pamela? Yes, it will be six years in January,' Caitlin said.

Like yesterday, her thoughts were all over the place. She couldn't get them straight. She felt unsure of what to do or say next.

He selected a pen from three standing to attention in his breast pocket and made some marks on a document.

'So if you could just sign here, here and here, I will

give you this envelope which contains keys along with various bits and pieces, and that will be all the hard work over.'

'Is anyone living in the cottage at Southdean at the moment?' Caitlin asked as she signed.

'No, no. It's been empty for at least ten years. From what I gathered from my father, for many years your grandparents only went there very occasionally for a short visit. A weekend or two per year. But more recently, not at all. There is a local woman who pops in every few days to make sure everything is all right, and gives the place a bit of an airing, cleans anything that needs attention, that sort of thing. But apart from that, the cottage has been uninhabited for almost twenty years.'

'I see.'

'You would probably get a decent price for it, if you decided to sell, it's in a highly sought-after area. Or, if you're not sure what you want to do, perhaps you could consider renting it out. That will bring you in a useful income and ensure the place remains in a good and liveable condition whilst you think it over. Go down there, perhaps, have a look at the place. It's in a lovely setting, a beautiful part of the world. Perhaps you could take a short break down there before you go back to work? Or...'

'Yes?'

'Well, you know, you could even live there, if you wanted to. Give up your job... Who knows? And with the proceeds from the sale of the house up here, and the lump sum... Just a suggestion.' He hesitated, seeming to feel he had overstepped the solicitor-client boundary. Then he added with a disarmingly boyish smile, 'I'd love the opportunity to get away from London and live down there in the country. Back to my roots. But of course, what appeals to one, doesn't always appeal to another.'

'Your partner might prefer city life.' Caitlin suggested, slyly taking the opportunity of finding out a bit more about this man with the gorgeous eyes.

'My partner? Yes, yes, he definitely prefers being in the city.' Henry responded with a solemn nod of the head, then as she fought to disguise her disappointment, he added, embarrassed once again, 'Ah, sorry, you meant... Ah, haha, no. For a moment I thought you were referring to my business partner, Colin. Haha! How awkward. No, no 'better half' at the moment, sadly.'

Slightly flushed, he cleared his throat and made a bit of a show of shuffling his papers. Taking this as a sign the appointment was over, Caitlin got up and held out a hand to him.

'Thank you so much for all you've done. It's—um...'

'Naturally I'll be in touch as soon as everything has gone through, but there's no reason why you shouldn't take possession of both residences and begin to make plans. If you require monies, I can give you an advance from the estate ahead of probate being granted. If you have any queries whatsoever, please don't hesitate to call. Here's my card. And here's your envelope. I'm very sorry about your grandfather, I didn't know him, but my father tells me he was quite the gentleman. But I know you'll enjoy your inheritance. Do let me know what you decide to do with the two properties. As I say, if you need any help at all, please don't hesitate.'

And then she was outside on the pavement, racing for her car as the heavens opened and torrents of icy rain descended.

In the car she placed the envelope on the front passenger seat. All the way home she shot glances at it, wondering. A thrill of excitement began to rise within her.

*

Chapter Three

In just forty minutes, practically a record, she did the drive from Jago's office across London to reach the little terraced house that had been her grandfather's home for many years.

It was very strange using the key to let herself inside. She found herself halting inside the door to listen for Gramps's voice. The house felt silent, alien. It wasn't his house anymore, but nor did it feel like hers. Like an intruder, she felt she shouldn't be there. She half-expected someone to challenge her at any moment. The house already had a cold, empty feeling, like it was a shell. The feeling intensified as she went from room to room and found everything just as he had left it, yet now it was the house of a stranger. She was seeing the place as if for the first time. It wasn't a good feeling.

Her phoned pinged. It was Sonia, asking how things had gone with Mr Dreamy. Almost at the same time, Jen's message popped up:

How was sexy-bum Jago today? All ok?
Trust Jen! Caitlin hadn't even noticed his backside. The back of his jacket covered most of it.

She rolled her eyes, putting her phone back in her pocket. She'd call them later. It would be good to get together again for dinner or a drink if they could manage it. She took a deep breath. Right then, get on with it, woman, she told herself.

She averted her eyes from the stairs, stepping quickly past the spot where Gramps had lain for so long before being found. At least he had fallen onto thick carpet and not a stone floor or rough wooden boards, nor chilly modern laminated flooring. Although it didn't matter how good the carpet was, seeing that he had fallen from the top of the stairs, the effect wasn't too much different to falling onto a floor with no carpet at all. But she didn't want to remember that.

She was supposed to be checking the condition of the property with a view to selling it, and she had to carry out an inventory, deciding what to keep, what to sell, what to give to charity, and what was, in the end, just junk, needing only to be boxed up and taken to the tip.

Instead she wandered around the house, relaxing a little now as she relived memories of her happier visits, touching this, straightening that. After about twenty minutes, just as she was shaking herself awake and reminding herself there were things to get done, there was a soft knock on the front door.

A woman was standing there; she was probably about sixty years of age, Caitlin guessed, and she was wearing a sad expression.

As soon as she saw Caitlin, the woman grabbed her hand and said, 'Oh my dear, I'm so, *so* sorry. Such a *nice* gentleman. As soon as I saw your car, I said to my Terry, that'll be Caitlin, I said, and I've just *got* to pop round and tell her how sorry I am, I said.'

In spite of the sad face, her mouth quirked up at the corners as she spoke. She was clearly relishing the whole thing. Caitlin felt a flash of annoyance but pushed it aside, forcing herself to smile at the woman. Then finding it difficult to know what to do with the visitor's clutching hand, Caitlin shook it, and when it didn't fall back to the woman's side, Caitlin was aware of a compulsion to take a step back to increase the distance between them.

The nosy neighbour stepped forward and Caitlin, feeling crowded, stepped back again. And now the woman was right in the hallway, then pushing past, she went to ogle the stairwell.

'Is this where it happened? Oh my!' All this said in a theatrical mock horror, her mouth still tipping upwards in spite of the dramatically wide eyes and shocked tones. She added, 'There wasn't any blood then? Well, let's be thankful for small mercies, that's what I always say. Through here, were you?'

And now the woman was in the kitchen and Caitlin was fighting feelings of outrage.

'I'm sorry, Mrs... er...?'

'Cahill. Brenda. From next door. Me and Terry have lived in that same house for forty years, since we first got back from our honeymoon in Weymouth. Mind you, house prices have shot up, haven't they, good thing we got in when we did. Of course, wages have gone up, too, but even so you can't keep up, can you, not when you're on a pension. I'm so sorry we didn't go to the funeral. I expect you've had it by now, haven't you? Only we didn't know when it was or anything. I kept hoping we'd see you and be able to ask, but you haven't been here for a while, have you? Must be hard, coming back after what happened...?'

Caitlin had to stop her, had to break in with, 'Mrs Cahill, I'm afraid I'm really very busy, so I can't really...'

'Well, tell you what, Ducks, I'll pop the kettle on and then after a nice cup of tea, we'll get started. What say we start with Dickie's bedroom and work our way down?'

Dickie?

For a few bewildered seconds, Caitlin just stared at the busy form of Mrs Cahill, filling the kettle and setting it on the gas ring, then easily locating cups and saucers and even the teapot. Coming to a sudden decision, Caitlin pulled herself together and said firmly,

'I'm sorry, Mrs Cahill, but I only popped in to check there were no letters. I'm leaving again immediately, I'm afraid.'

And without waiting for Mrs Cahill's response, Caitlin turned and left the room. By the time she reached the front door, the neighbour was catching her up.

Clearly disappointed, she was saying, 'Oh? Coming back to tackle it all some other time? I don't blame you dear, all those personal items, and all those memories coming flooding back. Very upsetting for you, I should think?'

'Yes, very true.' Caitlin said, opening the door and indicating Mrs Cahill should precede her.

'Well of course it is, very upsetting, I should think. And you all on your own too, no husband to look after you. It would be upsetting, what with you being all he had in the world, and visiting him every week in your little blue Corsa, regular as clockwork. A right good 'un, you were, never missed a week, did you? In all these years? Me and my Terry used to often say

The Cousins

how good you were, coming round in all weathers...'

'As you say,' Caitlin said coldly. 'I was all he had.'

Somehow she managed to close and lock the front door. With a quick 'Well, thank you for your kind words,' she hurried back to the car and got in. As she drove away, Mrs Cahill was standing on her own doorstep, clutching her beige cardigan about her and waving Caitlin off as if she was a favourite niece.

Caitlin wondered how she would get the house cleared in peace with that busybody interfering and talking nonstop whilst she enjoyed someone else's misfortune.

She was just putting the key in the lock of her own front door when she remembered the kettle.

Rage and misery swept through her in roughly equal measures. She went into the kitchen in her own flat and leaned against the counter, wondering what on earth to do about it.

If only she could be sure.

If only that bloody woman hadn't kept talking on and on at her and moving around the house touching Gramps' stuff and calling him Dickie and knowing where everything was and all there was to know about his life. And Caitlin's, too.

No husband to look after you.

Stupid woman, Caitlin grumbled, pressing her hands to her temples. What in the name of hell should she do now? She sighed. She knew perfectly well what she had to do, but...

She fumed to herself. Had the woman turned on the gas under the kettle or turned it off? Had she put it on at all? Or...? Caitlin remembered Mrs Cahill filling the kettle and placing it on the stove, but what had she done next?

A glance at her watch showed it had been almost

an hour since she had been in the kitchen with that woman. By now the kitchen–no, the whole house–could be full of steam. Which wasn't really a problem, but the kettle would quickly boil dry... Her mind was filled with a vision of lines of fire engines all with their sirens blaring, and a dozen or more firemen playing torrents of water upon the whole street to dowse the flames caused by this one small piece of neglect. The nine o'clock news would cite her as the one who had endangered a whole suburb with this one thoughtless act.

Had that stupid, stupid, *stupid* woman turned off the gas under the kettle before following Caitlin from the house? Or not?

Caitlin huffed. Raking her fingers through her hair, she looked about the room, as if that would provide some enlightenment. She gave a strangled groan of rage and frustration and thumped the countertop. There was only one way she was going to be able to be certain.

She had to go straight back to Gramps' house again.

Now a sense of urgency made her snatch up her keys, phone and bag, tearing out of the flat, fumbling frantically to lock the door, fumbling, shaky-fingered, with the keys, dropping the bunch in her haste, then bumping her head on the door as she straightened up.

She got the door locked then pelted down the block's four flights of stairs and pushed the building entry door wide as she ran out to her car parked in its spot on the far side of the residents' designated parking area.

In another thirty seconds she was driving out of the tiny parking area, turning left onto the main road and once again heading for her grandfather's house, ignoring the concerned beeping from her car as it reminded her she had yet to fasten her seatbelt.

This was probably a complete waste of time, but she had to be sure. She couldn't just assume everything was okay and leave it. She'd never be able to relax if she was worrying the whole house might burn down. Or the whole street. She halted for a red light and put on her seatbelt.

'What shade of green are you waiting for?' she muttered under her breath at the car in front. Gradually, with excessive caution, it pulled away and she was able to move off once again.

But she felt idiotic. She agonised over whether it was better to park near the house or further away. If she parked nearer, Brenda Cahill—the nosy old bag—would see the car—*your little blue Corsa*—recognise it, and no doubt come round immediately, desperate to know what was going on.

It would be better to park further down the road and hope she could enter Gramps' house undetected. The only problem with that scenario was if the neighbour realised she was there, Caitlin would have further to go to reach her car and escape the dratted woman's questions and urge for salacious details.

Caitlin decided she would risk parking further away. She entered the road from the opposite end to the Cahills', and once parked up, made her approach quietly, keeping as close to the houses as she could, before slipping stealthily into the shelter of the house's front porch in the manner of an experienced burglar.

Carefully she placed the key into the lock and turning it, opened the door as slowly and as silently as she possibly could. She accomplished this more or less soundlessly and the tiny amount of noise she did make was easily drowned out by the loud theme tune of the TV show the neighbours were watching.

Caitlin stepped inside the hallway, closed and then re-locked the front door. Next she pulled the big old curtain across the doorway to block out not just any draughts but also prying neighbours.

She hurried into the kitchen. The kettle was cold, the gas was out, and as she had half-known it would be, all was well. Caitlin heaved a huge sigh of relief and sank down at the oak table. She felt ridiculous, but she knew she'd done the right thing. She'd had to be sure. Thank God everything was all right!

Now that she was there, she decided she may as well have that cup of tea, and she set the kettle to boil.

In a little fit of spite against Brenda Cahill, Caitlin snatched the teabags out of the teapot the neighbour had made ready, plopped one into a cup and the other in the waste bin. She put the teapot back in the cupboard along with the second cup and saucer, feeling that in her own small—petty, she admitted—way she had her revenge on Brenda Cahill for upsetting her and making her have to come back to check the kettle wasn't boiling.

She inspected the contents of the fridge: there was half a carton of milk, still just in date, but otherwise only a few other sorry bits and pieces. She put everything except the milk into the waste bin, turned off the fridge and pulled the plug out of the wall socket.

Gramps had no freezer, so that was one thing among many she wouldn't need to worry about.

She sat at the table to sip her tea. The silence closed about her, and she grew calm. She looked around. This room, like all the rooms, was full of knick-knacks, ornaments and stuff. Clearing the house was going to be a huge job.

She'd forgotten to charge her phone, as she discovered when she went to make a note on there. So she went over to the dresser to rummage for a piece of paper and found only a writing pad of old-fashioned smart blue notepaper, the kind straight out of the 1970s, with the lined sheet you slipped underneath the top sheet so you could keep your handwriting in a neat straight row as you wrote. It would have to do, she told herself, no sense in saving it, Gramps would not use it now. She dug in her bag for a pen and sat back down.

She headed up several sheets of paper with the names of the rooms, and beginning with the kitchen, began to note down everything the room contained.

As she sipped her tea and made her list, she thought about her cousins. Seeing that they had been closer to Gramps than she had been aware of, perhaps she ought to call them to check if they wanted any keepsake or item of furniture from the house. She would do that later. Or maybe tomorrow.

She continued making her list, ending up by going through everything in the kitchen, every cupboard, drawer and shelf, noting the contents in greater detail. When she added anything to the list she thought might be valuable, she added a little pound sign in the margin, and if there was anything she wanted to keep, she wrote 'ME' in the margin. Anything useful to either charity shop or anyone else, she put a little triangle next to it for want of a better idea, and lastly, anything that she thought worthless she put an X beside.

She emptied the larder, removing two unopened bottles of wine to take home with her, and consigned all the other items—half-full jars of marmalade and mustard, a bottle of brown sauce, some pickles, the mouldy tail-end of a loaf, a small, half-empty box of breakfast cereal, salt, pepper, a tiny tin of mackerel in tomato sauce, a packet of stock cubes and two cans of baked beans—to the bin, and then she removed the bin liner, tied up the top and left it by the front door with the wine bottles, ready to take it with her when she left so she could drop it into her own big wheelie bin when she got home.

She washed up her cup, dried it and put it away, and then decided she needed to go home. Her head ached and she felt drained and weepy. But at least she had made a start.

Whether or not Brenda Cahill heard her leave—and it had been difficult to juggle bin bag, wine and her handbag, and lock the front door at the same time without making a little noise—there was not so much as a twitch of her dreary net curtains.

Caitlin made it back to her car unmolested.

*

Chapter Four

Her grandfather's death certificate arrived in the following day's post. It seemed so weird to read the words there in black and white. It was a legal document announcing to all officialdom that Richard Reginald Mitcheson was dead. The main cause of death was given as cardiac failure following a fall, with the wound on the head listed as a contributory factor. Holding the document in her hand made it all seem so final, so undeniable. He was gone.

She had seen many certificates over the years in her capacity as a genealogist, usually stamped 'not for use as identification' or 'copy', and a large number of these had been death certificates, with deaths caused by any number of terrible occurrences: from the sadly all too common whooping cough in the case of the young babies of previous generations, to the odd case of phthisis, now called tuberculosis, or softening of the brain, usually known to modern medicine as dementia. But this was the first time she had seen one for a member of her own family.

Her parents had been killed in a traffic collision on the motorway. It had been the first day of their New Year break and they had set off early that day, in good spirits and ready for a well-earned rest, having talked about it endlessly with her for months beforehand. Her father had been newly retired from the armed forces, and they were looking forward to the changes that would bring to their lives: a fresh start, they'd said, with the opportunity for travel and new experiences.

But halfway through their journey the weather had deteriorated rapidly, and they had run into a fog bank, only to find themselves careering into the backs of several other vehicles. They hadn't been able to swerve in time, and vehicles had piled into the back of them. Caitlin's father had been killed outright, her mother had survived long enough to reach hospital but had died on the way to the operating theatre.

The shock of losing her daughter and her son-in-law had profoundly impacted Caitlin's grandmother Isobel, and she'd had a massive stroke, dying from it just six days later.

All of these tragedies had been dealt with by Gramps with very little support from Caitlin. She had been nineteen years of age, abroad at the time of her parents' deaths, on a month-long backpacking trip to Australia. When she had finally received the terrible news about her parents, she had returned home in a state of shock, arriving in Britain only to discover her grandmother had passed away that morning.

Now, eighteen years later, Caitlin was unprepared for the sense of finality it gave her as she held in her hand the death certificate of her grandfather.

There were three copies—she would need two to

send to various government departments relating to Gramps' pension, tax, and so on, to inform them of his decease and provide them with the evidence they needed for their records. And of course, she'd need to lodge a copy with Henry Jago, to enable the process of probate to get moving.

A mountain of tasks piled up in her mind, and again her solution was to grab a notebook—the blue bonded writing paper from Gramps' house—and begin making a list to ensure nothing vital was forgotten.

The post had also brought her copies of the forms she had signed at Jago's office. Caitlin toyed with the idea of ringing him to let him know they had arrived safely and to thank him for sending them, she dismissed this tactic as much too desperate. But it would be nice to see him again. She dithered, but in the end decided to leave the poor man alone.

Working on her list reminded Caitlin of another thing she had to take care of. No need to delay, it was something she could take care of now. She rang both her cousins and left voicemail messages, saying she hoped they were keeping well, and asking if they thought there was anything they would like from Gramps' house. She left her number for them to call her, even though it would show up on their screens.

Michael rang just a few minutes later. He said he'd like a photo, if she could spare one but other than that he didn't want anything. He asked how she was, and she began to tell him all about going to Gramps' house and the nosy neighbour. He seemed to find it funny, but before he rang off, he reminded her of his offer to let him know if she needed any help. He added that he and Becka could come over at the weekend if she could wait until then.

She promised to think about it and let him know,

touched by his concern and feeling for the first time how good it would be to get to know her new family, who seemed like nice people.

She messaged her friends. She had coffee and toast. She sat in her little dining-room overlooking the communal garden. Leaves were yellowing and falling, the ground was wet, the sky a dreary greyish white. She sighed. If only it was spring, how pretty all this would look, how nice it would be to see the sun again. She promised herself she would start planning a holiday soon, she needed to get away, have a change of scene. Her money worries were at an end, barring any probate issues. She could hardly dare to allow herself to think about how much money she would now have.

'You'll be a millionaire!' Jen had squealed with delight, hugging her.

'Not exactly!' Caitlin had protested, but thinking about it now in the cold and rather more sober light of day, Jen wasn't far out, she realised. She felt guilty about the twinge of excitement she had then. It wasn't—shouldn't be—about the money.

She felt horribly depressed at the thought of having to go back to Gramps' house today to carry on listing and sorting. But it had to be done. Best get it over with. Reluctantly she galvanised herself into action, got ready and left the house.

On the way to Gramps' house, she stopped at a storage facility and asked about prices, then she bought some cardboard boxes and was on her way again.

Now all she had to do was get into the house again without being noticed by Brenda Cahill.

Luck was with her. As she left her car and started walking along the street, she saw the couple come out of their house, complete with a little red shopping bag on wheels. For a few seconds, she halted in her tracks, horrified, but with relief saw they turned in the opposite direction. So long as they didn't turn and look behind them, she would be safe.

She made it to the house, slipped inside quickly and once again locked the door behind her, pulling the curtain across the door as she had the previous day. Then she stopped dead. There was a faint scent on the air. Something she couldn't quite identify. But faint though it was, it told her all she needed to know. Everything looked just the same, nothing appeared to have been moved, nothing was missing so far as she could tell, but one thing remained:

Someone had been in Gramps' house.

It was three days before she found the photographs. She had finally got around to tackling her grandfather's bedroom. It was the last room she had to sort through; she'd put it off and put it off until there was nothing else left to do.

She'd forgotten the words he spoke just before he died, in spite of the fact they were almost his last, and had puzzled her so much at the time.

But then she opened the top drawer of the tall-boy and found not clothes but, pretty much everything else, it seemed. Then his words came back to her along with their sense of urgency. She remembered the painful grip of his hand, strong for someone who had such a short time to live. Desperation, perhaps, to make sure his message was heeded. She remembered how strange those words had sounded at the time, and that she'd realised he'd thought he was talking to his wife.

The drawer contained a huge array of old tat: bits of string and wire, neatly coiled and held in their coils by the wire closures from packets of sandwich bags or the plastic tags on loaves of bread. Old—and very attractive, very *collectable*—tobacco tins, pastille and lozenge tins full of fuses and fuse wire, washers, nails and screws. This, Caitlin realised, was Gramps' man-cave. He had no garage, and the tiny overgrown patch behind the house didn't allow for a shed, and so this drawer was where he had squirrelled away all the odd bits and pieces he wanted to keep. For whatever reason he had kept this stuff, with the usual old-fashioned urge for thrift of the earlier generation who had lived through the privations of the war and no doubt numerous economic declines since then.

The little slice of cardboard wrapped round with fuse wire bore the legend *Is 6d* in the top corner. She'd heard of shillings and old pence, but this was the first time she'd actually seen such an old price written on anything, so the wire dated back to before decimalisation in 1971. There were obsolete batteries of varying sizes, and tiny light bulbs. There was a small manual for the fridge downstairs in the kitchen, along with a receipt for its purchase in 1995. All manner of small 'treasures'.

And then there were the photos. There were probably a dozen packets of photos, mostly black and white, mostly of her grandmother, her mother as a child, her parents, even of herself as a child. These she had seen a few times before. But one of the packets, shoved right to the back of the drawer, contained a set of perhaps six photos, again all black and white, depicting an unfamiliar group of young people.

Caitlin took this packet and moved to perch on the end of the bed, and as she did so she shot a glance from bed to tall-boy, and she remembered how in the hospital that night he had gestured weakly with his arm, and said something along the lines of, 'I've still got a photo here somewhere...'

She spread the photos out on the covers and looked at them. Each picture showed a group of young people, boys and girls, probably in their teens or twenties. They were all outdoors. In one, a couple of girls sat on a brick wall, the wide skirts of their dresses spread out against the brickwork, the flowery patterns seeming fresh and vivid even in their shades of grey, their little peter-pan collared white blouses gleaming in contrast against the dark trousers and jerseys of the boys standing behind them. In another, the positions were reversed, the boys kneeling or reclining on the ground in front whilst the girls stood behind. Another photo showed a blanket spread on the ground and remnants of a picnic lay about. In the background a pretty little stream ran by. In the next picture a couple of bicycles leaned against trees and in another, a lovely windmill was behind and to the left of the group of youngsters.

Although they were in black and white, the photos seemed so alive, perfectly encapsulating the moment in which it was taken, the laughter, the fun. All of them smiled at the camera or held up bottles of what was probably ginger beer in a kind of salute. They were all squashed together to pose for the camera, and back across the years Caitlin smiled too, infected by the happy images from long ago.

She flipped them over to look at the backs in case there were any details written, but the only legend they all carried was a date, *14th May 1963*. No other information was given, so Caitlin felt that she still knew nothing. She gathered the photos up, replaced them in the packet which she put in her bag to take home with her, along with all the other family photos, then with reluctance, she returned to the task in hand.

Much to her relief, she had not encountered the nosy neighbour again, although she had caught a soft sound that might have been a knock at the door a couple of times, but she had ignored it. To be on the safe side, she had kept the door locked.

She was convinced that someone had been in the house again; there was that same odd scent hanging in the air, like perfume or something, though very faint, and although she couldn't be sure, she had a vague uneasy feeling that things had been moved or were not quite as they had been before, but here too, she had no definite proof.

No doubt the neighbours had a key, she thought. A spare key, in case of Gramps locking himself out or to facilitate a delivery if he had been out. Not that he ever went out, not really, she admitted. But regardless of how the intruder had got in, she didn't feel like going to ask the neighbours for the spare key. It was easier to call a locksmith.

So she made arrangements to have the front door lock changed and a lock and new bolt fitted on the back door. Hopefully that would be enough to keep out the unwelcome visitor, whoever it was.

The next day, a Saturday, she opened up and ushered her two cousins into Gramps' house.

She'd decided to put the sale of the property in the hands of Michael, who was, after all, an estate agent. In exchange for the listing, he promised to give her a discount, even though she'd said it didn't matter. To him, it clearly did, no doubt, she thought, it was a pride thing. He wanted to be able to help, and to tell people he had done so.

'I still need to go through everything and make sure there's nothing else I want to keep,' she told him. 'But if there's anything either of you would like

The Cousins

to have, feel free to just take it. Otherwise, I'll be hiring a clearance firm to empty the place so that it can go on the market.'

'No need,' he said quickly. 'We can handle the house clearance too, you know. Save you a lot of bother.'

She smiled. 'Thanks. Do you mind if I think about it for a few days and let you know? Not quite ready yet.'

'Sure, okay.' He shrugged, and she thought he seemed a little disappointed.

As she showed them round the tiny house, she pointed out the one or two nice pieces of furniture that weren't to her taste or were too big for her flat but that could be valued by someone else. Eventually all that was left to do was to finalise the price and other details with Michael.

Eventually, everything settled, she handed over a spare set of keys to Michael, so that he could come back to make a note of the details of the house, and once everything was agreed, to show clients round. She didn't expect, or want, ever to set foot in the house again. But nevertheless, she was surprised by an unexpected wave of sorrow, and embarrassed, she had to wipe her eyes with a tissue Laura gave her.

But they were so understanding. They invited her to join them for a pub lunch.

For some years her only 'family' had been her friends Jen and Sonia. Otherwise, she had been alone except for Gramps. Or so she had thought. But she had never been aware of being lonely. Already, though, she was growing to like her newly found cousins and the thought of not staying in touch made her feel sad. They seemed to enjoy seeing her too, and had been quick to offer her help if she needed it. So, with only a slight hesitation, she said,

'I'm planning to go down to the cottage in Southdean next weekend. I haven't been there since I was little, but now that it's mine, I'd like to see it again. Not that I remember it. Anyway... I wondered if you'd fancy coming down with me. If you want to, of course, feel free to say no, if you're busy or are just not interested,' she added hastily.

'Hell yes, count me in!' Michael laughed and Laura leaned across the table to give Caitlin a quick, awkward hug.

'We'd love to,' she said with her gentle smile. 'Are you sure you want us to come with you? If it's the first time you've been down there for ages, are you sure you don't want to be alone?'

'Well...' said Caitlin, considering this. 'I'm not sure, I mean, would you mind if I went there first and you came down the next day? The thing is, I haven't got a clue what kind of state it's in, or how big it is. I don't know if there will be room for all of us to actually stay there.'

'There'll be places to stay in nearby Rottingdean or even Brighton if the cottage is too small, or damp or whatever,' Laura pointed out. 'Why don't you go down, and then phone or text us and let us know for sure when you've had a chance to suss it out? We could come down the next day, if everything's okay.'

'Perfect,' Caitlin grinned at her, reassured.

Michael said, 'Would it be all right for me to bring Becka? I know she'd love to see you again.'

'Of course!' Caitlin exclaimed. 'I assumed you would bring her, and Gareth's very welcome too,' she said to Laura. 'That would be lovely.'

She sat back. She felt happy, excited. She could hardly wait to get down to Sussex.

*

Chapter Five

After a long dreary week, it was a relief to pack up her car and leave London on Friday afternoon.

It seemed like half the world had the same idea, she realised as she sat in traffic, trying to remain alert though only inching forward towards the junction. She put the radio on, found a station that played 90s music and leaned back against the headrest and relaxed, humming along with an old song by The La's.

Because of being away from today, she'd had to have Friday-night-dinner with the girls on Thursday night instead. She'd hope to persuade at least one of them to go with her to Sussex, but neither could get away at such short notice. Sonia was a teacher, so any time off outside of school holidays was next to impossible to organise, and Jen's manager was away this week, so she had to step up: they couldn't both be off at the same time. So here Caitlin was, unsure about going to see the house with no gal-pal back-up.

She'd text and send photos, they could keep in touch, even if it wasn't the same as being there together.

Although she was only going away for a long weekend, it was like being at the start of a full two-week holiday. She was grateful to be able to choose her own hours of work, as her council contract only stipulated a minimum. After all that had happened recently, she needed the break to recharge her batteries. But at the same time, she was nervous about visiting the cottage.

The more she thought about it, the more it seemed odd—she let off the handbrake and began to roll gently forward a few yards only to halt again—it seemed odd that she remembered going to the cottage as a small child but not since then. She had all but forgotten its existence. Henry Jago had said that the house had remained empty for a long time. Caitlin's parents and her grandmother had died sixteen years ago, and the cottage had obviously remained in the ownership of the family all this time, but she could remember no visits in her teens, only ever seeing her grandfather at the house in London, either with both her parents, or after they had died, alone. She couldn't even remember the last time she had seen her grandmother. She couldn't remember her grandfather ever mentioning the cottage, or going to stay there, or even leaving the house in London for anything more than a few hours at a time. Had he been to the cottage even once since those early days?

Her father had been in the armed forces, but unlike most soldiers, his work was not of the sort that meant he got sent here, there and everywhere. She had not been an army brat in the usual sense of constant upheaval and new starts. When she'd said to him once in a stroppy teenage fit, 'What do you even do?', he'd just laughed and come out with the usual cliché of, 'I could tell you but then I'd have to kill you.'

Now she wondered. She knew he'd been in finance admin rather than a battlefield-type of military operations. Their life had been stable. He'd come home for dinner most evenings, rarely worked overnight or at the weekend, and only occasionally going off to some conference or another, usually only away one or two nights at the most.

So his work wasn't the reason they had seen so little of her grandparents. Nor could it have been why they never returned to the cottage during her later childhood years.

In fact she couldn't recall the cottage even being mentioned by her parents after she was about, what, six years old? Eight, perhaps? Had she just forgotten? Or was there another reason? Perhaps they hadn't enjoyed going to the cottage, or perhaps it had been rented out to tenants to bring in an income as Henry had suggested she could do? Perhaps the adults had not all got along well? It was quite common for people to not get along with their in-laws, wasn't it? Or was the place derelict, or just too small for guests? Maybe life had simply been too busy to allow time to go down to Sussex even for a weekend break?

But they'd taken holidays. Her parents had taken her all over Britain and much of Europe for vacations, and for her eighteenth birthday they had surprised her with a trip to New York. For her twentieth, they had paid for her to go to Stockholm for a few days with a boyfriend she had been madly in love with at the time. She recalled he had slept with a barmaid the day after her birthday celebrations and that had been the end of her first great romance. Ash, that was his name. Ash Egerton. The knob. He was now balding, overweight and worked as a civil servant in some boring job, and was on his third marriage, according to social media. Not that she spied on him or anything.

And after that, her parents had died, and she hadn't had a family to spend time with. Apart from the weekly duty visit to her grandfather. Such a relief she needn't do that anymore.

The car in front had moved on, opening up a small gap and Caitlin slowly closed up behind it again. She was still musing on that holiday with Ash–and could vividly recall him gripping the armrests in terror as the plane had dropped several hundred feet in an airpocket. She remembered she had relished the thrill of it, like a rollercoaster ride, but Ash had hated every minute of the flight and been horribly sick. She remembered she had been scornful and unsympathetic, telling him he was a baby. Obviously, it had not been a match made in heaven after all.

With these and many other reminiscences, she bore with the seemingly endless stream of traffic and at last found herself on the motorway where the traffic was comparatively free flowing.

It was not a long journey by any means, but with the volume of evening traffic, she was already twenty minutes behind schedule. She should still be in the Rottingdean area for dinner at a pub by about seven o'clock.

She turned her thoughts to the aim of her journey and wondered again exactly what she would find when she finally got there. What if the cottage was really small and dark, or damp and mouldy? Maybe the roof was caving in or falling down, or... What if there weren't really roses around the door and a 'welcome home', happy-ever-after feeling waiting for her at Brook Cottage? What if she really hated the place?

'Then I'll sell it,' she told herself firmly and out loud, and felt better.

The envelope with the keys Henry Jago had given her also contained a piece of paper bearing the name Katherine Green, along with an address and a phone number. Caitlin assumed these were the contact details for the lady who had cleaned the cottage and kept an eye on things for Gramps all these years. Caitlin had already left a message on Mrs Green's answering machine—like Caitlin, she still had a landline—saying that she was coming down to the cottage this weekend and that Mrs Green should not be alarmed if she saw lights on in the house.

Her phone rang. According to the sat-nav screen it was Jen calling. Thank God for hands-free. Caitlin answered, but immediately Jen's voice came to her, excruciatingly loud one second, dying away the next with every small obstacle along the roadside.

'Are you there yet? Is it amazing?'

'I'm still quite a way off. The traffic's been horrendous. What are you up to?'

'Rob wants to go out for dinner. His sister's birthday. I forgot, actually, so I don't feel like I can get out of it. I'll have to grab a card and some flowers on the way.' She sighed. 'I'm so pissed off that I forgot all about it. And that's with him reminding me too!'

'Don't worry about it. You've had a lot on at work, and you've had me to worry about and support. I'm sure Rob won't mind.' Caitlin wasn't a fan of Jen's boyfriend Rob but he seemed to make Jen happy, most of the time, so Jen's friends had to put up with him.

They talked a little more then Jen had to go and

get ready. Rob was picking her up—they had talked about moving in together but not done it yet.

'Don't forget to send photos!' Jen said before ending the call.

That distraction aside, Caitlin continued worrying away at her previous thoughts. She couldn't keep from speculating over the reasons for keeping on a property that no one visited. It had to be simply that it was an investment, and that the money from renting it out—if it *was* rented out—was a useful income for her grandfather. And of course, if it was rented out, then Caitlin and her family wouldn't have been able to keep popping down there to stay.

The logic of this possible explanation brought her a sense of relief. She let out a deep breath. Why had it been worrying her so much? Perhaps, subconsciously, it had just been yet another loose end for her to attend to, niggling away at the back of her mind. She had a tendency to examine everything, turning it over and over in her mind, working away at any puzzle until she found the solution, overthinking every simple occurrence. Knowing that didn't stop her wondering how long it had been since anyone had been in the house longer than the time it took to check the pipes hadn't frozen. Apart from Mrs Green, that is.

Nerves niggled in the pit of her stomach, so she gave herself a little pep-talk. She was just going down for the weekend, she'd be home again on Monday. No nee dot make so much of it, it was just one item on a list of stuff to deal with, and if she hated the place, she could soon get it on the market. And if when she arrived she found she didn't like the cottage, or if, say, it was damp or too small for her and her cousins and their partners to stay there this weekend, well then, they'd just have to stay in a hotel in the area. It was near the south coast, there would be dozens of hotels, guesthouses, and Airbnbs available. If need be, as a last resort, she could easily contact her cousins to let them know not to bother coming down. Everything, she reminded herself yet again, was going to be fine.

By the time she reached Southdean itself, the afternoon sun was fading, and day had already become evening. And already dark at only ten minutes past seven, it felt as if summer was gone forever, and autumn was truly taking a misty-breathed hold, even though it was not October for another week. There was a damp chill in the air, and as Caitlin parked the car behind a nice-looking pub, she was only too glad to grab her jacket and slip it on, feeling to make sure her phone was still in the pocket. She locked the car and headed into the pub, realising that in a few short weeks the clocks would go back and it would be even darker, colder. All downhill to the year's long-awaited end.

She shook her head to shake away the gloomy thoughts and went inside, the warmth and the noise a welcome change.

The food was good, the ambience perfect and she felt a slight reluctance to leave the bright noisiness of the pub to drive the last little bit of the journey to the cottage.

Outside an hour later it was even colder, darker, and she shivered as she walked back to the car. They had rooms here at the pub, perhaps she should book in for the night and go on to the cottage in the morning?

But no, she couldn't do that. She'd promised Michael and Laura that she'd phone them later tonight to tell them whether or not they would all be able to stay at the cottage.

She drove along dark twisting and unfamiliar lanes. Even with the best efforts of her satnav, she missed the turning for the cottage but had only gone a couple of hundred yards before she realised her mistake; it was easy enough to turn into field entrance, turn, and go back the way she'd come.

She followed the narrow lane carefully back, glad of the headlights' full beam as the trees on either side of the lane loomed overhead and almost met above her, making her feel as though she was travelling through a tunnel.

This time she found the entrance easily. A painted sign nailed to a gatepost showed her where to pull in. The part of the sign that had the name of the property had been broken off, leaving no indication of what the cottage had once been called. Not very helpful, she grumbled to herself. Caitlin slowed the car, turned in at the gate then came to a halt. It was very dark here, surrounded on all sides by trees. She reminded herself it was partly the gloomy weather and the time of day, most definitely not the location or the house itself that made it seem more than a little spooky.

She grabbed her bag and rummaged inside for the front door key, drawing her phone from her pocket and turning on the torch app to find her way safely to the door without twisting an ankle. As she drew nearer to the cottage, with relief she noted that the overarching trees seemed to fall back from the path, leaving a clear area in front of the building. And there it was:

A chocolate-box cottage of beams, whitewash, thatch, with roses and ivy in a tangle together scrambling up the left-hand corner and across the centre of the house, spreading out to frame windows upstairs and down.

With a shock of realisation, she recognised the cottage now.

She fumbled to fit the key in the lock and was relieved that it turned easily and with a loud and very definite *thunk*. She pushed the door open and bent to grab her handbag and her holdall.

She shone the light from her phone inside the door, searching for the expected light-switch. The entrance hall was inky black and forbidding. No light shone in from the deserted lane. She told herself if she couldn't find the light-switch, then she was simply going to get straight back into her car and return to the pub and wait until the morning to explore or take possession of the cottage. Why hadn't she come to the house first before going for her meal? Hindsight, as always, came just that little too late. If she'd planned it a little better, she could have found her way in the last vestiges of daylight instead of fumbling like an idiot in the complete darkness.

But to her relief, the switch was right there. She pressed it down, there was a reassuring click and the hall was illuminated by a somewhat inadequate single bulb. Only then did she step across the threshold and close the front door behind her.

The hallway was far longer and wider than she had expected, practically a room in its own right.

As she stepped inside and set her bags down, she looked around. She couldn't tell if these were half-forgotten memories surfacing after many years or if she was just registering the common details of other old country cottages such as she had seen on TV or in magazines.

There were stone tiles or flags on the floor, with a large rug faded into soft pinks, browns and golds spread across them to create a warm and cosy feel to an otherwise gaping, chilly space. A pair of upright chairs sat either side of a small occasional table bearing an old-fashioned big black telephone, and a small sofa covered in the same rich, burgundy-coloured damask as the chair seats was set back against the opposite wall which was white-washed with solid black beams the same as the exterior of the cottage.

She could immediately see that the stairs ran up behind that wall, rising from the right, but she didn't want to go up there just yet. First, she wanted to explore the rooms downstairs.

To her left was a doorway with one single step going down. As before, she paused before entering the room, groping with her hand for the light switch on the wall beside the door. Lights glowed into warmth, brighter in here than in the hall.

It was a long sitting-room with a tall, curtained window, or possibly doors, at the far end overlooking the garden. At least she assumed there was a garden. Peeking out now, she saw that it was much too dark to make out anything more than the vague shapes of tall shrubs or trees against the not-quite-black sky.

At this end of the room, there was a window with a padded window-seat beneath it, the cushion of which was covered in the same burgundy damask she'd seen in the hall, but this time with the addition of some decorative gold-threaded needlework.

These colours, the deep red and the gold, were repeated here and there throughout the room, so that in spite of the white walls and the black beams, the room retained a cosy feel. Another rug covered this floor, and like the hall rug it appeared old and faded yet still held some mellow tones. Where the floorboards were visible around the edges of the rug, these were stained to the colour of honey. She wondered if the original flagstones lay beneath these boards.

There was a large fireplace, and the grate was laid out ready for a new fire, whilst a wicker basket beside the grate was full of chopped wood and crumpled sheets of newspaper. The brass surround of the fire gleamed, as did the tongs and poker that hung on brass hooks that had been knocked into the wall. Now she noticed with a sense of gratitude that there wasn't a speck of dust anywhere. Clearly Mrs Green knew her stuff and did it diligently.

Forming the other three sides of a square with the fireplace, three sofas had been positioned, upholstered in the same damask as the window-seat cushions and other chairs. In the centre there was a wooden coffee table with a clean, polished top. To one side, between the fireplace and the tall window at the far end, there was a half-empty bookcase. That was the entirety of the furniture in the sitting-room.

There were no pictures on the walls, no vases of flowers, no ornaments, no family photos in elegant frames to grace the mantelpiece. This place will be a doddle to inventory, she decided, but it didn't look as though there would be much in the way of knick-knacks for herself or the cousins to keep as mementoes if they wanted to do that.

Her phone beeped in her jacket pocket, and she pulled it out in time to see the notification on the screen stating that *Henry Jago Phwoargoeous Solicitor Extraordinaire* had messaged her. With a grin, she decided she'd have to change the name she'd given him before someone else saw it. Imagine if Henry himself saw it! OMG!

His message ran: *I wondered if you had decided when you were going to go down to view the cottage in Sussex yet? Sorry, I should have said, this is a message from Henry Jago, solicitor. Please do feel free to let me know if you require any further assistance.*

She immediately texted back: *Hello Mr Jago. As a matter of fact, I'm there right now. I've just arrived from London a few minutes ago.*

She smiled to see that he immediately sent another text. Had he been waiting to hear back from her?

Oh interesting. And what do you think of the place? Do please call me Henry.

In reply, she said: *Not sure yet. It's a bit gloomy. It might look better in daylight, though I'm not too sure.*

Ah. Shame. Not a keeper, then? he responded immediately.

I'll have to think about it. Your Mrs Green has done a brilliant job keeping it clean and tidy.

Good. Glad to hear it. Well, I'd better let you go. As I say, do let me know if I can be of any service. H.

Feeling vaguely disappointed that it appeared to be the end of the conversation, she sent him a thumbs up emoji then shoved her phone back in her pocket.

Returning to the hall, she crossed to the opposite doorway that ran under the stairs, again feeling for the light-switch and found herself in a sparsely furnished dining-room.

The room was a small square, with two doors on the far wall, and one small window giving out onto what was presumably a view of the garden at the side of the house.

In the centre of the room stood a large oak table, very similar in appearance to the one in Gramps' kitchen in the terraced house in London. There were four chairs arranged around the table, one on each side, with a further two chairs standing back against the wall in case the table's central leaves were opened up to accommodate additional diners.

The bare walls and surfaces seemed more noticeable in here, and the rough, whitewashed surface coupled with the lack of furniture made the room seem cold and unwelcoming. The stone-flagged floor echoed her every step, no colourful rug here to soften her tread.

She crossed the room to the two doors on the opposite wall, reflecting that the room only needed a few candles or some cushions and so on to give the room a nice warm glow, to soften the harsh lines of the black beams against that ubiquitous whitewash. Something to think about if she kept the house either to live in or to rent out.

She opened the door on the left and as she reached to find the switch to turn on the light, she caught sight of a movement directly in front of her in the dark.

She screamed.

Immediately the light flooded the room with brilliance, she realised her mistake and laughed a little hysterically, feeling foolish. Relief rushed in as she saw it had been her own reflection in the glass of the kitchen window ahead that had scared her.

She stood there clutching the door frame and took a few deep breaths, glad no one else was there to see her make a fool of herself. Finally calm, she stepped into the room to look about her. It was a kitchen, very old, and not particularly practical or pleasing to the eye by modern standards. It was just about functional, she thought, and she could probably put up with it for a day or two, although it would definitely be the first thing to be remodelled by whomever ultimately purchased the property.

Yet it felt so warm and familiar. She leaned back against the door frame and looked around her. In her mind's eye she saw a well-scrubbed wooden table in the corner and herself drawn up to it on a big chair, her legs dangling. There were cereal bowls, white with a broad royal-blue stripe and a big fat milk jug in the same pattern. She remembered a woman, dark-haired, standing at the sink in a ruffled apron, yanking on the pump handle to draw ice-cold water to fill a kettle which she set on the stove to boil.

I know I've been here before, she thought, but that's a new memory, and so vivid. She tried to remember more, but the image had gone, the spell broken, and this was just an old shabby kitchen. She crossed to the sink. The pump had gone, replaced by a modern mixer tap above a huge Belfast sink, presumably fed by a decent supply of hot water from the gas boiler in the corner on the far wall.

Beyond the sink a half-glazed wooden door led outside. But she didn't bother to unlock it, it would be pointless right now; she could look at the garden in the morning.

She returned to the dining-room and the other door. She opened it, felt a draught of cold air seep out over her, and she put on the light, mentally reminding herself not to freak out if she caught her reflection in a window in this room too. She found a room not quite as big as the kitchen or the dining-room, but still a decent size. It was completely bare. There were no curtains at the window, no furniture, and no carpet. Just bare flagstones. And it was freezing in there. She saw that one small top window was slightly open, and in spite of her tugging at the handle, it refused to budge.

There was a fireplace. It had been swept clean, presumably by Mrs Green, but had not been laid ready to use again. The surround was not as grand or highly polished as the one in the sitting-room. The mantel was a solid black beam identical to those in

The Cousins

the other rooms though not so large; the grate was a simple iron one set into a brick alcove with a narrow flue above it. There was a battered blackened shovel, tongs and brush set on a stand.

The whole room had an air of sad emptiness, and Caitlin, feeling she had seen everything there was to see, was only too glad to turn and leave, putting off the light and firmly closing the door.

The sound of her own feet in the heavy silence was beginning to work on her nerves. She went back into the hall and hesitated at the bottom of the stairs. She felt for a light switch but couldn't seem to find one and there was not enough light from the hall to see it. She needed the torch again. As she began to rummage in her pocket again for her phone, it startled her by suddenly ringing, and she dropped it on the floor. Luckily it hit the edge of the rug and the screen wasn't damaged.

The screen showed, *Laura calling* and so when Caitlin had quickly swiped her finger across the screen, she said a breathless, 'Hi Laura!'

She heard Laura chuckle. 'You sound out of breath! Did you have to run to get to the phone?'

'Yes,' Caitlin fibbed, trying for a light-hearted chuckle, not wanting to admit her nerves were rattled.

'Are you at the cottage yet? What's it like? Do you still want us to come down tomorrow? Or not?'

'Oh God. Erm—yes—yes, I'd love you to come down...'

'You sure? You don't sound convinced. Is there something wrong?'

'I only got here a few minutes ago. Traffic. I don't know why I didn't leave London earlier to make sure and get here in daylight. It's fine, it just feels so creepy being here all on my own in a strange house. I don't want to tell you guys to come down here for nothing, but...'

'What?' Laura prompted.

'I know it sounds really stupid, but I think I'm too scared to stay here tonight. I think... Yes, that's what I'll do, I'll go back to the pub where I had dinner earlier and stay there tonight then come back here in the morning when it's a bit brighter and a lot less *Nightmare on Elm Street*. Sorry. I have to say the place is pretty empty—just a few basic items of furniture, and old at that. But not in a good way.'

'Maybe there's an attic?' Laura suggested. 'Or a cellar? Maybe all the old junk has been shoved into the cellar out of the way?'

'A cellar. Or an attic,' Caitlin said with a shaky laugh. 'Just what every bijou residence needs.' She looked around her at the shadows and blank windows. 'Great. Er, look, I'd love you all to see the place, so why don't you come down as planned? You can come and take a look around, and then it might give us all a sense of closure, and we'll have seen the family seat, as it were. Maybe you four can come up with some suggestions about what I should do with the place?' She felt as though she was babbling and made herself shut up.

'All right, Caitlin, we'll see you tomorrow. Don't sweat it. Go and find yourself a nice, noisy pub to stay in and we'll see you at about eleven o'clock tomorrow. Is that okay? Nighty night.'

They said goodbye, and Caitlin stood there a moment looking around her. She took a few photos and sent them through to her friends, with the caption, *Spooky as hell! Going to a pub for the night. Coming back in the daylight tomorrow. Hopefully the ghosts will have gone by then!*

It wasn't even a quarter to nine, but it felt like the

middle of the night. Feeling ridiculous, she steeled herself to go back to the dining-room, the kitchen and the sitting-room, turning off all the lights again, and then finally she turned off the hall light, grabbed her bags, jumped outside, banged the door shut and locked it, and almost ran back to her car.

The radio came on as soon as she started the engine and the haunting melody of Sade's *No Ordinary Love* made her leap out of her skin, swearing as she bit her lip. Normally that was one of her favourite songs, but now she snapped the radio off, backed the car around so she could drive out into the lane nose-first, and she headed back to Rottingdean, civilisation, and the pub she had only left thirty minutes earlier.

*

Chapter Six

The pub's bedroom was a reasonable price and very comfortable. Caitlin had a good night's sleep, though by the following morning she felt beyond ridiculous for letting childish fears get the better of her.

What had she been thinking? If only she hadn't blurted it all out like a moron on the phone to Laura. She cringed at the memory of it for the zillionth time over her breakfast. What must Laura have thought of her? And what would she have said to hubby Gareth or to her brother and his partner? Were all four of them laughing at her, thinking her flaky and over-imaginative? She was dreading seeing them again, especially Michael, the super-confident salesman.

She finished her bacon sandwich and coffee, paid her bill, and loaded her stuff in the car to drive back to the cottage.

The sun was still not shining but at least there was actual daylight. Surely the house would look better now? She wouldn't need to stand in the doorways, groping for a light-switch so she could see where she was going or enough to enter one of the rooms.

As she pulled into the little parking area in front of the cottage, she could see all the lights were on in the house. Had her cousins arrived much earlier than expected? But if so, how did they get in?

She left her luggage in the boot of the car and just grabbed her phone, hurrying to the front door and reaching for the handle. The door swung open and, surprised, Caitlin stepped inside, calling out,

'Hi guys! I didn't expect you this early!'

There was no answer, and she went from room to room downstairs but found no one. She was puzzled. The house even *felt* empty, and now she remembered that of course, there had been no cars outside when she had arrived.

Of course, she suddenly thought, Mrs Green! Relief flooded her. Presumably Mrs Green had received Caitlin's message and thinking Caitlin might be arriving this morning, she had popped in from some nearby house to put all the lights on and make the place a bit more welcoming. Though it was a shame she hadn't stayed long enough to say hello and set Caitlin's mind at rest about the front door being unlocked and all the lights on.

Caitlin was back in the hall now. She halted at the foot of the stairs, peering up. There was now no reason why she shouldn't go upstairs and check out the rest of the house.

But she continued looking up the stairs. They seemed almost as dark and forbidding as they had done the evening before. But at least she could now see the location of the light-switch.

She clicked it. Nothing happened. She clicked it a couple more times, then realised. Of course, with all the other lights are on, this one should be on too.

Clearly then it was a simple matter of replacing a lightbulb that was either broken or missing altogether. Nothing serious. Nothing to get worried or upset about. No reason not to go up to the nice bright rooms above and have a good look round.

She couldn't stand here like a baby, like an idiot, she had no choice but to force herself to go up the stairs in the half-light.

'Right then,' she said, but softly.

She took a deep breath, annoyed with herself for being such a coward. She took the first step, then second, and then it seemed a bit easier. The stairs didn't creak, nor did they echo her steps alarmingly: the thickly cushioned carpet muffled all sounds and made everything seem normal and comfortable.

Halfway up the steps she suddenly wondered why the front door had been unlocked. Surely even if Mrs Green had wanted to make the place bright and welcoming for her and her cousins, she would have still locked up when she'd left?

At the top of the stairs, Caitlin found herself in a square open landing, with a small window on either of the two long sides of the building looking out to the front and to the back of the house. Even without the lights on, it was light and airy up here, though the light didn't penetrate down into the dark stairwell very efficiently. The huge space was open right up to the roof, and all decorated in the same way as the rest of the cottage, with whitewashed walls and black beams which gave a much-needed sense of brightness.

It was clear there would be no attic or loft space though, as the ceiling was the roof. So maybe there's a cellar, Caitlin thought, and didn't know if that was better or worse than the idea of having an attic to tackle.

At either side of the hallway, on the short walls of the cottage, were the doors leading to the two bedrooms and a bathroom. She would look at them in a moment, she decided. She continued to mentally make note of what she could see, trying to ignore the prickling of her senses and the urge to just get out now and never come back. When had she become such a wuss?

There was an old chest beneath the landing's front window, with a long lace doily on top upon which stood a vase of dried flowers of uninspiring, somewhat faded colours. There was a little rug in this area but otherwise the place was bare and the boards uncarpeted; her footsteps echoed loudly as she crossed the space to reach the furthest door.

It stood partially open, and through the crack she could see the end of a bath, with the taps, and the chain of the plug hanging straight down. The bath appeared to be full of water. An eerie silence was broken every few seconds by the loud dripping of one of the taps. Why was the bath full?

Silence enveloped her, broken only by the regular *drip drip drip* of the tap. She felt paralysed, too afraid to move, for no real reason.

She stood by the door, with her hand on the pink-glazed finger-panel above the handle. Taking a deep breath, she steeled herself then pushed the bathroom door wide open, staring at the bath with terrified eyes, half-expecting to find someone drowned in the bath.

It was empty.

This was ridiculous. *She* was ridiculous, she told herself.

Again, annoyed with herself for letting her nerves get the better of her, she stepped briskly across and yanked the chain to pull the plug out of the hole and the chilly water began to drain noisily away. The ordinary sounds helped to steady her nerves once more.

Drying her fingers on her jeans, she turned, left the room and still with that brisk impatience with herself, went to throw open the next door. This revealed a large pleasant bedroom, complete with generously-proportioned double bed, made up with fresh linen and a cosy-looking counterpane. There were rugs on either side of the bed, and another chest similar to the one in the hall bearing another vase of dreary dried flowers occupied the place at the foot of the bed.

There was a modest, clean fireplace, with an old cauldron full of chopped wood and newspaper, and a box of matches on the mantelpiece. Beside the window there was a clean, well-polished rocking chair with two brightly coloured cushions.

'Nothing scary about this at all,' she told herself aloud, partly with a sense of relief, and partly for the reassurance. She turned to go back across the hall to fling open the remaining door to reveal a second bedroom the image of the first but a little larger. Even the décor was the same colour, with an identical chest and vase, a rocking chair and two cushions. Perhaps not very exciting or glamorous, but everything was clean and pleasant. Suitable for the cousins to use for a night or two.

The ordeal over, she turned back to go back downstairs, feeling a sense of accomplishment, feeling relaxed now. Then she halted at the bottom of the stairs.

The front door was standing wide open.

She came forward slowly and looked outside expecting to see her cousins or the cleaning lady in the process of arriving. The drive was still empty apart from her own car.

'Hallo?' called Caitlin.

She hurried to shut the door and did yet another walk-through of the house, but just as before, no one else was there. This time, her rattled nerves remained unsettled. She tried to think of explanations. Clearly the house was a little 'quirky', so possibly the catches didn't work properly on the door but no doubt she would get use to that in time and remember to make sure the door was properly closed every time it had been opened. No one responded to her call, for which she was grateful, but the sound of her own voice cutting through the silence restored her confidence again, and so to continue bolstering that confidence, she declared loudly to the house:

'Time to take a look at the garden, I think.'

She went through to the kitchen, then there was a short delay whilst she fumbled for the keyring and went through the small bunch to find a likely-looking key. She found it, slotted it into the lock, turned it, and was relieved to find it turned easily and without any melodramatic screeching. The door swung open inwards.

She stepped through and saw ahead of her a long, wide expanse of lawn dotted with fruit trees and rose bushes, still with many blooms alive with colour, the same pinks and reds of the interior of the cottage.

But right in front of her was a courtyard which captured the now strongly shining morning sun beautifully, making a perfect picture. She was captivated and immediately went over to take a closer look.

There was an aged bench leaning back against the wall of the house in the full glory of the sun. In the centre of the courtyard was a well that was hung about with flowering baskets of summer flowers still blooming, and beside the well was a small round table with a couple of chairs.

Caitlin remembered the well as soon as she saw it. She remembered how as a small child she had been both frightened by it and fascinated. There was a heavy wooden cover over the mouth of the well, and another basket brimming with flowers reposed on top of this.

The bucket and winding handle had been removed many years earlier, but she was glad to see the brick and wooden canopy above the well remained, still in perfect order. The top of the well's wall was a little higher than her waist, but she remembered that when she was a small child, it had seemed very high, and she had stood on tiptoes, searching for toeholds with her sandalled feet, so she could lean up and drum her fists on the wooden cover with a delicious sense of daring.

Now she pulled out one of the chairs by the table and sat down. She dumped her phone on the tabletop, twisted round to settle her back against the warm brick of the wall, and gazed up at the cottage.

This would be a lovely spot for a cup of coffee, or a bottle of wine shared with friends, she thought. And just as she was thinking that, voices from the front driveway caught her attention. The sounds of car doors slamming told her they had arrived, and she went eagerly to greet her newly discovered relations.

They came in, all smiles and excitement, and immediately Caitlin's fears melted away.

With a slight sense of ownership, she showed them around the place, and they all exclaimed and commented favourably.

As she held back in the dining-room and allowed

the others to precede her into the kitchen and the empty room next door, Laura took her arm and in a soft voice said, 'So how are you this morning? Recovered from your nerves?'

She sounded concerned, and the fact that she had lowered her voice made Caitlin grateful for not being embarrassed in front of the others. She nodded and with a rueful smile, said, 'I think it was just my imagination getting the better of me. I must have been more tired than I thought by the time I got here.'

'Well, you've been through so much lately,' Laura reminded her, 'what with your grandfather passing away and having to make all the arrangements, then the funeral, and dealing with the house and everything, so, it's hardly surprising that you've got worn out. You probably needed the break. Maybe this weekend could be a chance for you to relax and recharge your batteries a bit?'

'Yes, you could be right,' Caitlin said. 'Now, what do you think of the house?'

'It's nice...' Laura said, but a little hesitantly. Caitlin looked at her closely.

'You don't like it?'

The others came back before Laura could answer. Michael immediately said,

'Who doesn't like it? Laura? Surely, you're not saying you don't love this gorgeous cottage?'

She hesitated again, clearly not wanting to say anything negative about the house.

'Well, I mean, it's just a bit...well, *old*.'

Michael laughed but Becka slapped him playfully, and said she agreed.

'It's a wee bit spooky,' she said to Caitlin.

'Nonsense!' Michael said. 'It's a lovely place. Just delightful. It's so clean and nicely kept. With none of that clutter you normally get in period properties. You know, you'd pay a fortune for a lovely place like this. It's the perfect retreat so many people are looking for. Erm—anyway, sorry, went off into salesman mode for a moment there. And sorry to interrupt, Caitlin, but did you say the door to the garden is locked?'

'Oh yes, here's the key,' Caitlin said, handing it over. She turned back to Laura, 'Actually, the garden is really nice. There's a lovely little courtyard.'

They all followed Michael out into the courtyard and stood there oohing and ahhing as they gazed about them.

'This *is* really nice,' Laura said.

Becka wrinkled her nose and pointed at the well. 'Is that a real well, or one of those pretend ones?'

'It's real,' said Caitlin. 'I remember it from when I was little. I was always a bit scared knowing that beneath that cover there was a long drop and then some deep, cold water. And there used to be a hand-pump in the kitchen to bring the water in from there. But obviously that was all done away with as there is a proper tap now.'

'God,' said Becka as if she could hardly imagine such a primitive way of life. 'I bet the water was freezing!'

'It was!' Caitlin laughed.

Michael said, 'It's not just the one tap now still, is it? Just one cold tap?'

Caitlin nodded. 'No, no, there is at least a boiler for the hot water, and a modern tap. But as for the rest, well, there will obviously be quite a bit of extra work to do to get that kitchen up to modern standards.'

He nodded thoughtfully. Then shrugged. 'It would be well worth it, though, from an investment point of view.'

'What's that door over there?' Laura asked. She pointed to a door in the wall a few feet away from the kitchen door. Caitlin hadn't noticed it before, but she immediately guessed what it was.

'Oh, that must be the cellar. Remember when we were talking last night, and you said there would be either a cellar or an attic? Well, there's no attic. So I'm guessing this is the cellar.'

Gareth jogged across to it and tried the handle. 'It's locked. Looks like a small yale key, if you've got one of those on the bunch?'

She had. She gave it to him and he ran back again to fit the key in the lock. It turned easily enough but the door had warped slightly, no doubt due to the damp weather and it took him and Michael a couple of minutes to prise it open. Caitlin and Laura had joined them when they finally pulled the door wide open to reveal a set of dark concrete steps leading down into the ground.

'Yes, this is it! The cellar.' Caitlin said but couldn't help a slight shiver.

'Oh no, you won't get me going down there!' Laura said and fastened her hand through Caitlin's arm. 'You men can go down there if you want, but us girls are staying right here.'

They gathered by the doorway, holding their breath to see what the men discovered.

Michael, equipped for all eventualities as any good estate agent should be, pulled a small torch from his pocket.

'Cissies,' he said with a laugh. 'There could be a really useful space down here if you got some electricity put in.'

He proceeded slowly down the steps, one hand on the wall to steady himself in lieu of a handrail. Gareth went down behind him, and as they went,

Michael said over his shoulder to his brother-in-law,

'Mind the step just here, the edge has crumbled away, I don't want you to slip and take us both right down to the bottom.'

'Be careful, for God's sake!' Becka snapped at them.

'That settles it,' Laura said to Caitlin. 'I'm definitely not going down there. Knowing me I'd probably trip and break my neck.'

Caitlin agreed she'd probably do the same, and she watched anxiously over Laura's shoulder as the two men carefully made their way down the steps in the dim torch-light and finally reached the bottom. They jangled through the keys, turning the torch this way and that to light them so they could see which one was the most viable candidate.

Laura was still gripping Caitlin's arm tightly, and her other hand hovered in front of her mouth as she watched her husband and her brother descend.

Caitlin was slightly irritated by Laura's tendency to grab at her and clasp at her all the time, especially as her display of nerves was jangling Caitlin's own just when she was fighting to keep control of them. Caitlin was just about to turn away when suddenly Laura gave a strangled little half-scream and yanked hard on Caitlin's arm.

'Oh my God, was that a *rat*? Oh my God!'

Caitlin hadn't seen anything, but Laura had a clearer view than she did. At the bottom of the steps Michael shone the torch around him, illuminating his feet.

'There could well be rats, ladies, so be careful when you come down. Also, the steps are not all that safe, so again, just take a little extra care.'

'It's okay,' Caitlin assured him. 'I think we'll just stay put up here.'

'Oh God, another one! Gareth, Michael, come back,' Laura called.

Gareth was glancing around warily and not looking too happy. He called up to his wife, 'Don't worry, love, we'll only be minute. Unless I see a rat, in which case I'll be back up there immediately!'

'What's down there?' Caitlin called. 'Anything interesting?'

Handing the torch to Gareth, Michael unlocked the door, and Caitlin heard a slight screech of hinges. There was a moment's silence as Gareth waved the torch around and they both craned their neck to see inside.

'There's nothing here,' Michael finally called back up to them. 'Unfortunately. Just a smallish room. They probably just used it to store extra fuel in winter. It's not very big, no light, no window and the floor looks a bit unsafe in places. Okay then, we're coming back up. A bit disappointing to be honest. What a shame.'

They locked the door, then turned and began to come back up the steps, moving more quickly now that their eyes were accustomed to the gloom.

'So nothing to get excited about then?' Becka asked from over Caitlin's shoulder, making her jump.

'Sadly no, but if Caitlin does decide to sell the cottage, it might be one of those little extras that appeals to would-be buyers. It could be converted into a nice little games room or gym or something. Or perhaps a nice wine cellar.'

They stood in the courtyard. Gareth locked the outside cellar door and handed the keys back to Caitlin.

Laura said, 'I suppose you haven't had a chance to think about that yet, have you?'

'Whether I want to sell the place?' Caitlin asked.

'No, I haven't really given it much thought. I suppose I will have to sell it. Sadly. I had kind of hoped it would be a dear little place and that I would fall in love with it.'

'Well, that might still happen, Caitlin,' Becka said. 'You just need to spend some time here, get to know it better. I bet it's gorgeous in the spring, with all the apple blossom and then in the summer you'd have the roses. And even in the winter—picture this courtyard and the trees all covered in snow, think how lovely they would look. Don't rush into anything.'

'Sorry to interrupt, ladies,' Gareth said. 'But I was wondering what we're going to do about somewhere to stay. There are only two bedrooms here, after all.'

'Well, I can't go back to the same pub tonight,' Caitlin told them. 'They've got a band playing there tonight and they've booked out all the rooms for the artists and the crew. I was thinking we could all stay here. You four could have the two bedrooms and I could sleep in the sitting-room on one of the sofas. What do you think?'

'We could do,' Laura said, exchanging a look with her husband, who gave a nod and a shrug. 'But are you sure you'll be comfortable enough on a sofa?'

'Yes, I'm sure I'll be fine.' Caitlin said. 'Anyway, it's only for a night or two. We'll need to pop out for supplies though—there's no working fridge and I'm not too sure about how to work the Aga either.'

'We could go out to a pub for a meal this evening,' Becka suggested.

Laura added, 'And we really only need a few bottles of water or something for this evening and tomorrow morning.'

'Water? Some beers or vodka more like!' Michael said, giving her shoulder a playful squeeze which made her wince and swat him in retaliation.

Becka looked a bit annoyed by his suggestion but any reply she might have given was lost as she happened to glance up at one of the bedroom windows, and pointed, exclaiming, 'There's someone in the house!'

They all glanced up and sure enough they could make out the outline of a head and shoulders, of a woman's long hair. The person was standing just by the window of the first bedroom.

'What the hell?' Gareth muttered, and with a nod at Michael, the two men ran into the house. The woman at the window hadn't moved. She appeared to be observing them from an oblique angle, as if she was next to the window and looking out sideways.

'Could it be the cleaning lady?' Caitlin suggested. 'There's a Katherine Green comes in from time to time. I did let her know we were coming. In fact when I arrived earlier...'

But before she could finish, Becka let out an agonised scream and, clutching at Caitlin for support, began to massage her ankle.

'What did you do?' Laura asked anxiously, hurrying to Becka's side. She and Caitlin supported Becka to one of the garden chairs. Above them, Gareth was opening the window and looking out, puzzled.

'There's no one here? It was definitely this room, wasn't it?'

At that moment Michael opened the window in the second bedroom and also leaned out, calling to Gareth. 'There's no one in here. It must be your room.'

'But that... that's crazy,' Gareth blustered, shaking his head, glancing about him in confusion. 'There's no one in here. Everything in here is perfectly normal. I'll go and check the bathroom.'

Caitlin was shaking her head and trying to make them listen, but they didn't hear her saying, 'If it was the cleaning lady, she's probably just come back downstairs.'

Michael was looking down at the women in the courtyard below.

'Was it this one or that one?'

Caitlin and Laura pointed to the other window. Then they bent to look at Becka's ankle but apart from a red mark on the surface of the skin and the fact that she was still in pain, Caitlin thought it didn't seem too serious. Becka rubbed the sore area. 'I think I must have just twisted it.'

Michael reappeared at the window where Gareth had been only a minute before. Gareth was now looking out of the bathroom window. They leaned out again so they could see each other and the three women, but they both shook their heads.

Michael said, 'Nothing here. Not a thing.'

'Oh my God!' Becka said in horror. 'That can only mean one thing—the house is haunted!'

*

Chapter Seven

They all trooped back indoors to the sitting-room. With all five of them there, the room seemed crowded. Caitlin wished there were a couple of extra armchairs; she felt a little too close for comfort to Michael as they squashed together with Becka on one of the sofas. Technically, she supposed, the sofa was a three-seater, but Michael was a big man with massive shoulders and a tendency to sprawl, so a bit more room would have been welcome.

But even then, she knew she would probably not feel comfortable. Not just because of feeling squashed, and not just because of the odd incident which seemed to have really upset Gareth, Laura and Becka. Caitlin thought the reason she felt so awkward was because the other four were two couples. They were all older than her, at least in their early forties, although she had already worked out that Michael must be slightly more. But they were such distinct couples, with the two women habitually clinging to the arms or necks of their partners, added to which they made such overly pronounced efforts to include Caitlin that she actually began to feel more excluded.

Later, she felt bored, too. They seemed to have nothing better to do than to sit all afternoon in the same place, just talking. No longe interested in looking over the house or garden, they all sat in the same spots for almost five hours and just talked. And not even talking about anything interesting. By five o'clock she didn't know any more about any of them than she had at ten-thirty that morning. They just talked about the weather or things they had seen on TV or the drive down to Sussex, or people they worked with. A host of minor and uninteresting topics.

She was aware she was becoming irritable and withdrawn. She just wanted them to leave. And she felt horrid because of it—compensating by guiltily trying to pay closer attention to the endless trivia.

It was obvious that they knew one another really well, and Caitlin had to remind herself to make allowances for that. But they seemed to have no interest in getting to know her or finding out anything about her, nor did they seem to want to share any meaningful information about themselves. Whenever she asked a question, it was partially answered, then somehow the subject was changed, and her original question was forgotten during the relating of a dull tale about someone she didn't even know, and most likely never would.

But they were so nice and so keen to include her in this dreary afternoon, she felt ashamed of her bad temper and churlish behaviour. She told herself she was just being irritable and expecting too much. It took time to get to know people, you couldn't expect to do it in a single afternoon. She tried to pay more attention to their long-winded stories about complete strangers and reminded herself to smile in all the right places.

Afternoon gradually became evening, and at long last the question arose once again of what to do about an evening meal.

There was a little mock-bickering between Laura and Gareth. Laura was trying to persuade him that he and Michael should go out and pick up a takeaway for everyone. Gareth was trying to get out of it, though it seemed fairly clear to Caitlin that he planned to agree all along, he just enjoyed irritating his wife. No one seemed able to get a decent phone signal to be able to order on any apps. Caitlin's phone battery was about to die, and she was conserving the last ten percent for any emergency that might crop up. She fumed to herself over forgetting her charger.

Meanwhile, Becka pulled off her shoe and pop-sock to examine her ankle. Michael massaged it for her and declared that she would probably need to be shot to put her out of everyone else's misery. Everyone roared with laughter at his 'joke', whilst Caitlin cringed and just wished Becka would put her shoe back on. From where Caitlin was sitting, the ankle looked perfectly normal but it was still too painful for Becka to put any weight on it, and every time she got up, which she did several times for no reason whatsoever, she hobbled about supported by Michael in a way that made Caitlin have a stern but silent word with herself about patience and people not all being the same.

In the end, just as Caitlin was beginning to think she could take no more wheedling and grumbling from Laura, Gareth agreed to take a run to the takeaway, and Laura said she would go with him to make sure he didn't mess up the order. Michael said he'd grab a lift with them and pop into an off license to get some beers and wine.

Caitlin wasn't sure if she liked the sound of that but as always, she didn't want to upset anyone so she just smiled, nodded and said she would be fine with whatever he brought back, and at the same time, wondering just how much they planned to drink. It made sense for Caitlin and Becka to stay behind. While Becka remained in her seat, Caitlin wanted to start a fire going as the house was cooling rapidly now the autumn day was drawing to its end.

As the others were leaving, Becka yelled, 'And don't forget chopsticks as there isn't any cutlery here!'

She turned sideways on the sofa to put her ankle up to rest it.

'I'm so knackered,' she complained, and at the same time she began to massage her forehead with her fingertips.

'Headache?' Caitlin asked, trying to be sympathetic even though she felt like shaking Becka to make her pull herself together and stop being so irritating.

'Yes, a terrible one. I get migraines, you see.'

'Ooh, nasty,' said Caitlin, thinking, of course you do. She was beginning to think Becka was one of those people who enjoyed ill-health. No doubt she had an entire repertoire of health problems.

'Oh it is. Sometimes when I get one of my heads, it lays me out for days. And sick—I get so ill when I have a migraine.'

'Yes, I've heard other people say...' Caitlin said, but Becka was warming to her subject now.

'And doctors can't do anything to help me, you know. I'm on that many different tablets, and then of course I'm very sensitive...'

Caitlin smiled sweetly. I'll just bet you are, she was

just thinking to herself, when from above their heads came an odd banging sound.

'What the hell...?' Becka said, sitting bolt upright. Caitlin was just thinking the same. They both sat up straight and listened.

The sound came again, a soft banging. Becka leapt to her feet with great theatricality and began to limp across to the hall, saying as she went, 'One of those stupid men must have left a window open and now it's banging. I'll just pop up and close it. Otherwise, that noise is going to drive me mad. With my head, I can't deal with banging.'

Caitlin belatedly realised she should offer to go, and she jumped up to follow Becka, trying to persuade her to go back and rest her ankle. Becka shook off her offer with a saintly smile.

'It's alright, honestly. I'm not in any really terrible pain, it's more of a niggling twinge. It will only take me a minute.'

There was another bang as she said this, and Caitlin, thinking, 'You're a niggling twinge,' let her go, turning back to attend to the fire, kneeling to put a few more bits of wood on the little licking flames and thinking what a lovely scent was giving off.

As she waited for Becka to return, Caitlin wandered over to the front window and was vaguely surprised to see two cars still parked outside, hers and Michael's, but then she remembered he'd said he would go with the others in their car. She just hoped they wouldn't be too much longer.

Becka was now hobbling back down the stairs. She grabbed at Caitlin's arm, groaning in pain as she reached the hall, and Caitlin found herself attending Becka back to the sofa.

'Was the window open?' Caitlin asked. Becka nodded.

'Yes, the window in the first bedroom, above here. Wide open it was and banging back and forth. But not to worry, I've closed it now.'

They sat in the deepening gloom, the only light coming from the fire. Seeing it was almost dark outside, Caitlin got up to put the light on, then she went into the hall to put the light on there too, to help the others find their way in when they came back. The bulbs weren't very powerful ones and the rooms still seemed rather dim. She returned to the sitting-room and sat back down on the other sofa opposite Becka.

Becka said, 'It could be nice in here, you know. It just wants a few homely touches, and a bit of colour.'

Caitlin nodded. 'True,' but then said, 'But I don't know if I'd really be happy here. It's just so...'

There came another violent bang from upstairs, making them both jump out of their skins. And as they both sat there, alert and listening, there came the sound of footsteps walking across the floor of the room directly above their heads, slowly and deliberately, then there was a silence as if the steps had halted, before walking back across the room again.

Caitlin felt chills running down her spine, and she looked down to see the little hairs on her arms were standing up on end. She wondered what to do, but Becka had no such concerns. She leapt up, her injured ankle forgotten, and with a shriek she ran to the door, saying, 'I'm not staying here. This place is definitely haunted! Oh my God, oh my God, I've got to get outside! It's not safe!'

But in the doorway to the hall, she stopped dead and with a panicked flap of the arms, she turned and raced back to collect the handbag she'd forgotten. She halted, looked at Caitlin and said, in a pleading voice,

'What shall we do? I don't know what to do. I mean, we can't stay here, can we? Not when things are walking around and opening windows. But...'

'Let's just settle back down,' Caitlin suggested. 'The others will be back soon, and then we can all decide what to do together.'

'Okay,' Becka said, with a glance at the ceiling. Then almost immediately she began fidgeting and darting anxious glances towards the hall. Caitlin's own nerves began to feel even more stretched taut. She fervently hoped the others would be back soon, she really didn't think she could cope with the house or Becka much longer. Especially Becka.

'Oh, I do wish they'd hurry up!' Becka wailed.

Caitlin murmured something in agreement but was drowned out by a sudden banging from above their heads.

'Oh-God-oh-God-oh-God!' moaned Becka in terror. She was huddled in the corner of the sofa now, hugging herself, wide eyes fixed on the doorway.

Caitlin didn't know what to do. She was pretty frightened herself and didn't want to go upstairs and investigate, but she felt so stupid just sitting there shivering with fear. She hoped and prayed the others would be back soon, but by her watch they'd only been gone about twenty minutes. Surely they'd be at least the same amount of time again, if not more?

Footsteps again walked slowly and deliberately across the floor above them.

'No wonder this damned house has been empty for years,' Becka whispered. 'You'll never sell this place. You couldn't let anyone buy it without telling them. Something really horrible must have happened here.'

Caitlin was about to refute that, gently, by saying

that it was just old and a bit creaky, but then a voice popped into her head. Gramps lying in his hospital bed, just before he died. Without thinking, Caitlin said, 'Whatever happened to the boy?'

'What?' Becka asked, suddenly, as if pouncing on Caitlin's thoughts.

Caitlin shook her head. 'Nothing. Sorry. Just... I don't know. I mean, I don't remember ever hearing anything weird about this house, no rumours, no stories. Except...'

'Except what?'

'Just before Gramps died, when I was sitting with him in the hospital, he woke up and saw me, and he said...'

'For God's sake! What did he say, Caitlin? Please, you've got to tell me!' Becka begged her, rocking in her seat, her hands clenched in her lap. She looked close to tears, Caitlin thought, and no wonder, they were both feeling the stress of this place. And in the tiny, tiny pause before Caitlin could reply, the footsteps walked back across the room above their heads again. Becka's eyes, wide with fear, stared up at the ceiling again as if tracing the movements above their heads.

Caitlin tried to suppress a shiver but failed. 'It can't be haunted,' she said, though more to herself than to Becka. 'It just isn't possible. There's no such thing...'

'What did he say, Caitlin? You have to tell me!' Becka pleaded and slipped across the gap to sit next to her on the sofa, grabbing Caitlin's arm. 'Please!'

'Becka, it's not anything very...' Caitlin sighed. Then she just gave up, and pushing aside her fear, she said, 'He'd been asleep, and when he woke, he saw me sitting there, and he thought I was my grandmother—his dead wife—apparently I resemble Isobel quite a lot. And he said... oh, it's probably nothing really... but he said, 'You didn't say anything about the boy?' That's all.'

"The boy?" Becka was puzzled.

A bang from upstairs made them jump, repeated immediately by another. Caitlin, trembling but determined, half-rose, saying, 'Don't you think we ought to—if we go together...'

'No!' Becka almost leapt to her feet, but sat back down again, perching on the edge of the sofa. 'No. We should wait for the others. Please don't go, Caitlin.' Becka pulled Caitlin back down onto the sofa beside her and again gripped her arm tightly, ensuring Caitlin couldn't leave. She reached forward to massage her ankle with her one free hand. 'It's too painful for me to keep moving about. But tell me about the boy. What boy? It doesn't make any sense.'

Caitlin reluctantly had to agree. It really made no sense at all, it felt like just half of a story, like a one-sided phone conversation overheard. 'He wasn't in any fit state to explain himself, he was just rambling really, I mean, he *was* dying. Just that he thought I was Isobel, and he said something like, do you remember when we were young, then he said about the boy, that she hadn't said anything about the boy, had she. Oh and then, oh sorry, I'd forgotten this bit, then he said, 'I know you didn't tell anyone, just like you promised. No one knows.' It just sounded super mysterious, that's all.'

'A boy as in a child? Or what? Was it a childhood friend? Never told anyone what?' Becka asked, still puzzling.

With a touch of irritation, Caitlin repeated, 'Like I said, I don't know, it wasn't clear. All I can do is tell you what he said. I don't know what it meant. It was just a bit weird, that's all.'

'Hmm. I suppose so.' But Becka didn't really sound

convinced, and she was obviously losing interest in the story now.

There was another spate of odd creaks and soft thumps from upstairs, and Becka suddenly burst out again with, 'Oh God! I can't stand it! Let's wait outside for them. I don't care if it's dark or cold. I'm so scared in here! I can't take it anymore!'

'No, it's okay,' Caitlin said, patting her arm. 'They'll be back soon and we're better waiting in here where the light is on, rather than outside in the cold. Just hang on, it won't be long now.'

In fact, it was just a few minutes later that the cone of light from the car's lights swept across the hall and into the sitting-room, beaming across the ceiling, and almost immediately the banging of doors announced they were back, and it felt as if everything was all right again.

A huge wave of relief washed over Caitlin as she hurried to follow Becka out into the hall to greet the others as they came in the front door.

Michael stopped dead, which meant Laura and Gareth, arms full, careered into the back of him and cursed.

'What's happened?' he asked, ignoring the others behind him. Laura's protests fell silent, and she glanced from Caitlin to Becka and back again, awareness lighting up in her.

'What?' she demanded of her brother. 'What do you mean, what's happened? Why would anything have happened?'

Becka broke into overwrought sobs and flung herself into Michael's arms. 'There was a ghost.' She sobbed with the abandon of a child.

Caitlin, still awkward with these near-strangers, watched this from the sitting-room doorway. Michael hugged Becka as she wept on his shoulder. He patted her back soothingly, and over her head, his eyes met Caitlin's.

'What is all this?' he demanded, and his tone made Caitlin feel defensive, as if he somehow blamed her for not taking care of his partner. She shrugged, folded her arms over her chest and said,

'We heard some odd noises, that's all. And a window was open and banging.'

But before she could elaborate, Gareth, on his way through to the kitchen with the takeaway bags, said over his shoulder, 'Bloody nonsense.'

Becka sobbed even harder and between sobs managed to gasp out, '...N–not n-nonsense...we heard f-footsteps. And b-banging. Upstairs. B-but n-no-one there.'

Michael began guiding her through to the sitting-room, shushing her gently and murmuring to her. Laura hung back in the hall, setting down a couple of bottles of wine on the telephone table, and taking Caitlin's arm, said in a low voice,

'Seriously? Did something really happen while we were out?'

Nodding, Caitlin told her everything that had happened, and Laura's eyes grew large and anxious. When Caitlin had finished, Laura rubbed her hands over her eyes and forehead in a gesture of worry.

'God, it sounds horrible. I'm surprised the two of you didn't run out into the lane to wait for us.'

'It's a bit too cold and dark for that,' Caitlin told her. 'Though we thought about it.'

'Shall we go upstairs together, you and I, just to check everything's all right?' Laura suggested. 'I mean, it's okay if you don't want to, but I don't want to go up there on my own, yet we really ought to make sure everything's all right.'

'Well, I...' Caitlin was reluctant but then thought better of it, and said, 'Yes, sure, that might be a good idea, let's just take a quick look. If nothing else, it might set my mind at rest.'

'Mine too. At least you're not going to be sleeping up there tonight.'

'True.'

'No offence,' Laura said at the foot of the stairs, 'but I'm not exactly looking forward to spending the night here as it is, and if it's haunted, well, you can forget it. I'll make Gareth drive me back into Rottingdean, and if we can't find a pub or a guesthouse, I'll happily sleep on the beach or even in the car if it means I don't have to stay here.'

By now they were near the top of the stairs. Caitlin felt butterflies crashing about in the pit of her stomach, and she was trembling, yet scolding herself yet again for being an idiot. There couldn't possibly be anything to be scared of, that was just ridiculous.

Laura, one step in front, hesitated, and Caitlin, seeing her querying look, pointed to the left, saying in a whisper,

'It came from that one.'

'Right. Here goes nothing,' Laura said, and grabbing Caitlin's arm, stepped forward, her hand outstretched for the door handle. She gripped it, turned it, and together they warily pushed the door wide open. An icy blast met them. Laura reached out to turn on the light. Immediately they saw the window was standing wide open. Laura seemed relieved. She let go of Caitlin's arm and hurried across the room to close the window.

'Well, I'm not surprised there was banging,' she said. 'It's that window that was making all the noise, caught by the wind.'

Caitlin joined her by the window and examined the

catch. 'Yes, but Becka came up and shut it. So how did it get open again?'

Laura turned to give her an appraising look. 'She closed it?'

'Yes, she did.'

'And afterwards, both of you still heard banging?'

'Yup!'

'Oh my God! That's...' She halted abruptly as if having second thoughts. Then, 'But maybe the catch is loose or...'

'It's not, I just checked it. It's actually quite stiff,' Caitlin said.

They spent a couple of minutes experimenting with opening and closing the window. It didn't matter what they did, they couldn't get the window to open by accident. They stared at each other.

'And in any case, that doesn't explain the footsteps,' Caitlin said.

Laura looked panicked. '*Footsteps?*'

'Didn't you hear Becka telling Michael? When we were sitting downstairs, we could hear footsteps coming from up here, they were going across the room, pausing, then going back to the window again.'

'That's enough! Let's get out of here.' Laura turned abruptly and practically ran to the door. The door slammed shut just as she reached it. Laura let out a squeal of surprise and wrenched frantically at the handle, but she couldn't get the door open.

'It's locked!' she said, her voice rising in fear.

'What?' Caitlin ran to her side and pounded on the panel of the door.

'Michael! Gareth! We're locked in! Michael! Help! Gareth!' Laura yelled.

They heard the sound of someone running up the stairs, heard their approach along the hallway then Caitlin pounded again so they knew which room they were in.

'It's okay,' Michael called through the door, sounding surprising nearby. 'You can come out, there's no one here but us.'

Laura wrestled with the door handle again, sobbing with fear and frustration.

'It's still locked, Michael. Stop messing about and unlock the bloody door! I want to get out of here!'

Michael's voice was one of surprise as he said, 'But there's no key in the lock on this side. I thought it must be on your side.'

'For God's sake, why would we lock ourselves in, you effing idiot? We'd hardly be stuck, would we?' Laura snapped.

'Ah, erm—no, no I suppose not.' He sounded a bit sheepish. 'But then where's the key?'

'I don't care where the... Just break the bloody door down!' Laura snarled. 'Get me out of here! Now!'

'What? But—well, Caitlin, what do you think?'

'It's all right, Michael,' Caitlin called through the door. 'You can break the door down if you have to.'

Laura tried the door handle again and this time there was a click and the door slid gently open.

The two women gaped at the other three on the other side of the door.

'Wh–what happened?' Michael asked, confused.

'I don't know—it was locked fast, but then it just—opened.' Laura said.

Gareth began turning the handle this way and that. The catch didn't stick once. He drew the key out of the lock and examined it. 'There's nothing odd about it. I don't understand what happened?'

Laura broke into overwrought tears and Becka, pushing past the men, wrapped an arm round her and led her downstairs, murmuring soothing words no one else could hear.

Caitlin and Michael looked at each other. Caitlin didn't know what to say, but she felt idiotic, suspecting he thought they had just become hysterical and girly and had somehow forgotten how to simply open a door.

'Let's go downstairs and get some food while it's still hot, maybe things won't seem so bad once we've eaten,' was all he said, and Caitlin was only too happy to go along with this. They left Gareth up there still testing the door.

In the kitchen Becka and Laura had started unpacking the take-away. Caitlin noticed Becka's hands were shaking as she carried out the task and Laura was still sniffing and dabbing at her eyes. She opened a can of beer, and as Caitlin watched, downed almost all of it in two long draughts.

They started to carry everything through to the sitting-room, Gareth reappearing now to take a six-pack of beers from Caitlin to lighten the load she was carrying, and he grabbed an extra beer for himself.

No-one alluded to the strange events for a while, until suddenly, whilst they were all concentrating on their food, there came the sound of a bang from upstairs and Laura, starting violently, dropped her food on the floor.

Becka gave a whimper and clutched at Michael, who set down his food on the coffee table to put his arms around her. He shot Caitlin a straight look.

'Is that what you heard earlier?'

She nodded. 'And then we heard the footsteps.'

'Not on my watch!' Gareth declared. He jumped up and ran from the room. They heard him bounding up the stairs then his steps paused, presumably on the threshold of the room. They heard a muffled curse from him, then the sound of him crossing the room followed by the banging of the window. Clearly it had been open again.

He started to come back downstairs, and immediately they heard another bang above their heads. Michael went into the hall to meet him coming down. The women heard Michael say,

'It's doing it again.'

'It can't be, I literally just shut the fucking window!' Gareth exclaimed.

'I'll come up with you,' Michael said, and they heard them go back upstairs, across the hall, into the bedroom, and across the room to the window. They heard the window being shut with some force this time, then the sound of their voices as they came back down again.

They hadn't even sat back down when there was another bang from upstairs.

'That's it!' shrieked Becka, on her feet. 'I'm going home! I'm not staying here another minute! Michael, are you coming?' She was grabbing her bag and her jacket.

There was another bang from upstairs. Becka visibly jolted, the shock forcing a curse from her lips. Michael seemed unsure what to do. He glanced at Caitlin.

'Well, I mean, what else did we need to do? I can't think... We've seen the house. There's not really anything else, is there? Or was there anything else you wanted me to do?'

'Michael! Come on!' Becka urged.

Caitlin shook her head. 'No, I just wanted all of you to see the place, but obviously it's not the kind of place to feel sentimental about. Was there anything any of you were interested in keeping, only...'

'No!' Becka almost shouted, then jolted again as another loud bang sounded from upstairs. But this seemed to calm her slightly and she had the grace to look a little ashamed. 'I'm so sorry Caitlin, you've been sweet, you really have, and I know this is not your fault, but I can't spend another second in this godawful house, I've got to get out. You do understand, don't you?'

'Of course I do, don't worry.' Caitlin rose to give Becka a hug, and suddenly they were all saying their goodbyes.

Michael invited Caitlin to go back with them, saying their home was only an hour and a half's drive away, but Caitlin declined.

'I'll stay in the pub again tonight and drive home in the morning,' she assured him. 'I think the sooner we get this place sold, the better. It's just a nightmare.'

'Such a shame,' Laura said. She gave Caitlin a farewell hug and kissed her cheek, promising to call her in a few days. Gareth also gave Caitlin a quick hug, wishing her a safe journey.

They carried out all the food containers and bottles to put it all into the boot of Laura and Gareth's car, poured water on the sitting-room fire, turned off the lights, came out of the house and locked the front door.

With a sigh of relief Caitlin got into her car, and watching the others to go ahead of her, she pulled out into the lane and turned back towards Rottingdean. With a flash of her headlights, she bade farewell to her cousins and turned to head into the town, as they turned in the opposite direction to head towards the motorway and the safety of their own homes.

Caitlin drove directly to the pub where she had spent the previous night.

*

Chapter Eight

Feeling edgy and exhausted, Caitlin pulled into the pub car park, noting as she did so that it was pretty packed. A huge van bearing the legend *Buns and Poses* on the side, along with a picture of an electric guitar reminded her why.

'Dammit!' she said to herself. Of course, the band! This was why she hadn't been able to book a room for tonight. She hesitated for a moment, unsure, then decided to at least get something to eat, her barely-touched curry was now cold and lying in the boot of someone else's car whizzing down the motorway at probably more like 80mph than 70.with just one chair

She locked the car and went into the pub. The landlord confirmed he had no vacant rooms available and that there was a forty-minute wait for food. She wasn't too worried about the wait, she was hungry but too stressed to try finding anywhere else to eat, craving the reassurance of noise and company. She found an empty table in a corner well away from the band, and she sat there with her half pint of cider and the pub's copy of the local newspaper, making a supreme effort to relax.

When her food finally arrived, a comforting homemade cottage pie with carrots and peas, she tucked into it with relish and was soon feeling much better. But the band was getting loud, and their supporters boisterous, so as soon as she had finished eating, she went back to her car.

She got in, turned on the engine, put on the headlights, fastened her seatbelt and then she stopped. Where the hell was she going to go?

She didn't want to go home to London. She had already promised herself a conversation with the cleaning lady Katherine Green the next morning, and she still hadn't made a full inventory of the furniture and other contents of the cottage.

The mere thought of returning to the cottage filled her with anxiety, but if she went round it really quickly in the morning, in broad daylight, hopefully she'd be in and out before any more odd or scary things happened.

She didn't want to drive all the way back to London only to return in the morning, even if it was only a two-hour journey each way. She didn't feel like driving all over Rottingdean or even down into Brighton to try to find somewhere to stay, though it was only nine o'clock at night. But it felt later, and she was tired. But she couldn't stay at the pub and could hardly sleep in the car park.

She recalled what Laura had said earlier about how she would sleep on the beach if she had to. Was that a possibility?

She headed the car towards the seafront. There was a long scantily-grassed area for parking. She pulled the car into a space, turned off the engine, unlatched her seat belt and tipped her seat back a bit. She grabbed her jacket and spent a couple of irritable minutes trying to arrange it over herself to give as much coverage as possible for a short garment. She closed her eyes, and after a little more fidgeting to get into a more comfy position, she was asleep.

A banging on her window woke her in a fright, and for a moment she thought she was in the haunted cottage again. But through heavy eyelids, she saw the face of a police officer peering at her. She opened her door a crack rather than turn on the engine to open her window.

'Sorry love, you can't sleep here. Regulations. I'm going to have to ask you to move on. Or else it's a hefty fine.'

She nodded, apologising, and casting aside her jacket, she righted her seat. Fumbling to get her seatbelt done up, she started the car. She dropped the window, the cold air helped her to wake up a bit. She gave the constable a rueful smile and wondered as she pulled away where on earth she could go. The glowing dial of the car clock showed that it was now a quarter past eleven—she had slept for almost two hours before being chased away, but now she was drowsy and slow-witted.

She couldn't face that drive home.

The cold air streamed in and revived her sleepy brain a little. She sighed and made the turning to go back through the little town. There was nowhere else to go. She could park outside the cottage and sleep in the car.

She drove slowly along the lane, it was too dark and unfamiliar to do more than crawl along, and she was glad she was going so slowly when a badger was suddenly right there in the road in front of her, shocked by the headlights, and even at that slow speed she had to brake to allow the animal to amble across the road and disappear safely into the hedgerow opposite.

As she made the turning into the driveway, she immediately saw something was wrong. There were lights on in the cottage!

She knew they had turned off all the lights. Out of sheer terror she almost slammed the car back into reverse and back out into the lane to head back to the bright lights—relatively speaking—of Rottingdean.

But then she saw the cars.

Michael and Becka, Laura and Gareth had come back to the cottage. Their cars were parked on the drive under the trees. She stared in disbelief. What the hell...?

Caitlin turned off the headlights. She left the car in the driveway entrance, and slipped out of her seat, and as she went, things began to assemble into a new shape in her mind. She crept across the grass and up to the cottage, keeping off the overgrown gravel in case it crunched under her feet, moving as quickly and silently as she could. When she reached the sitting-room window, keeping well into the shadows, she peeked through the ivy and rose leaves to look inside.

They were there, the four of them, laughing and talking, empty food containers littered on the coffee table. She couldn't hear what they were saying but they were all obviously perfectly relaxed and happy. Laura raised her glass of wine and said something, and the others laughed and raised theirs, clinking the glasses together.

'To us!' they cheered in unison and drank their toasts. 'And fuck Caitlin!'

Caitlin's first instinct, as she stood there watching them laughing at her expense, and drinking a toast to themselves, was to rush in there and confront them. But then as the first heat of her rage began to die away, it was replaced by a cold hard sense of betrayal.

And now she had to know *why*.

She watched them for a few more minutes, her emotions wavering as she tried to determine what to do next.

It was obvious that all the terror about the so-called 'haunting' was a lie. The noises, the window and door problems had to have been stage-managed somehow by her cousins, and it was equally obvious that they were all in it together. They had to be. The footsteps they'd heard from the room above their heads. Becka clutching at her, petrified. All lies. A charade.

What clever little actors and actresses they all are, she thought. Her anger began to build.

She remembered Gareth's outrage as he had raced upstairs to try to find a solution to the mysterious noises. Then there had been the so-called locked door of the bedroom. Clearly Laura had only been pretending not to be able to open it. Caitlin herself hadn't tried. If someone has their hand on the doorknob and says it won't open, she reminded herself, you believe them, don't you? You don't assume they are lying or somehow incapable of turning the knob. It was all a sham.

She felt overwhelmed by humiliation. She had been an absolute prize idiot. They had run rings around her, and she had been—ugh—so gullible, so stupid! The way Laura and Becka had both clutched at her, grabbing her arm, upset, even weeping with fear.

'And now look at them,' Caitlin muttered again.
The mysterious woman at the upstairs window. It had to be another of their ploys to frighten her, obviously.

She felt so many emotions all at once, she couldn't sort them all out. Hurt, betrayed, humiliated. How could they? And then, hard on that, yet again, *why*? Why had the four of them tricked her? Surely it wasn't just a stupid prank? They weren't kids, it had to be more than a mere joke. It had been a calculated, malicious attempt to get her out of the house, to genuinely frighten her and to make her leave.

But again, why? What possible reason could they have to do this to her? What had she ever done to them? She barely knew of their existence until a couple of weeks earlier. How had she hurt or injured them? What grudge could any one of them, let alone all of them collectively, possibly have against her?

Cautiously she retraced her steps, desperate now to get away without drawing attention to herself. They could not know that she *knew*. That would be giving away her only advantage. Even though she had no idea what this was all about, that much at least was patently clear. The slightest noise might give her away. And she couldn't bear to face them now that she knew how they had tricked her.

She sat in the front seat of her car, the door open, still not sure what to do. She had the urge now to drive back to London and stay there, in the safety and comfort of her own little flat.

A glance at the dashboard clock showed her it was now twenty-five minutes to midnight. Apparently, her cousins and their partners had decided to stay at the cottage after all. Even as she sat there, she saw a light go on in one of the bedrooms—the 'haunted' one—and almost immediately Becka appeared at the window to close the curtains.

It was a relief that Becka didn't happen to glance down and see an extra car parked there. Caitlin prayed she wouldn't be noticed, even though she was sitting very still there in the darkness.

The curtains were now closed, she felt safe again. But at any moment she could be caught. She had to get out of there.

Now, where to go?

When she had arrived yesterday, she had taken that wrong turn and been forced to pull into the gateway of a field to turn around to go back. If she was in luck, the gate might still be open, and the field still empty of livestock. She would pull in there and park up, then get a few hours' sleep in the car. Then in the morning she could decide what she was going to do about her cousins.

As quietly as possible, she reversed the car out onto the lane, thankful that there seemed to be a total absence of traffic on this road. Under the cover of the hedgerow, with the car now facing away from the cottage, she put on her headlights on low beam and drove the short distance along the lane until she saw the gap in the trees which marked the entrance to the field.

As she swung the car in off the road, she saw the field was empty except for the tall silent stalks of harvested maize, waiting to be cut down or ploughed in at some point in the near future. The stalks created a perfect screen for her arrival.

She pulled the car in parallel with the lane then killed the engine, leaving her window open a crack for ventilation. On one side, the trees, hedge and undergrowth shielded her from the road, and on two of her other sides, the maize provided cover. The remaining side was fine because it was away from the road.

Her anger and sense of betrayal had begun to die down now, leaving only a deep sense of hurt and a need to know the reason behind it all. She settled back in her seat and as before, arranged her jacket over her as a cover. She felt as safe as any small wild thing in its burrow and knew she could sleep safely for a few hours at least, it was unlikely anyone—especially her cousins—would find her there. In the morning, she would once again review the situation then decide what to do next.

As she closed her eyes, her phone began to ring. She fished in her bag for it and felt a jolt of dismay when she saw the words *Laura calling* on the screen.

For a moment she thought about ignoring the call. But then she decided she would answer, though her battery would no doubt die mid-conversation. She forced herself to sound bright and bubbly.

'Hi Laura! Is everything okay? Are you back home now?'

'Yes, we are, thank God! What a fucking nightmare! I've never been so glad to leave a place in my life. D'you know, up until now I've never even believed in ghosts! I'll never doubt again!'

'Me either,' said Caitlin, more fervently than she could have believed possible.

'So where did you end up staying?' Laura asked her.

'Oh, I finally found a little B&B on the outskirts of Brighton. It's a bit basic,' she said, feeling a twinge of guilt over the lie, but then she remembered her cousins' trickery, and hardened her heart. 'But it's only for one night, so I can put up with it.'

'Well, anything's better than staying at that hellhole of a cottage. Okay, well so long as you're all right.' Laura sounded as if she was genuinely concerned. Lying cow, thought Caitlin, and marvelled once again at what great actors they all were.

'Yes, I'm fine, and what about you?' Caitlin asked again. 'I'm so sorry you came all that way for nothing, not to mention all the strange stuff that happened. You must be so glad to be back home again?'

'Definitely. I'm never going back to that place again. No offence, Caitlin, but it's a ghastly place.'

'No, none taken, I completely agree with you,' Caitlin assured her. 'What a nightmare! I was so disappointed. I had really hoped it would be a lovely little holiday home for us all.' Then for effect, she added, 'I thought I would pop in there quickly in the morning on the way home, just for a last look round and to make a note of a few things.'

She thought she heard a soft gasp of dismay at the other end of the line, but she couldn't swear to it.

'Do you really think you should?' Laura asked. There was an edge to her tone, and Caitlin could almost hear the others nearby shaking their heads and trying frantically to get Laura to talk her out of it. Sure enough, Laura said, 'Oh Caitlin, you can't! You can't go back there all alone! It's not safe, I'm absolutely convinced! Please promise me you won't go back there on your own, I won't be able to sleep a wink tonight worrying about what might happen! Caitlin, please!'

Caitlin felt no compunction about lying through her teeth. She happily fell in with Laura's wishes, saying, 'Yes, actually, you might be right. I'd better wait until I can go there with an estate agent. Do you think Michael would still be able to handle the sale for me, after everything that happened today?'

There was a second's delay then Laura, sounding relieved, said, 'Oh, I'm sure he will. I'll ask him for

The Cousins

you if you like. Shall I give you a call back tomorrow?'

'Perfect!' And Caitlin thanked her and rang off. She sighed and sat there for a few minutes.

But now she needed the loo. She got out of the car and walked along the hedgerow for a few yards before squatting down to pee. Fortunately, she had a tissue in her jeans' pocket.

As she stood up and fastened her jeans again, she saw lights through the trees. She walked along a little bit further and realised what they were. It was the back of the cottage. The field ran along behind the rear garden. She stood there for a few minutes and then, feeling cold, she turned and went back to the car.

She settled down for a few hours' sleep.

It came eventually, but she didn't sleep well or deeply. She drifted in and out of uneasy dreams and woke at dawn to find she was cold and her neck stiff. Outside a light rain was falling.

She needed the loo again, then ran back to the car to grab her jacket, and turned to walk back along the line of trees and hedges until she could see the cottage. She pushed her way through the undergrowth until she reached the crumbling wall that enclosed the garden. Protected from view by apple trees and an evergreen of some kind, she jammed her toes into crevices between the bricks, just as she had as a child when she wanted to bang on the cover of the well, and she was able to wedge herself in a corner on the top of the garden wall, where she had a great if slightly patchy view of the back of the cottage through the foliage.

The curtains were all still closed, and she could hear no sounds of activity from indoors.

If only I had a cup of coffee, she thought to herself. And some stake-out doughnuts. She shivered a little and rubbed the sleep from her eyes. She fished her phone out of her pocket and swiped the screen. The time was almost a quarter to seven. And she had five whole percent of battery life. Use them wisely, she told herself.

The birdsong alone was worth getting up for, she had to admit. She stood a few moments to listen. She turned back to look towards her car, satisfied to see that from the road, it would be completely hidden from view.

Her thoughts wandered over and over the events of the day before. And no matter which way she turned or how she looked at what had happened, she still found the same question beating in her brain.

Why?

*

Chapter Nine

She prowled about restlessly before walking back to her car. But after sitting in the front seat for a while, bored but with nothing else to do, she returned to her vantage point peeking over the wall at the cottage. She was still fuming and upset but at a complete loss to know how to deal with the situation. She shrank from confronting them face to face, not being the type of person who enjoyed emotional situations, but had no clue as to the most calm, clear-headed way to deal with the situation.

A couple of times she made up her mind to storm round to the front door of the cottage and tell them exactly what she thought of them, and once she decided to just drive away, even getting as far as starting the engine of her car, but reason—or possibly fear or just plain old human curiosity—prevailed and she turned off the ignition again and sat there feeling defeated and stupid, gnawing her thumbnail as she tried yet again to decide on her next move.

A little after half-past eight, she finally saw and heard the first tell-tale signs of life from the cottage—water running in the pipes, curtains opening.

At about ten past nine, she raced to take refuge in her car from a downpour of rain, but could hear the sound of car doors slamming and engines starting up. The cousins were on the move. Doubtless afraid she would go back on her word to Laura and return to the cottage, they were making a timely getaway to ensure they didn't get caught.

Again she contemplated confronting them. She imagined pulling her car across the entrance to the driveway to block them in, action-thriller style, or simply tailing them along the lane to see where they went. But in the end, she just didn't bother. She couldn't bear the thought of seeing any of them again, they had betrayed her trust and colluded to make a fool of her. She was relieved they were going; she need never see them again.

She waited until she heard the two cars driving down the lane, waited another ten minutes for them to put some distance between the cottage and themselves, and then she drove back around to the front of the cottage.

She pulled in cautiously at entrance, even though she knew there was no one there, she needed to be extra sure. It was a huge relief to see the driveway was empty. The cousins had really gone.

The lights were off, the front door locked, the food containers and drink bottles all cleared neatly away. Apart from the slight scent of curry on the air, you'd never know anyone had been here, she thought, which was what they had obviously, *obviously* intended all along. She had half-expected to find the lights blazing and the door or an upstairs window unfastened as they had been the previous morning.

And now the penny dropped, and she understood about that too. Suddenly, the unlocked front door, the lights unexpectedly on, all the mysterious events, *all of them*, over the past twenty-four hours looked a lot less mysterious, and a lot more pathetically malicious.

Presumably the cousins had arrived a lot earlier than they'd admitted yesterday. Surely they had done so purposely to start setting up the 'haunted house' premise to scare her away? It could hardly have been a spur-of-the-moment silly prank. Which meant it had to have been planned in advance, and executed according to a precise plan, step by step, with all of them complicit in the project to scare her out of her wits. They'd have known she'd be unsettled or at least puzzled to find the lights on and the door unlocked, seeing that she hadn't left the cottage like that on Friday night when she went back to the pub. So this whole thing must have been their intention from the outset. Had they even driven past on Friday evening? Been aware of the time she arrived? Watched or waited to see what she would do, then returned first thing the next morning to carry out their charade?

All this planning meant there was malice here, and a serious sense of purpose. They had wanted her scared, wanted her to run away. But in any case, whatever they had done, it all came back to that same old question.

Why?

She went round the cottage, no longer scared now that she knew the cousins had been to blame for the 'haunting'. It seemed warm and quite cosy now. She moved around with confidence now that she wasn't afraid. She found the place was growing on her. She caught herself thinking of things she would like to do to it, of colour schemes, or possible renovations, even soft furnishings, and small mundane things like where to put her favourite cactus, Spike. Knowing she would have the money to carry out her fledgling schemes helped, of course.

Upstairs everything was just as neat and tidy as the sitting-room and kitchen. The windows were closed. Everything was in perfect order, and if she hadn't already seen with her own eyes that they had been there, she could not have found out. There were no signs that anyone had been there for the night; they had left the house just as she had found it on Friday.

For some time she stood in a daydream looking out of a bedroom window at the garden. She could just about make out the spot where she had stood watching only half an hour earlier.

From downstairs she heard the sound of a knock at the front door. For a moment, she felt all her old fears flooding back, but she went down and opened the door, peering cautiously around the doorframe, half-expecting to see Michael or Laura there wearing a big insincere smile.

'Caitlin?' said the older lady who stood there, smiling. 'My, but you're the image of your grandmother, it's real uncanny. I'm Katherine, Katherine Green, your grandfather's cleaning lady.'

As Caitlin beamed at her in welcome, much relieved, Katherine came into the cottage out of the rain, removing an ancient headscarf with seaside images on it and the slogan, *beside the seaside* as she did so, and shaking raindrops off on the step.

'I'm a bit later than usual,' she said. 'Because I saw the cars there and thought as you might have visitors. But they left quite early, didn't they?'

Pulling herself together, Caitlin agreed the visitors had left very early considering it was Sunday. She wasn't quite sure what else to say.

Katherine Green, 'Call me Kath, everyone does', was already bustling off into the kitchen and removing a thermos flask from her old-fashioned wicker shopping basket.

'Now, I don't know if you've had your breakfast, but I always like to start off with a nice cup of tea. Do you fancy a cup?'

Caitlin certainly did, but automatically she began to politely decline. The flask was one of those with both an inner and an outer cup, and ignoring Caitlin's protests, Kath poured them both a cup of steaming tea.

'Do you usually work on a Sunday, Mrs, er, Kath?' Caitlin ventured to ask.

'Oh no, but I can't come tomorrow, and I was hoping I'd catch you, in case there was anything you needed to ask.' Kath waved a hand around her head. 'So what do you think of the place, then?' She settled herself at the dining-room table, and Caitlin joined her.

'Is it haunted?' Caitlin asked immediately, wrapping her fingers about the little cup and as the heat seeped into her skin, realising now that she was not quite warm enough. But she'd left her jacket in the car and couldn't be bothered to go to fetch it.

Kath burst out laughing, a big comforting sound. 'Haunted? Bless you, love! I'm sorry to laugh, that's mean of me. It is quite an old house, that's true, but no, my lovely, it's not haunted. Nor has no-one ever died here except they was old and what my old granny used to call 'full of years'. Not sure what it means, but I always take it to mean having lived a good full life and being glad to be off at last. Something like that, anyway. Your grandmother died here, I suppose that's true, and she wasn't so terribly old, but neither was she no spring chicken neither and at least it was fairly sudden, no lingering on in pain for months or years on end, no sorrowing for her lost loved ones. It was your mother, wasn't it? And your father? You lost your parents at the same time, didn't you? I was so sorry to hear that. It must have been a terrible shock.'

'Yes, it was. Thank you for the tea, I needed that,' Caitlin added.

She was warming to Kath. She appeared to enjoy a good gossip, and Caitlin had the distinct feeling that Kath had stored up a lot of questions about her and was seizing the opportunity to satisfy a long-held curiosity. But at least she was straight and open about it. Plus, she had brought Caitlin a really good cup of tea.

'And now your grandfather too, I was sorry to hear about that,' Kath said, looking at Caitlin with shrewd eyes.

'Yes.'

'Does that mean you're all alone in the world?' She meant a partner, Caitlin knew, but didn't want to get into that.

'Apart from my cousins and their partners. It was the four of them who stayed here last night.'

'So where did you sleep, then? On the sofa?'

'It's a long story. But the house is definitely not haunted?'

'No, lovey, not at all. Don't you let anything like that worry you for a minute. Now do you want me to make a start? Or have you got things to do, because I don't want to get in your way, you know. I can always pop back a bit later. Whatever works best for you.'

'Honestly, now is fine. Please just do whatever you'd normally do. I'm not exactly busy, though I'm going to make an inventory. I'm—erm—I'm thinking

of selling the house, as you probably guessed.'
Kath nodded. 'Well, I did think that might happen. It's yours now to do with as you want. And no doubt you've already got your own place...'

She got to her feet and took off her coat to reveal an old-fashioned pink nylon housecoat underneath. She folded her coat carefully and lay it over the back of the chair, then went to the cupboard under the kitchen sink and brought out a plastic box with a handle, not unlike a toolbox, but containing cleaning supplies and cloths. She hauled out some large yellow rubber gloves and pulled them on, workmanlike, ready to tackle her first task.

'I'll start upstairs. Just give me a call if you want anything.' And off she went.

Caitlin found it comforting to hear someone else moving around the house, humming and singing, but not bothering her as she went about making her lists. By the time Caitlin had been through the whole house and was reluctantly contemplating going down to the cellar, it seemed Kath was ready for her next break.

On an impulse, Caitlin told Kath she had to go down there. It must have been clear from her face and the tone of her voice that she didn't exactly relish the idea, because Kath's shrewd eyes fixed on Caitlin's face.

'You haven't been down there yet?'

Caitlin shook her head and said, 'No, but my cousins went down there yesterday morning and said there wasn't anything much worth seeing. It was dark and small and a bit unsafe. And then there were the rats.'

'Rats!' Kath, lips pursed as if she were either annoyed or insulted, or quite possibly both, leapt to her feet, found her own bunch of keys, similar to

Caitlin's, and beckoned Caitlin to follow her.

'Come on, I'll take you down there.'

Caitlin stood up and went after her, still uncertain.

'There's nothing for you to worry about,' Kath told her. She sounded so positive that Caitlin believed her. They went outside. Caitlin was vaguely aware the rain had stopped, and the sun was trying to come out, poking prettily between silver and white fluffy clouds.

At the bottom of the steps, which Caitlin could now see looked pretty sound, Kath unlocked the door then before opening it she reached to click a switch on the wall on her right so that a light came on and illuminated the steps with bright, white light.

'They said there was no light,' Caitlin said. 'They used a torch.'

'Did they, now?' was Kath's only comment, and she waited for Caitlin to descend the steps to join her. 'Mind the edge of this one, it's a bit funny. I must get someone in to sort that out.' She said it softly almost as if it were a memo to herself.

Intrigued, Caitlin realised that once again, her cousins had deliberately deceived her. They had tricked her in so many ways. She vividly remembered how only yesterday Michael and Gareth, with a torch, had edged their way down the steps as if it had been a perilous undertaking, when as Caitlin saw now, there was a good strong handrail, the light-switch was readily accessible and the steps were perfectly safe and even, with the sole exception of the slight break on the edge of the one step near the bottom that Kath had pointed out to her.

She remembered the way Laura and Becka had clutched at her and turned her away at just the right moment, with all their little screams and cries of alarm or hurt ankles. Now, as if she was watching a movie, she saw all the ways in which they had worked on her, manipulating what she saw and how she saw it.

The men had said it was small, dark and contained only old broken furniture. An old fuel store, they had said. But as Caitlin now saw, that couldn't have been further from the truth. Admittedly at the bottom of the steps, until Kath put the rest of the lights on, it was a little dim inside, but once the lights came on, she looked in astonishment and saw it was a large, clean space, well-decorated and beautifully furnished.

It was hard to take in what she was seeing. Upstairs the furnishings were so simple as to border on bare, but down here everything was lavish and elegantly beautiful.

The area extended beneath the entire cottage. The floor was covered with a really handsome carpet, admittedly a little faded, but it was clearly very old and for the most part the rich warm colours shone through. It was similar in style and colour to those much, much smaller carpets and fabrics upstairs.

The walls were painted a soft peach, and the one huge room was furnished very much as a gentleman's drawing-room in an old country house would be furnished, with large squashy leather armchairs and sofas, tables, lamps, bookcases. In fact, Caitlin decided it resembled nothing so much as a gentleman's club like you'd see in a drama on TV, rather than a room in a private residence. Certainly, it was neither gloomy, cramped nor dangerously uneven, and there were definitely no rats. There was even one of those old globes which contained a selection of posh liqueurs and tiny crystal glasses.

Kath was watching Caitlin. She noted her total amazement with a knowing smile. Kath slipped off her shoes at the bottom of the steps and Caitlin, seeing her do that, did the same.

'He didn't like people to wear their shoes down here—that carpet is some kind of antique. He once told me it was worth more than the house, but I think he was just pulling my leg. But he was my boss and if he wanted me to be careful of the carpet, then I was careful of the carpet.'

Unlike in the cottage, here there were even paintings on the walls, hung in great ornate frames of mellow gold. The pictures themselves were so deeply mired in the grime of generations that the subjects were all but hidden from view. What a dreary lot, she dismissed them, but then hard on that thought, the sudden possibility. How lovely they will look if I have them cleaned, she thought. Even better... I wonder how much they might be worth?

And above the door to the steps hung a pair of samplers of the kind sewn by young girls learning both their stitches and their scriptures in the nineteenth century—or perhaps even longer ago than that. The samplers were framed and covered by glass so that the colours had been beautifully preserved. The stitches, neat and simple, were worked in reds and greens and blues with tiny flashes of gold and brown on a white muslin background. Little leaves, birds, stars and roses decorated the corners. The one hanging on the right read: 'I have wounded them that they were not able to rise: they are fallen under my feet. Ps 18: 38'.

'Charming,' Caitlin commented ironically. The one on the left was a bit more of a familiar text for samplers: 'Then were there brought unto Him little children, that He should put His hands on them, and pray. Matt 19: 13'.'

'Not exactly the normal light and fluffy bits you

usually see: 'There's no place like home' or 'The Lord is my shepherd',' she commented, and Kath nodded, her lips pursed in disapproval. The samplers made Caitlin shudder, but she was all too aware that like many domestic and crafted antiques, these were now considered highly collectable and might fetch a good price if she could find the right auction. Though they would pass through Gareth's hands at his auction house over her dead body, she told herself angrily.

In the surface of a lovely little side-table, there was a chessboard inlaid in what looked like ivory and stained walnut. As she bent to take a closer look, she found a shallow drawer underneath the board, and pulling it out, found all the little chess pieces, also in ivory and walnut, snuggly fitted down into velvet-lined slots. It was an exquisite set. On top, beside the chessboard was a 1930s celluloid or possibly Lucite cigarette box, its lid a pearly gold, again highly desirable to a collector of vintage artefacts.

She was shaking her head over it all. So much style, so many collectable items, possibly items of a very serious value.

She turned to Kath, who was still watching her and waiting for her reaction. 'It's incredible,' Caitlin said. 'You'd never in a million years think...'

'Bit of a surprise, isn't it? I was the same, first time I came down here. He wanted to show it me and tell me how I was to clean it all, you know, and well... gobsmacked doesn't begin to cover it.'

Caitlin shook her head again, wonderingly. 'No, it doesn't.'

'He told me, your grandfather did, that all this was got up to look exactly like his father's study at their old place before they lost it. All this stuff is from there, donkey's years old some of it, and I think he would just come down here and shut the door and forget he was now living in a little cottage on the edge of a village instead of still being at the manor.'

'Amazing,' Caitlin said again. 'Gramps certainly knew his stuff.'

'Gramps? Oh, my word, yes, I remember you calling him that when you was little! Ah such a sweet little girl, you were. And it was sad you were the only little one that ever came along for your mum and dad. Of course, there are your great aunt's children, your grandmother's sister Pamela, she died young, but at least she saw them grow up, which is a mercy. Though in many ways, it's not been a very lucky family, this one hasn't.'

Caitlin had to agree with that. Few surviving children, and all female at that. Apart from Michael, anyway. But anyway he was from Granny's side of the family, so didn't count as a direct blood descendent of Gramps.

Caitlin went to sit in one of the armchairs. It was like falling back into a soft eiderdown. She stroked the buttery leather with a tentative finger.

'This is lovely.'

Kath nodded again.

'All this stuff, from his father, and *his* father too, it was so important to your grandfather. Obviously once upon a time, at the manor, they must have been really well off.'

'I've brought some old photos with me,' Caitlin suddenly remembered. 'I was going to show them to my cousins, if it seemed as though they might be interested.' She thought about what Kath had said about her being a little girl. Kath had been here many years. 'When we go back upstairs, can I show them to you? You might recognise some of the people.'

'How old are these photos?' Kath asked.

Caitlin tried to do the sums in her head. 'They've

got the date on the back of them, May 1963. So—what, sixty-one years old? Something like that.'

'I would have been a baby then. Oh, May? No, I wasn't born until the December.'

'I don't suppose your mother kept house for the family back then, did she?' Caitlin asked hopefully. 'I'm just clutching at straws. I feel as if there's a mystery of some sort about that time.'

'No, my mum was too busy raising six children and doing all their laundry. But I've lived in the area all my life, and I know lots of local people. So even if I didn't know them back then, I might still recognise them. Let me have a look, you never know.'

Caitlin was still looking round and marvelling at the lovely space that had been created down here. Bit by bit she began to talk to Kath, telling her all that had happened. She began by describing for Kath again the way Michael and Gareth had come down here yesterday morning and what they had said about it, and then from there she ended up telling her everything. She told her all about the 'haunting' last night, and what had happened afterwards, including where and how she spent the night and what she had seen when she had come back to sleep at the cottage, only to find her cousins had returned before her.

Kath was angry and disgusted.

'You poor pet, going through all that! No offense,' she said, 'but these cousins of yours don't sound very nice. A right bunch of... Why would they try to frighten you away? That was a really horrible thing to do. What were they up to?'

'I don't know,' Caitlin had to admit. 'That's what I've been asking myself. Why?'

Then, after another moment, she was telling Kath about Gramps' last moments in the hospital and the strange things he had said. It took a while but Kath listened without comment, her arms folded and her expression one of deep concentration. Caitlin greatly appreciated her interest and her attention. She really liked this motherly woman who knew so much about the family she herself barely knew. Caitlin ended with a shrug, adding, 'Now I just don't know what to do about any of it.'

'You need to try and work out *why* they've done *what* they've done. Is there some reason they wanted you out of the house? Why would they be drinking a toast to getting rid of you?'

'I can't think of anything. I mean, all that's happened is they made me feel so uncomfortable here that I decided that I would sell the place. The only advantage to them in all this is that Michael will get a nice little commission as the estate agent handling the sale. But that's hardly enough to make their fortunes. In any case, I'm going to use another estate agent now and cut him out of his commission completely. Bloody well serve him right for being such a knob.'

'It certainly does serve him right, I'd do exactly the same in your shoes,' Kath said, still fuming over the way Caitlin had been treated.

Caitlin got up and took a walk about the room, examining the furniture with gentle looks and strokes of her fingers, and all the time thinking out loud.

'I suppose if they convinced me there was nothing down here, they could have come back sometime once the cottage was officially up for sale, and they could have stripped out everything and either kept it or sold it. I'd have been none the wiser. It's all good stuff, altogether probably worth quite a bit. But then, I asked them down here specifically so that they could choose a few things they wanted. Though I probably wouldn't have been too happy if they'd wanted to take everything, I must admit. I suppose I was just thinking they might take the odd knick-knack for sentimental reasons. But how far would the amount they'd get for this lot go between the four of them? Although in actual fact it would probably be divided by two, half for each couple, but even so...' She was shaking her head, still puzzled.

'You don't think it's worth their time?' Kath asked. She flicked a duster over a picture frame out of force of habit. Then licked her thumb to rub at a tiny mark.

'No, not really. I mean, it would be a nice little sum, but again, it seems like a lot of effort for a relatively small reward. Unless the most important thing was having a laugh at my expense and the money was just icing on the cake.' She sighed and ran a hand over the cool smooth curve of the globe-shaped tantalus. *Here be serpents*, she saw painted in a cloud-shaped bubble, and she smiled wryly at that.

'There's naughty ladies inside that,' Kath said with a nod and a grin at the globe.

Caitlin lifted the lid and saw the inside of the domed cover was decorated all over with naked Victorian ladies, very tastefully posed behind curling ostrich feathers and drapery, with just the odd glimpse of a cherry-pink nipple or a pale curvy buttock.

'It's beautiful! That must have been very naughty in its day! I'll bet it's worth a bob or two,' she exclaimed.

'Must be,' Kath agreed but this seemed to only bring them back to the beginning again and Caitlin felt she was getting nowhere.

'But I still don't feel it's enough. Do you think

that's everything, or are there any other secrets? Is there a buried treasure or something? A secret passage stuffed with gold? A hidden fortune?'

'It would be nice if there was,' Kath said sadly, 'but there's never even been so much as a suggestion of hidden treasure. I don't think meself there's anything like that. But who knows?'

By mutual consent they went out to the bottom of the steps and put their shoes back on. Caitlin turned out the lights, locking the downstairs door, and they went back up the steps to the garden, Caitlin locking the upstairs cellar door behind them.

Back in the kitchen, she dug in her handbag for her phone, only to find it had now officially died. She was longing to speak to her friends.

'Is there anywhere round here where I could buy a cable for my phone, do you think?' she asked Kath.

'That looks like the same make as my Eric's. You could have a lend of his, no problem. I bet you're lost without your phone, aren't you?'

'I am a bit,' Caitlin admitted with a grin. Then she caught sight of the cardboard packet. 'Oh those photos I told you about!'

Fishing them out, she presented them to Kath, who in turn rummaged in her bag for her reading glasses.

'Well, that's obviously your grandfather,' Kath began, indicating a tall young man in a jacket and tie, lounging against a wall. Caitlin looked eagerly over Kath's shoulder. Kath then pointed out two of the girls. 'That one, with the long hair, that's your grandmother, Isobel. She looks just as she did when I first met her, only younger here, of course. So I reckon that's likely her little sister Pam next to her, as she's the littlest one there and Pam was about ten years younger than Issie, I seem to remember.

Shame she died so young.'

'Yes, it is,' Caitlin said. 'In fact, I'm beginning to think everyone in our family died young.'

'Well, she lived long enough to marry and have children, though I think they were only school-age when she died. You probably know more about that than I do. I didn't really know her or her husband well. They got married here in Southdean, and I seem to remember he was a local man, though I can't seem to remember his name. Did it begin with an L?' She thought for a moment or two then shook her head, frustrated. 'It'll come back to me, I expect. Anyway I think they moved away for a time. Not very far, just you know, in those days anywhere that was outside your own village was 'away'. Then she came back a year or so later, and I seem to remember she was widowed then, though she was quite young still, such a shame. I never knew your cousins, apart from just to recognise them and smile and say hello. A boy and a girl, did you say?'

'Yes, older than me by a few years, possibly as many as ten years older. Michael and Becka. They are descended from Isobel's sister Pamela.'

Half to herself she said, 'So these are my grandfather, my grandmother and my grandmother's sister, my Aunt Pamela. There are a total of three boys and three girls in these photos if you include the one taking the photos. That seems to vary, they all must have had a turn except Pamela.' She nodded to herself as she said it, then a little louder, to Kath, said, 'As you say, Pamela's not really quite old enough to be part of the group.'

'No, she was most likely just tagging along. I'm not sure,' Kath said, peering at another of the photos, and turning it this way and that to get more light on it, 'But this one looks a bit like Barbara Kennett. Of course, I never knew her, she died when I was just a little baby, but I know someone who's got a photo of someone that looks just like this, and that's who it is. She was a local girl, and her family had a farm not far from here. If it is Barbara, then one of the boys might be her brother Stanley, I'm not sure what happened to him. There used to be a story years ago. I can't quite remember it now.'

Kath thought for a moment, took another look then shook her head and handed them back to Caitlin. 'I don't think I can help you any more than that. Sorry, lovely.'

'It's all right,' Caitlin said, looking through the photos herself one last time. 'It's just nice to know which ones are Gramps and Grandma. I wasn't absolutely sure before.'

Kath got up and went back to her cleaning. Caitlin sat daydreaming, gazing out at the garden, lost in thought. An hour later, Kath found her still sitting there.

'I just thought I'd let you know I'm off home now.'

Caitlin came back to reality with a jerk. Seeing the rain was falling again and heavily now, she got up and stretched.

'Let me take you home, you'll get soaked otherwise.'

'Well, I don't mind saying, I'd be very grateful for a lift if it's no trouble,'

Caitlin assured her it was no trouble, and they went out together to Caitlin's car. Kath's instructions directed Caitlin further along the lane until she came to a little huddle of four terraced cottages. Caitlin went inside for a moment or two and met Kath's husband Eric and their elderly golden labrador, Sarge.

She was relieved to be able to borrow the charger

cable for her phone from Eric. 'Not that I use my phone much,' he told her. 'I'm not one for technology. Plug it in now, while you have a cup of tea, that'll give you a bit of charge to be going on with.'

So the phone was plugged in and for the next forty-five minutes, she sat and listened to their good-natured bickering over their cups of tea. And was gratified to see how annoyed he was when Kath told him about the cousins and their tricks.

Eventually she left, taking the charger with her and promising to return it the following day. Without forming any particular plans, Caitlin had decided to stay at the cottage for a few days, so she drove to the nearest supermarket Kath had directed her to, and stocked up on a few basic groceries and kitchen items to see her through the next few days in a cottage with a dodgy old Aga she had no intention of even attempting to get to grips with.

Whilst she was in the supermarket her phone rang. The screen showed *Michael calling*. She hesitated, toying with the idea of ignoring him, but was convinced that would be pointless. Sooner or later, she'd have to speak with him.

'Where are you?' he demanded before even asking how she was, or anything else for that matter. Caitlin was glad to be able to say in all truth that she was in the supermarket getting some groceries.

'Oh, okay, only I called your landline a couple of times and got no answer. Though I must admit, I was surprised you even had a landline these days.' He sounded terse and not particularly friendly. She waited. His manner didn't endear him to her on top of everything else that had happened, and she was trying to figure out his reason for calling.

'Laura said you wanted to put the cottage on the

market. So I thought I'd give you a buzz, let you know I can go down tomorrow to take some measurements and so on and a few marketing photos, normally you'd be talking weeks before I could do anything, but I've just had some time open up in my schedule. And as it's for family...'

Oh now he apparently had some family feeling! Or maybe he just wanted some extra cash? Caitlin pondered for a second. Did she still want to sell the house?

'Caitlin? You there?' he bellowed. He was so loud and pushy, suddenly she was full of loathing for him. She felt no guilt about lying to him or manipulating him. Serve him right to get a bit of it back.

'Yes, yes, sorry. Oh—er—tomorrow. Um...'

'I know it's a bit soon, but you might as well get on with it, no sense waiting too long. Besides it's the only day I'm free for quite some time. I just thought you'd be pleased to get cracking.'

Caitlin assumed that most of what he said was unlikely to be true, but at that moment she couldn't think of anything to say in objection to getting started with the cottage. And this might help her to get closer to what her cousins were really up to.

'Okay, that will be great,' she said. 'Thank you,' she added with emphasis. Then, unable to resist, she added again, 'Won't you find it a bit creepy being here on your own?'

'Hmm. Well, I'm certainly not looking forward to it,' he said. 'But hopefully I'll be in and out so quickly there won't be time for anything weird to happen. Erm, listen, I don't think we ought to mention the place is haunted to any prospective purchasers. Don't want to frighten them off, do we?'

'We certainly don't,' Caitlin agreed with a hearty laugh.

'Okay then, well thanks for the business, and I'll be in touch soon. Bye.'
'Er, Michael?'
'What?' He sounded impatient. Moron, she thought.
'What time do you want to meet at the cottage?'
'Meet? You're coming down?'
'Well, you'll need me to let you in. How else will you be able to get into the cottage to take your photos and measurements and stuff?' Caitlin asked with a smile in her voice, and felt as if she'd scored a point. He gave an embarrassed laugh. Because of course he couldn't admit that he already had some means of getting in without her.
'Of course! What an idiot I am, I'd forget my head if it wasn't screwed on! Erm let's see, half eleven okay for you?' He forced another laugh.
Caitlin smiled to herself, enjoying his discomfort. Small pleasures.
'That would be lovely. Thanks a lot, Michael.' She clicked the end call button before he could say anything more.
In the corner of the supermarket was a little kiosk where you could get keys cut and dry-cleaning could be dropped off and collected. Caitlin asked the man behind the desk if he knew of a locksmith in the area.
'I'm a locksmith myself, love,' he told her.
'Perfect.'
She arranged for him to call at the cottage at half past eight in the morning to change the locks of the front, back and cellar doors. She was taking no more chances with her beloved cousins.

*

Chapter Ten

Caitlin had a moment of panic the next morning. Michael was due at half past eleven, but she didn't especially trust him to arrive when he said he would, based on how things had gone the last couple of days. She was sure the nice locksmith would run out of time because it had taken him seemingly forever to change the lock on the front door, saying something about the angle being wrong, and the wood being extra hard due to its age. Or was it too soft? She hadn't been paying attention, just mentally urging him to get on with it. But, she'd thought, fingers crossed, he would at least finish that one crucial lock before Michael arrived, even if he was still doing the others. Then to her intense relief, he was finished and paid by five to eleven and departed, leaving her feeling that her plan just might possibly work.

She had been torn in so many different directions as to the best way to handle the meeting with her cousin.

To begin with, she'd been tempted to not show up at all. She had seriously considered going out and not being there when he arrived. Or just staying inside the cottage, not opening the door and waiting to see how he reacted when he tried to get in then realised he couldn't. But what was the point of avoiding him? How would that help her to get to the bottom of what was going on? Sadly, she had to discount avoidance as an option.

But she wanted to feel she had achieved a certain amount of vengeance, so, deciding to try a combination of approaches, she had hidden her car down the lane earlier in the morning, then after the locksmith had gone, she stayed inside the cottage—the new front door securely locked, of course—made herself a cup of tea, and stood back behind the sitting-room curtains, sipping her tea and watching for Michael. He arrived a few minutes early, just as she expected, and looked around furtively, seemingly relieved she wasn't there yet, and then drew out his 'secret' key and slipped it into the lock. The look on his face when the key didn't fit was hilarious, and hiding back behind the curtains, she almost choked on her tea.

He stood there for fully five minutes looking baffled, and then, and only then, did he finally seem to figure out what must have happened, and he raised his hand to knock on the door.

She went to let him in, taking care to pocket the front door key. He came into the house warily, clearly nothing like as relaxed as she was, and as she beamed at him in welcome, she knew he realised the game had changed, though he said nothing to give himself away. Once a bluffer, always a bluffer, she thought. He seemed to be full of questions that he hesitated on the brink of asking. She was pleased she had finally been able to knock some of the wind out of his sails.

'I'm in the kitchen,' she called over her shoulder as she turned to go back. 'I've just made a cup of tea, if you want one?'

He accepted gracelessly, and she smiled to herself. Of course, he couldn't ask her about the locks because he couldn't admit he had somehow obtained a key, but she could see it was killing him to hold back.

'Milk and sugar?' she asked him brightly. He nodded.

Finally, he found his voice. 'You look as if you've been here forever,' he said. And stared significantly at the cardboard box of groceries on the table, the cups and saucers. 'Did you really only arrive just now?'

She used the act of pouring in his milk to cover her little debate with herself. She could say yes, she'd been here since moments after he and the others had left the previous morning. But on the other hand, she still needed him to tip his hand, so she decided to continue lying.

'Well not just now, I got here just before nine. After last Friday, I really expected the traffic would be a lot worse, so I left early. But it wasn't that bad and I actually got here quicker than last time.'

'So did you have your key with you, then?' he asked, oh-so-casually.

She looked at him as if he was crazy. Did a careless shrug as she chucked his teabag into the sink to dispose of later. And with a slightly confused but polite smile, said, 'Well, yes, otherwise how would I get in?'

He nodded and smiled back. 'Just wondered.' He couldn't hold back. A second or two later, he couldn't help asking again. 'So you didn't have any trouble getting in, then?'

'Why would I? There you go.' She handed him his mug of tea and enjoyed seeing him wince as the hot china burnt his fingers. She knew she was being malicious, but then remembered he and the others toasting themselves, laughing at her, and she hardened her heart. She decided to play for time. 'The cleaning woman was here when I arrived, so she let me in. She seems very nice and efficient. Kath Green, her name is. Nice lady.'

He wasn't interested in the cleaning woman, though. However, it was obvious he didn't feel able to keep on asking her about the key, so he let it drop and moved on to his new topic.

'Not scared to be here on your own, then, after the other evening?'

'That was a bit scary,' she admitted with a smile. 'So far, though, nothing spooky has happened this morning. But it has only been a couple of hours.' She made a show of tapping the tabletop. 'Touch wood.'

She sipped her tea and watched him over the rim of her mug.

He forced a laugh. 'Yes, it was bloody spooky the other night, wasn't it? Never experienced anything like that before. Too weird for words. You wouldn't catch me spending any time here all on my own, I can tell you.'

'Good thing you persuaded me to come down here this morning then, isn't it?' Caitlin pointed out. She set down her mug. 'Now, where do you want to start?'

She trotted after him, still all smiles, as he went all over the house. She deliberately held back to allow him to go first, agreeing with everything he said and all his suggestions, and generally allowing him to recover his composure.

When he was ready to take photos of the back garden, she was glad she had already thought of that. She had bolted the garden door but not locked it, so for the moment the issue of keys didn't arise. She slipped back the bolt and allowed him to precede her into the courtyard.

Of course, when he had taken a couple of snaps with his high-end estate agent's camera, he was ready to go down into the cellar. Caitlin had already made up her mind to allow the illusion to persist that she had not been down there and had no idea it was anything other than the dark and dangerous gloomy store he had described to her.

He tried the door handle. Found the door locked, of course, then he wondered aloud if the key was still on Caitlin's bunch.

With an anxious look, Caitlin said, 'Do you really need to go down there again? What if you fall in the dark? You might hurt yourself. And anyway, I thought we weren't going to mention it to any potential buyers? In which case, do you really need to take any photos?'

He tried to think of a plausible reason, in the end coming up with the rather lame, 'Well, I just thought I ought to know the dimensions in case anyone should ask. You never know, someone might be interested in its conversion potential.'

'Of course.' she said, and set off in search of her keys, even though they were in her pocket. She wanted to make him sweat a bit. She came back with the new set of keys in her hand and passed them to him.

'You needn't come down,' he said. 'Obviously it's a bit risky going down in the dark, and the steps aren't very safe. And you just never know...'

The Cousins

She did a *no way* gesture with her hands. 'Oh, trust me, I'm not going *anywhere* near that rat-infested cellar, don't you worry.'

He smirked ot himself as he unlocked the door, and carefully shielding the light-switch from her, he made a show of laying the keys on the step whilst he pulled a yellow plastic torch out of his pocket and used it to light his feet as he went forward into the darkness.

Caitlin called an anxious, 'You will be careful, won't you?' She waggled her fingers at him in a little wave and turned to go back into the kitchen. She heard his steps quicken now that he didn't have to pretend. He was not one of life's brainiacs, she thought. When she was sure he was right out of sight, she lightly skipped down the steps, grabbed the keys and pocketed them. If she let them out of her sight, he would slip them off the keyring or make an impression of them in a bar of soap or something equally ridiculous, just so he could get himself a spare set on the quiet.

When he finally returned, he found her in the kitchen rinsing the mugs.

'Did you—er—bring the keys with you?' he asked, trying to sound as if it didn't really matter.

She looked up with another of her bright smiles. 'Oh yes, I did, sorry. Force of habit. Shall I pop out and lock up?'

'Er—well, I can do that, as you're busy.'

'Oh, it's no bother at all.' She hurried away and returned almost immediately.

'How big is the cellar?' she asked him, keen to convince him she still hadn't peeked inside.

Caught off-guard he blustered a bit. 'Oh, well, I should say it was about eight feet by ten feet, at the most. Quite small.' Then seeing her querying look, he added, 'Well I couldn't get right to the far end because of all the crap that's piled up down there. Firewood and old broken chairs and so forth. That's probably where the rats are nesting, to be honest. But someone might find that area is a useful little space. A home office, perhaps. People love to work from home these days. But anyway, I'm a pretty good judge, after all these years, when comes to estimating the size of rooms.'

'I'm sure you are.' She beamed at him like the adoring little cousin he thought she was.

'Well, I'm all done, then,' he said. 'I'll just take a couple of nice shots of the front of the place. I'm sure we won't have any trouble at all securing a sale. Buyers are just queuing up for exactly this type of character property in need of a bit of TLC. Of course, because of the condition of the place here and there, you do realise we won't be able to quite ask the top price for the property, don't you?'

'I understand,' she said solemnly. 'Don't you think we ought to tell them it's haunted? After all, it doesn't seem very fair not to tell people.'

'Well, wait and see if they ask anything. In an older property, potential buyers would expect a few, shall we say, 'quirks', don't forget. And remember, many people find the supernatural fascinating, so we could be doing them a huge favour.'

He headed for the front door, so he didn't see Caitlin's expression at that last comment. He paused with his hand on the doorhandle. Clearly he wasn't going to use this occasion to spend more time with her than he had to. She'd half-expected the offer of a pub lunch at the least. But it wasn't to be.

'I expect you'll be going straight back to London?' he asked, seemingly innocently.

'No, I thought I'd stay until tomorrow. I need to go

The Cousins

and see the cleaning lady again plus I've got one or two other things to do. And I don't really feel like driving straight back today. Thank you so much, by the way. I really appreciate all this.'

'Not at all, my dear, you're most welcome. Keep it in the family, eh?' Then he looked a bit worried. 'But, Caitlin, you can't stay here all on your own tonight. Not after what happened last night. Laura would never forgive me if I let you...'

So now he was finally remembering such things as pretending to have family feeling, had he? She tried to look a little brave. 'Michael, I'm sure I'll be all right.' She bit her lip. 'Actually I might sleep in the sitting-room tonight. It's the upstairs that's a bit... you know.'

He shook his head. 'I don't think you should. I really think you should stay at the pub again if you absolutely insist on staying down here. Really, for your own comfort—and for my peace of mind. If nothing else this cottage is a bit remote, if anything should happen. In fact, why don't you go back to London. After all, it's not so very far.'

'Hmm. Perhaps you're right.' She allowed herself to sound a little uncertain. 'I suppose at least I will have the comfort of sleeping in my own bed. And as you say, it's not that long a journey.'

He was watching her closely, his salesman smile becoming fixed. She could sense him willing himself to be patient and let her come round to his way of thinking. She knew he wanted to urge her to hurry up and make up her mind. He so much wanted her out of the way, he just had to have something planned, she was certain.

Finally she said, hugging her arms across her chest as if cold, or scared, 'Yes. I think you might be right. Perhaps it would be best if I went back home after I see Mrs Green. Everything else can wait, there's nothing urgent. The pub wasn't really all that comfortable, to be honest, and the noise. *Buns and Poses* were on, and they had a lot of fans!'

She kissed his cheek and thanked him once again for his time, and after watching him take a couple more photos, she waved him off. As he pulled out into the lane, he called back to her, 'Don't leave it too late to get off, will you, there's supposed to be a heavy fog later.' And off he went.

Caitlin went inside and closed the door, relieved to be alone again.

'Wow,' she said to herself. 'He *really* wants me to go back to London tonight. So obviously I'd better stay put.'

As the afternoon wore on, Caitlin tried to think what might be going to happen. She also puzzled over when it was going to happen. She had to assume it would be after dark. Even if Michael believed she was going back to London tonight, he knew that she planned to go to see Kath at some point that afternoon, and so he would—surely?—leave a decent interval. For that reason too, she knew that whatever he and the others had planned, it would likely be put into action tonight: they'd need to wait a little while, but not so long that they ran the risk of her spoiling things by arriving back at the cottage the next day.

She tidied the house, packing up everything she'd brought in with her and stowing it in the boot of her car. The house looked as empty now as it had on Friday evening when she'd first arrived. But as she locked up and dropped the key in her bag, she was aware of new feeling about the house: it was familiar now, and friendly. She stopped just short of calling it home. But wryly admitted to herself that it wouldn't be long before she didn't want to leave it. It seemed unlikely this house would be sold anytime soon.

She drove into the town to get some lunch and to buy herself a small but powerful torch, a pack of spare batteries, and a bottle of water. Over her pub lunch she texted her friends to tell them a little more about what was going on. They both—predictably—urged her to come straight back to London. As she set aside her phone, she wondered if perhaps they were right. Maybe she should stop messing about and just wash her hands of all of it: the cottage, the cousins, everything.

When she returned to the house, she edged the car along the lane anxiously in case she had misread Michael and he had returned whilst she was out. But she needn't have worried, the cottage remained empty.

Once again she left her car in its now-familiar hiding place in the field behind the cottage, then she realised that it hadn't occurred to Michael earlier to ask her where it was. She shook her head. He really wasn't quite as smart as he thought he was.

She'd made up her mind what she was going to do. She was going to wait down in the cellar. The lies they had told her about its condition made her suspicious. For that reason she felt this was the likely focus of her cousins' interest, whether because of the potential value of the furnishings, or for some other reason she didn't yet know.

As soon as it began to get dark, she let herself into the cellar, wincing at the noise of the hinges.

'I must get those oiled soon as,' she reminded herself.

She used her torch app instead of the lights to find her way. She locked the door behind her, went down the steps and crossed the admittedly quite eerie furnished room to the sofa on the far wall. The sofa was a huge handsome beast of leather workmanship, and its generously curved and padded back meant there was a decent–sized space between the back of the sofa and the wall. This would be her hiding place.

She ran the torch around the floor to check she hadn't tracked in any mud on her shoes that might give her away, then she stepped out of them, carrying them with her to the sofa. With a feeling of childish glee, she squeezed into the space, setting down the bottle of water beside her in case it was a long wait.

She had barely settled down when her phone rang. It was Becka. Caitlin was not in the least surprised. Checking up on me, Caitlin thought, making sure I'm out of the way before they do whatever it is they're planning.

She answered with a cheery, 'Hi Becka! How are you?'

Becka was fine, it seemed. She didn't sound fine, Caitlin thought, she sounded very tense. Becka asked, 'Where are you? I've tried your home number several times, but you're not home, are you?'

Caitlin had a mental picture of her poor rarely used home phone, inherited from a previous tenant, sitting on the corner of the kitchen counter, its little red message-received light flashing, forlorn and neglected in the empty flat. She smiled. She really should get rid of that landline and save herself some money on the line rental.

'No, I'm just on my way back home now, should be there in about ten or fifteen minutes. I've been down to Sussex. Michael was coming to do a walk-through of the house today and take some pictures ready for putting it on the market.'

'Oh yes, of course!' Becka said. 'Laura did tell me that, but I forgot.'

Caitlin felt sad that her cousin was lying to her. In the beginning, after meeting them at the funeral, she had hoped that they would all become such good friends. Was it just her imagination or did Becka sound a teeny bit relieved?

'If you like, we could get together this evening,' Caitlin suggested, knowing that if she was right about Becka and Michael and the others, there was no way she would accept. 'Why don't you pop over, we could have some wine, maybe get a film?'

With something like dismay in her voice, Becka hurriedly declined, saying she already had plans for that evening.

'Plus,' she said. 'I'm feeling a bit under the weather, I might have to cancel as it is.' She did a little cough as proof.

'Aww,' said Caitlin, all sympathy. 'Poor you! You ought to get yourself off to bed then, you don't want to make it worse by tiring yourself.'

'Well, I just wanted to make sure you're all right.' Becka said valiantly and added several sniffs and a dainty cough. She kept her voice weak and sickly.

After a few minutes more, pretending that the traffic-jam she was in was finally on the move, Caitlin was able to get away. The call had gone a long way to confirming her suspicions that they were keeping tabs on her. They wanted to make sure she was well away from the cottage. She only hoped that when they arrived, she would be able to hear them from her place in the cellar and have time to conceal herself and that they wouldn't walk in on her playing on her phone.

She needn't have worried.

Less than half an hour later, giving her plenty of time to get out of her space, stretch, guzzle some water from her bottle, and finally remember to turn off her phone and get back into position again, she heard the sound of banging doors then footsteps above her head. It sounded as though at least two people, possibly more, had just entered the cottage and were walking across to the kitchen. In a very few minutes, she thought, they could be down in the cellar. She wished she had hidden outside somewhere, anywhere, and not in here after all. She was sick with nerves, feeling vulnerable and exposed. Surely they'd guess her plan, wouldn't they? They'd immediately check behind the sofa and find her. She'd been crazy to think they wouldn't notice. And it came to her now that Michael—and probably Gareth too if he was there—did not seem like the type of chap who liked to be crossed.

And—how had they got in this time?

She turned the torch off and drew herself in tightly behind the sofa, trying to hold her breath, hoping fervently they wouldn't bother to check for hidden cousins. She hoped she wouldn't sneeze. Or cough.

Her excellent hearing picked up the sound of scraping from the cellar door. One of them must be trying to pick the lock. After a few more minutes of muffled cursing she heard the door screech as it was wrenched open, then the lights came on, and more than one person loudly stomped down the step into the room.

There was a pause, and Caitlin hoped they would take off their shoes and not track dirt all over that precious antique carpet.

She heard the sound of a sharp intake of breath.

'Oh wow! It's *gorgeous* down here! Like an old-fashioned gentleman's study, the sort of thing you see in stately homes!'

That was Becka speaking. It seemed the cousins' return to the cottage after getting rid of Caitlin the other night hadn't included a trip to the cellar. There were more footsteps, then Caitlin heard Michael say, 'I can't believe she'd even had the lock of the cellar door changed. That must mean she came in here after all.'

'Not necessarily,' said another male voice. Gareth, obviously. 'Maybe she just told the locksmith to change all the locks, and she didn't come down here to check at all.'

There were general murmurs of annoyance, then Caitlin distinctly heard Michael say, 'I'm telling you Becka, your cousin suspects something. She's onto us.'

Caitlin was puzzled by the way he said that. But immediately Becka replied with a laugh, 'Well even if she is, it doesn't matter, does it? After tonight it will be too late.'

'Look, let's get on with it, shall we, I don't want to stay here a moment longer than I have to. This place gives me the effing creeps.'

That was Laura.

There were some sounds of movement and some light banging. Caitlin hoped they hadn't come to move out the furniture: if they did, sooner or later they would find her hiding place.

Someone sat down heavily on the sofa Caitlin was concealed behind. And when Gareth spoke, he sounded far too close for comfort.

'I've got a feeling we won't find it. There won't be any important papers here, they'll either be in Henry's office or back at the house in London, or Caitlin's already got it and it's in her flat. Odds are she's found it already.'

'I can't believe this faded old thing is worth all the fuss you've made over it,' Laura said, ignoring what Gareth had said.

'It's an Aubusson, I told you, that's a massive make of carpet. What with that and this globe drinks thing, we'll make a fortune. Add in everything else and well, it's all grist to the mill as far as I'm concerned.' That was Gareth again. NO doubt his experience of working in an auction house meant he had a mental price tag on everything eh saw in the place. And now that she knew they were aware of the value of the furniture—or at least, some of it—it made sense that this was their main object.

'What time's your mate coming with the van?' Gareth asked then.

It was Michael who answered: 'Not till midnight. He's doing another job at some poof's place in Kemp Town first. Got to go and drop that off then come back for this lot.'

'What? Midnight! I'm not sitting around here for—what? Four and a half hours! I thought he was coming straight away.' Becka sounded furious.

Before anyone else could speak, Laura called out, 'There's no papers here. I've been through all these drawers twice. A couple of old letters and photos, a few old bills, but nothing that's any good to us. We're wasting our time.'

'Bloody hell! There must be papers for all this stuff. He was renowned for keeping absolutely every bit of paper, every receipt, every bill, every guarantee. It has to be here. Let me look.'

'God, Michael! I think I know how to look through a drawer. You don't have to mansplain every sodding thing to me! I told you! It'll be at the bloody house in London. That's why she's been there. That's why she changed the locks here. For God's sake, when are you going to listen to me? You moron!' Laura added. 'She's not as dim as you made out. Not if she's had all the locks changed. That means she knows something.

Or that she's already found it.'

There was a long silence. Caitlin heard someone moving. She heard Michael's voice soothing Laura and trying to calm her. It sounded as though he was moving across the room. There was the sound of drawers being opened and slammed shut.

'There's nothing here,' he said finally, earning him a furious exhalation from his wife. He went on, 'You're probably right. The papers are most likely at the other house. Or her flat. I'll try to get inside the other house again tomorrow. It shouldn't be difficult. If that nosy neighbour comes round again, I can just tell her I'm the selling agent and make a nuisance of myself trying to persuade her to sell her house.'

'Do we really need the papers?' Becka whined.

'Ye-sss,' Michael said carefully, as if he'd already explained it way too many times. 'Because they will help to authenticate the pieces which will mean we get a better price for them. Let's try the other house again, and then if we still don't find the papers, we'll have to think about getting into her flat.'

Back into her flat? Caitlin felt as though her heart bumped against her ribs. A cold niggle of worry poked at her. As soon as they had gone, she ought to get back to London and make sure things were all right at that end.

Someone sighed heavily. Probably Becka, Caitlin thought. After another moment it was Becka who said, 'I can't sit here and wait for your mate and his van for over four hours. Let's go to the pub, have a few drinks, get a curry. We'll still be back here in plenty of time for your mate. This stuff's not going anywhere, and I'm not freezing my arse off sitting here waiting.'

Eventually the others gave in, and they all prepared to leave, Michael annoying everyone by wittering on about how they had to make sure they were back by eleven o'clock "latest" to start getting everything ready for the van-guy and his mates.

They snapped out the lights, and slammed the door behind them, and she heard them stamping away up the steps. Caitlin, stiff and cold, gave them a few minutes more, then crawled out to feel her way to sit on the sofa, her mind in a whirl of fury and dismay.

Eventually she got to her feet, still clutching her shoes. She took the torch and used it to find her way across to the step where she put them on, then holding her breath again, eased the door open, checking to make sure the coast was clear. A glance over her shoulder towards the cottage showed the lights were all still on.

As silently as she could, she closed the cellar door. Michael and the others hadn't been able to lock it so there was no point trying to make it secure. In any case, it wouldn't be long before she was back. She crept towards the kitchen window, surprised but relieved to have remained undiscovered.

As she stood there she heard voices. Through the kitchen window she saw Becka cross to the sink and stub out a cigarette. They were all still there, talking, arguing.

She backed away to the cover of some bushes, and from there took out her phone and turned it on. It took a few moments but when it was ready, she made sure the flash was suppressed and took a few pictures of them. If only she'd thought to record some of their earlier conversation in the cellar, that might have been useful as evidence at some point in the future, but she had been more worried about receiving a message that would ping or make her phone vibrate and give her away.

She caught Michael's voice saying wearily, 'Fine then, fine, let's just go. So long as we make sure and get back in good time for later.'

Then she saw them all file out. The lights were all turned off and somewhere on the other side of the cottage she heard car doors slamming and an engine starting up.

Again, she gave them a few minutes' start then she ran round the side of the house. Gareth and Laura's car was still there: they had all gone in Michael's larger, more expensive vehicle.

Panic hit her now. She felt overwhelmed. There was no way she could let just let them walk off with her grandfather's furniture and carpet so they could sell the lot for the most money they could get. If she waited until tomorrow, the place would be stripped bare.

But what the hell could she do about it?

She ran down the lane to her car, and less than a minute later she was driving a little too fast to Kath Green's house along the lane. Fortunately, the lights were on in Kath's home, and she could hear sounds from the TV. She was in. Caitlin didn't bother to lock her car, just leapt out and ran to pound on the front door.

Eric opened it and peered out.

'I'm so sorry,' Caitlin burst out and pushed past him to go inside. Kath stared up at her from a chair by the fire. Immediately Caitlin began to pour out a garbled version of the events and asked if they had a number for the local police. It was at this point she realised she should have just stayed at the cottage and dialled 999 for the emergency services, but it was too late now. She impatiently answered Kath's questions, practically hopping about in her desperation for action.

She'd told the whole story all over again when Eric interrupted her with a quick, 'No time for the cops, I'll get Our Ern's pig-cart.'

'Wh-what?' Caitlin gaped at him. She didn't have the words to express her confusion. He smiled and patted her arm.

'It's a bit smelly but it's not too bad. He hoses it down regular. I'll phone Our Ern and get him to fire her up.' He disappeared into the hall, and Caitlin turned to Kath in dismay.

'What...?' she repeated.

Kath pulled her into a chair.

'Don't you worry,' she said. 'Those boys'll sort it out.'

'But what...?'

'Ern's pig-cart.' Kath said, speaking slowly and loudly as if to a visitor from another planet. 'It's his truck for taking his pigs to the abattoir. Eric's brother. Eric'll get it and go up to the cottage, load up all your grandfather's stuff and be out again before your cousins get back to nick it. Won't that be a laugh? Turn the tables on them good and proper. Shame we won't be there to see their faces, though. Why? What else did you have in mind?'

Caitlin stared at her. In her mind it all fell neatly into place.

'That's bloody brilliant,' Caitlin said.

Kath nodded complacently and picked up her knitting.

Our Ern's pig-cart turned out to be a rather nice Toyota van with gratings all down the sides. True it was rather smelly but even Caitlin had to admit it was more or less clean. In any case she didn't have the luxury of an alternative.

They were back at the cottage by half-past eight and had packed the van by half past nine. Caitlin couldn't believe her eyes. All she had to do was hold the cellar door open. Eric and Our Ern, along with Ern's sons Ian and Keith, went straight down there and immediately—and with remarkable efficiency, Caitlin couldn't help thinking—walked all the furniture up the steps and round the side of the cottage and into the van. They worked so quickly and methodically Caitlin began to wonder if they had done this kind of thing before.

Last to come was the carpet, carefully rolled up and slotted into the 'cart' on top of the sofas.

By a quarter to ten they were pulling the vehicle in behind the Greens' end of terrace house and away from prying eyes. And by ten o'clock Caitlin was tucking into a very strong cup of tea and a toasted bacon sandwich and trying not to think about Our Ern's poor pigs.

Just before eleven o'clock she was pulling her car into its now-familiar place in the field behind the cottage so that she, Ian and Keith could conceal themselves amongst the shrubbery in the back garden.

They had hardly been in position ten minutes when lights went on in the house. The 'cousins' had returned from their sojourn in the pub and were ready for action. Going over it all in her head again, Caitlin spared a second to wonder again about that comment Michael had made to Becka about Caitlin being 'your' cousin, rather than saying 'our' cousin.

Kath had insisted that Caitlin have Ian and Keith along with her for 'back-up' even though Caitlin had made it clear that she had no intention of engaging with her cousins, she simply wanted to watch. But she had been overruled. And she had to admit, it was nice to know there was some 'back-up' here if she should need it, as Ian and Keith, though only nineteen and twenty-one respectively, were sturdy young men and looked as though they'd be handy in a fight, six feet tall or more to her five foot two. They had brought along a rather nice old-school camcorder and had it in place ready to catch the fireworks.

As soon as the lights went on in the house, Ian whispered, 'Rolling,' to indicate he had turned on the camcorder. Caitlin saw the comforting little red glow by the viewfinder. On the front, he'd covered the red recording light with a blob of blue-tack.

The kitchen door opened, and the cousins piled out, going directly to the cellar door. She heard the tell-tale squeak of the hinges as it opened.

Here we go, Caitlin thought, and quaked a little inside.

*

Chapter Eleven

Ian's camcorder caught the action beautifully. Caitlin's only regret was that she hadn't been right there in the cellar to see their faces when they came into the room and saw the vast empty space. But it was probably a good thing she hadn't been there...

The shouts told her all she needed to know. They all went down to the cellar. There was a delay of a couple of minutes. Then the shouting started. Ian and Keith were sniggering, shoulders convulsing as they tried to hold back the laughter. Now the shouting had begun to die away, and Caitlin could picture them all down there, trying to figure it out, trying to make sense of what had happened. Any second now, she thought.

And then here they came. First Michael, furiously angry from his posture and jerking movements, then Laura, one hand out to him, fighting back tears of dismay, clearly trying to calm him down. Next came Becka, also beside herself with rage, flinging herself about with loud groans, waving her arms and shouting, then clasping her hands to her head, pacing up and down, shaking her head and cursing. Lastly came Gareth, of all things, laughing.

'So much for your plans, Mikey-boy!'

Michael turned on him. As Caitlin watched with bated breath, Michael strode right up to Gareth and just as she thought he was going to punch Gareth in the mouth, instead he just wagged a finger in his face and murmured something she couldn't catch.

Then Gareth said, 'I don't know why you're so upset. She's only done to you what you were going to do to her. She played you, *Mikey-boy*. And lest we forget, the stuff is actually hers, so... Look, I told you right at the outset not to underestimate her, but oh no, you 'knew what you were doing' and wouldn't listen! And now look where it's...'

But he broke off. From some distance away there came a muffled pounding sound. Michael ground out another string of expletives and ran back into the house.

Laura looked from Gareth to Becka, confused.

Becka reminded her, 'That'll be his mate with the van. Michael won't like having to pay him for doing nothing!'

They all went back into the house still cursing and complaining, Gareth tagging behind, a big grin on his face.

Ian turned off his camcorder and the three of them strolled back to the Greens' at a leisurely pace across the fields. Caitlin was again grateful of their company; she would never have found her way alone.

Kath made cocoa. Ian reran the recording for Kath and Eric to see, and when it came to the bit where Michael went up to Gareth and spoke to him very quietly, Ian reran it again with the volume cranked

The Cousins

right up. With all of them holding their breath, they were just able to hear Michael say to Gareth:

'You've got just as much invested in this as me. If I go down, you go down. And stop fucking calling me Mikey-boy. I'm not your lackey.'

Ian promised to forward it to Caitlin. She was already planning to send it to Henry Jago in case she needed to take legal action.

'I need to arrange for all the stuff from the cellar to be put into storage,' she said. 'Do you know of anywhere local? I might be able to get them to collect.'

Eric shrugged. 'There are a couple of places, leave it with me. I'll get Our Ern and the boys to help me shift it all when we've found somewhere for you. You'd better let me have your number so I can let you know.'

Gratefully, she dropped him her phone number and sat back reassured. At least that was the important stuff taken care of.

'So,' said Kath. 'Now you've just got to go through all the papers at Mr Mitcheson's other house to find whatever it is they're looking for so you can steal a march on your relations.'

'And do it pronto,' Ian said.

Caitlin was forced to agree. There was something urgent or important, and she needed to find it before they did.

She had outwitted her cousins twice, but now as she stood in the little sitting-room at Gramps' terraced house back in London, she knew she was too late. It was clear from all the mess that someone—and she had a good idea who—had been there. Every drawer was yanked out onto the floor, contents strewn everywhere. Cupboard doors stood open, everything tossed in heaps on top of the heaps from the drawers. The cushions were off the sofa, chairs had been upturned. Caitlin's only surprise was that the cushions hadn't been ripped open and stuffing thrown everywhere James Bond-style.

Every room was the same.

She'd handed him the keys herself, so why had he changed the locks? Why was he trying to keep her out? She only had to look about her to find the reason to that: the mess, the obvious signs of a search, the place looked like a scene from some gangster film. But it still made no sense. Michael could have just let himself in, had a sneaky look around, and left again; she'd have been none the wiser. Why the mess, the chaos?

While she was still surveying the debris, fighting back the tears, and trying to decide where to start, she heard a knock on the front door.

Caitlin felt a sinking feeling in her stomach. She knew exactly who that would be. But she needed to speak to Brenda Cahill anyway, to find out what, if anything, she had observed. So her visit was perfectly timed. Caitlin opened the door.

'Well, they came back this morning,' said Brenda without preamble.

She pushed past Caitlin and bustled into the kitchen, her sensible black acrylic trousers crackling with static. 'And I had my doubts straight away. I asked him what he was doing here but he just told me to mind my own business and eff off. I said to my Terry, I said, he says he's an estate agent and got permission, but if that's true, why's he got a locksmith with him to change the locks? Seems a bit drastic if you ask me, I mean, surely you're still allowed inside the place right up until it's sold? There's all this stuff to shift for starters. Tea?'

The Cousins

It took Caitlin a moment to catch up, but finally she said, 'Yes, please.'

The kettle was on the stove, the cups and saucers set out, the teabags deployed in record time. Brenda said, 'I'll just pop back home for some milk. I'll leave the door open.'

'Thank you,' Caitlin called after her a beat too slowly. She sat at the kitchen table and surveyed the mess. The gloves were off now, there would be no more pretence, no more, 'let's just have a takeaway together' like friends. Or family. These 'cousins' were not her friends even if they were her relations. She needed to formulate a new plan.

Brenda came back in carrying a jug of milk and a packet of chocolate digestives. She finished making the tea and sat down opposite Caitlin, setting a steaming cup and saucer in front of each of them. Fixing hungry eyes on Caitlin, Brenda said,

'My Terry said we should have called the police, but I wasn't sure. He might have been here with your permission. So what's going on?'

Caitlin felt suddenly too weary. She felt now that Brenda—like Kath and her family—had become her ally. Might as well bring her on board, too. So she began at the beginning and told Brenda everything. Brenda listened without interruption for which Caitlin was grateful, and when she finally came to the end, and sipped her now-cold tea, Brenda's only comment was,

'Well, they're not both your cousins.'

'What?' Caitlin gaped at her. 'But...' And in her mind, once again things seemed to shift and reform into a new pattern.

'No, Dickie, he told me. There's a girl, the niece of his late wife, but there's no boy. Not anymore, I mean. I mean, there *was* a boy, but he died, oh quite a few years ago now. Drugs, if I remember rightly. I remember your grandfather telling me about it when it happened. Such bad luck they had, always. Well, the whole family really. He always said that if he believed in such things, he'd think a curse had been put on you all. After all what we started out with, he used to say, it's come down to this place, he said, and the little cottage in Sussex, and his one granddaughter and a niece from his late sister-in-law. That's all he had left.'

Caitlin was trying to grasp the implications of what Brenda was telling her, but she still found it hard to make that fit with what had happened during the last week or two. She sighed and nursed her empty teacup.

'I just don't know what they are trying to get out of all this. I could almost understand them wanting to strip out all the good furniture and sell it for whatever they could get, but it all seems too elaborate, too big somehow for just a few thousand pounds.'

She got her phone out of her bag and found the footage Ian had sent her. She forwarded through the video to get to a decent image of Michael. 'Is this the guy who came this morning?' She held the phone out to Brenda.

Brenda squinted at the screen. 'Yep, that's him. For definite.'

Caitlin nodded. The final doubt was removed. 'Well, he is an estate agent, so that part's true. I was planning to get him to handle the sale, and I did think about him doing the house clearance too, once I'd been through the place again. But there's no way I'll use him now. It's true I gave him some spare keys, but he was only supposed to come and you know, measure up, take a few pictures, get what he needed to sell the place. He wasn't supposed wreck it...' She bit her lip, anger vying with bewilderment and hurt.

Brenda got up and cleared away the teacups, rinsing them under the tap, drying them and putting them away in the right place in the right cupboard. Over her shoulder, she said,

'You need to go to the police. Or at least tell your solicitor what's going on. Get some advice on how to protect yourself from whatever they might be planning.' She turned back to face Caitlin. 'What are you going to do with this place? Let him sell it for you and pocket his big fat commission?'

Caitlin shook her head. 'Not after this, no. I'll find another firm. But not until I've gone through this place with a fine-toothed comb.' She took a deep breath, got a pull on herself. She came to a decision. 'Right. I'll get the locks changed for about the third time in a fortnight, and then I'll move in here myself. It'll take a while to go through the place thoroughly, so it won't be up for sale for a while yet. I need to find whatever they were looking for.'

'If he hasn't found it already,' Brenda pointed out.

Caitlin nodded. 'Yes, that's quite likely. And yes, I need to talk to the solicitor about it, you were right about that too. I'll ring up Mr Jago and see if he can see me later today.' She surveyed the room and thought sorrowfully about the disaster-areas that were the rest of the rooms. 'I'd better got on with it.'

'I'll give you a hand to get it all tidied up, love. No, it's no bother, I'm glad to help.'

Catilin, humbled by her kindness, gratefully accepted. She and Brenda set to work clearing up the house. They put all the drawers and cushions back, took photos of breakages, returned items to the emptied cupboards, picked everything up off the floor. Caitlin then vacuumed while Brenda wiped down all the surfaces, and they put two large bin-bags full of rubbish and broken ornaments outside in the black wheelie bin.

Caitlin turned the fridge back on, read the meter and notified the utility company the house was now occupied again. She stripped the bedding off the bed in the spare room—she couldn't face the thought of sleeping in the front bedroom which had been her grandfather's room. She turned on the central-heating and opened the spare bedroom window a few millimetres to air the room.

After taking about fifteen minutes to say goodbye and a heartfelt thank you to Brenda, Caitlin finally got away. She drove to her flat, for once too preoccupied to be aware of a sense of homecoming, only to find a police officer standing beside her open front door, taking notes, his radio crackling softly on his chest. Caitlin's neighbour rushed over to greet her. Caitlin took a brief second to reflect that until the last two weeks she had never been so involved with next-door neighbours.

'So sorry, miss, I am out, taking my children to the school so I don't hear anything. When I come back, the door is open, but I knew you were away. So I step inside to see, but you are not here, and I call the police. I hope that's okay.'

'Thank you, Mrs Chen, that was very kind of you,' Caitlin said. Mrs Chen, motherly and concerned, lingered by her own door in case Caitlin needed any help.

'You the owner?' the police officer asked.

Caitlin said she was the tenant, not the owner.

Nodding, the officer waved a pencil at the doorway, 'I'm afraid it's a bit of a mess. I've got someone coming over from Forensics, but I doubt they'll find anything. Everyone wears gloves these days. I suppose you didn't leave a key under the mat or anything like that?'

Caitlin shook her head. 'No, but I think I might know who did this, and if so, they've had plenty of time to make a copy.'

'Ex-boyfriend, eh? You'd better get your locks changed.'

'Hmm. Fortunately, I now have two locksmiths on speed-dial,' Caitlin said.

The police officer stared at her. 'Happens that often, eh?'

It proved to be a hectic day.

Caitlin rang to make an appointment with Henry Jago, but he couldn't see her until six o'clock. She arranged the appointment anyway, not wanting to let any more time elapse before speaking to him and bringing him up to speed on what had been happening.

Then she had to arrange for a locksmith to come to both her flat and Gramps's house to change the locks. She groaned at the price—this was costing her an arm and a leg. Fortunately, the locksmith had a two-for-one deal going on this week. When she gave him the address of the terraced house, he said,

'But I was only there this morning. And I was there the week before last. Summink funny going on, I reckon.'

'Yes,' she said. 'I thought you might say that. If that man rings you again to get the locks changed, please don't do it. The police are on to him for trespass and criminal damage. You don't want people to think you're involved in that sort of thing, do you?'

He certainly didn't. He took the large tip with a solemn promise to respond only to her call, and to inform both Caitlin and the police if anyone else tried to hire him to change Caitlin's locks.

Next she rang Michael. This was the toughest item on her to-do list, and she had saved it to last. She really didn't want to do it, but she knew she had to.

'Hello Caitlin,' Michael said, his salesman's voice silky smooth, all animosity pushed into the shadows until needed.

That didn't bode well, but she took a deep breath and plunged straight in, her tone icy.

'I think we both know where we stand. Keep away from me, keep away from the cottage in Sussex, my flat up here, and my grandfather's house in Putney.'

'Oh!' he said mockingly, adding, 'I suppose this means you don't want me to handle either sale for you?'

'What do you think, you arsehole? Are you even an estate agent at all?'

He pretended to be shocked. 'Certainly I am! How dare you suggest otherwise!'

'Obviously not a reputable one. Well, I'm tired of playing these pathetic games with you. I know you're not even my cousin, so who are you? What is it you want from me?'

'Caitlin! Caitlin! I'm so hurt by your tone. How could you be so cruel? Such cynicism in someone so young! Of course I'm your bloody cousin—who else would I be? And as to what I want—I just want a share of your nice little nest egg. It's not much to ask.'

'You won't be getting a penny. And I meant what I said. Keep away from me and all three properties. I will call the police if you or any of the others come near me or any of my properties again.'

'Well, you can try, but you can't possibly be at all three places at once, can you?'

She was silent for a few seconds, not sure whether

to continue the conversation or simply hang up.
He continued, 'Just out of interest, how did you manage it? Last night's little vanishing act, I mean. I mean, great work, by the way, I take my metaphorical hat off to you. But just how did you know?'

Had it only been last night, she thought. Aloud she said, 'I was there, I heard what you had planned. I moved quickly.'

'You were there? Where?'

'Behind the sofa on the far wall. I knew you were up to something, you're not exactly gifted at subtlety. And I had a pretty good idea what it might be. And, FYI, you're not the only one who has a mate with a van. We just moved quicker than you, that's all.'

As soon as she told him, she was annoyed with herself for giving away her advantage. But in any case, she couldn't hide there again. At least she had kept the Greens and Ern and his boys out of it. She didn't want to make any trouble for them, they had been so good to her.

'Oh, I see. Very good. As I say, my hat is officially off to you, my dear Caitlin, it was a masterstroke. Really quite something. I'll admit I was angry at the time—but—well there was more than a little admiration too. Now I really must be going, I am very busy. But before I go, I'd just like to say this—get out of my way, if you know what's good for you, girlie. Don't you ever cross me again like you did last night, or I will make sure it's the last thing you ever do.'

Then he hung up.

Caitlin was left staring at the phone in her trembling hand. Her appointment with Henry couldn't come round quickly enough for her liking, she really needed to speak to someone about all this.

She longed to talk things over with Jen and Sonia, and managed a short three-way chat with them, which was better than nothing. Sonia had a family thing that evening: her sister-in-law's birthday party which she couldn't get out of, and Jen had a date with Rob-the-just-about-okay. Their outrage on her behalf when she told them what had been happening was cheering, helping to settle her emotions. They made arrangements for getting together at her place once she knew what her plans were for the next few days.

She contacted her boss and explained she'd need a bit more of her holiday time. As things were slack at the moment, that worked out okay, but once the schools closed for Christmas, it would be a different story: everyone would want time off then.

Next she decided to pamper herself with a long soak in the bath and catch up on her laundry. Then she went through the fridge and threw out all the out-of-date limp lettuce and squidgy tomatoes. She made up a shopping list, then reminded herself she was moving into Gramps's house, so she'd need to take some essentials with her—the coffee, the cereal, stuff she already had at her place so needn't buy again just now.

Before she left for her appointment with Henry Jago, she rang Kath in Sussex to tell her of her suspicions about the cousins not being who they said they were, then she told Kath what Michael had said. She asked Kath if she knew anyone who could house-sit for her. Kath said to leave it with her, and Caitlin relaxed, knowing she could indeed do exactly that. Kath and her family were staunch allies, and she knew she could absolutely rely on them.

'Don't worry,' Kath told her, 'We'll make sure those B-words don't get into Mr Mitcheson's cottage.'

Caitlin smiled as she ended the call and felt a lot happier. Now to talk this over with Henry Jago. She took Gramps' old photos which she planned to show him as well as the video from Ian's camcorder. She intended to tell him everything, just as she had Kath and Brenda. She needed his advice, and obviously he needed to know as much as she did if he was to advise her.

She reached the offices of Jago and Wilkes at five minutes to six and found it all in darkness. She parked at the side of the building and went to the door. Henry was standing on the front doorstep looking like Oliver Twist abandoned on the steps of the workhouse. He smiled a shy smile at her as she approached, and she immediately had to revise her opinion of him. Now he looked like one of the sad little puppies she had once seen at an animal shelter. Please adopt me. I'll be good, I promise, and I won't eat much.

'Is there a problem?' she asked.

He looked a bit coy. He fidgeted. 'Thing is,' he began with true legal caution, 'I know it's only six o'clock but I'm starving. Didn't get any lunch—I spent my lunch hour trying to persuade an elderly lady not to leave all her money to a dog's home.'

'That was a bit tough on the dogs,' Caitlin said. She tried not to grin at him too intimately in a desperate attempt to curb her tendency to fall in love with cute solicitors at the drop of a hat.

'Well, the existing bequest of two million pounds will certainly be enough to keep all the current incumbents of the home well-stocked with Doggie Chunx for the entire span of their sad little lives, and now Jago and Wilkes will be able to attend to the legal needs of another generation of the family too. For a fee, of course.'

'Nice work,' said Caitlin.

He beamed at her. 'I thought so. Hence the appetite.'

'I love it when a man uses the word hence in an actual sentence,' Caitlin said. 'Where are you taking me? Or am I taking you?'

'No, no. I'm—er—I'm afraid I'm a bit old-fashioned. I'm most definitely taking you,' he said loudly, and to her surprise and amusement, even with only the streetlight she could see he blushed deepest beetroot. In a lower voice he added, 'Well, obviously I don't mean that in the sense of...'

'No, it's fine.' Caitlin waved her hands at him to prevent any further awkward explanations. She was trying not to laugh, sensing that might make things worse.

'It's this way. I thought we'd walk, if that's all right, it's not far.'

She wasn't sure what to say, especially in view of his accidental double-entendre. But before she had enough time to think of anything to say, they had arrived.

'Oh! A pub,' she said, thinking she had had enough pub-grub for one week. Then she wished she'd managed to inject a bit more enthusiasm into her voice.

'I hope you don't mind,' he said, anxious again, his eyebrows arching with worry. 'I'm not very good in posh restaurants. Clumsy. And erm... And after all, you're wearing jeans and er—trainers. And you've got what looks like bath cleaner on your sleeve.'

She couldn't argue with the truth of that. She made a mental note to remember to behave herself as he stood back to hold the door open for her.

It was nice inside, not too crowded, not too showy or noticeably attempting to entice young and rowdy sports-fans with huge flat-screen TVs or slot machines. Also, she noticed with relief, there were no play areas for small children. It shouldn't get too noisy in here.

Henry found them a table in the rear of the pub, set in its own little alcove. He put down his briefcase, unwound his scarf—probably cashmere, thought Caitlin—carefully folded it then lay it on top of the briefcase. Then he unbuttoned his coat—also probably cashmere, she thought ruefully—and carefully folded that too, and lay it over the other items. Finally, he took his seat, loosening his tie and undoing the topmost button of his shirt. That was probably the most casual he ever got, she suspected.

By this time, Caitlin had plonked herself down, shoved her jacket back off her shoulders, and left it squashed down behind her and had already read half the menu.

Henry said, his tone low but earnest, 'Are you seeing anyone?'

Caitlin blinked at him. She had expected to build up to that question a little more slowly. In say, three or four months... 'Well, I—er...'

'It's just that I like you. And I'm single. And I'm hoping you might like me and also be single. But I realise it's quite inappropriate, and obviously if you'd prefer things to remain formal and business-like, I would perfectly understand, and I want you to know that I would never, ever do anything to make you feel uncomfortable, and of course you would be perfectly within your rights to curtail our business relationship and find a new legal representative elsewhere, and there is a formal complaints procedure that you may wish to make use of, and—er—If so, I can give you the details...'

'Henry!' Caitlin held up her hand in an attempt to

halt his manifesto of apology. 'It's all right. Yes, I do like you. Yes, I am single. But let's just see how we get on, shall we? Or have you got a pre-nup in your briefcase just on the off chance?'

'Well, I do have a blank—er—ah. You're joking.'

'Yes, I'm afraid I am. Is it always Henry or do you prefer Harry—or...?'

'No. It is emphatically always Henry,' said Henry, emphatically. 'Thank you. And you're always Caitlin, I take it? Never...? What is it, Cait, I imagine?'

'Caitlin's fine, thanks.'

'What would you like to drink, Caitlin?'

'A glass of rosé, please, nothing fancy.'

He nodded and headed to the bar. She sat back and smiled to herself. Ooh, look at me, I'm on an accidental date! It felt a bit odd, but comfortable, pleasant, nice. Rather like Henry himself. She had time to send a quick 'accidental date alert' to Jen and Sonia, then had her phone safely back in her bag as he turned around.

He returned with their drinks. He was having a glass of white wine. Caitlin somehow found that surprising, because although she didn't know why, he just seemed more of a red wine kind of guy. Though if he'd come back with a whisky, that wouldn't have surprised her at all. At least it wasn't a pot of tea, with a little dish of lemon slices. Or one of those brandies that cost more than an entire meal.

'You wanted to consult me on a legal matter?' He asked as soon as he sat down again. She nodded. She sipped her drink. Very nice. She gave another nod, of approval this time.

'Yes, I've got quite a lot to tell you, and then I need you to tell me what you think I should do about it.'

'Ah. Shall we order our food, then you can tell me whilst we eat? Only I don't think I can last much longer.' His cute smile did things to her insides. She wondered if she could get him out of those good clothes on a first date. She imagined him carefully folding each layer of clothing one at a time when all she wanted to do was rip his shirt off him. And that stupid tie. She shook her head slightly, forcing herself to look down at her drink. Just get through the meal, she told herself crossly.

'Good idea.'

Again, once they had made their selections, he noted the table number then trotted off to the bar to place their orders, returning with his hands full of paper napkins, cutlery and a small steel bucket of condiments.

'I wasn't sure what you'd want with your chicken,' he said. 'So I brought all of the sauces. Right then. Tell me everything.' He leaned forward above his folded hands and fixed her with all his grave grey-eyed attention.

At first she kept getting distracted by those lovely eyes with their long lashes, but then she got into her story and even when their food arrived, she kept going until she had told him everything that had happened right up to her call to him that morning.

When she had finished, she sat back and waited for his reaction. She looked down at her plate and saw with a sense of disappointment that she had finished her food as well as her story. Henry continued to tidily consume his bream. He didn't say anything, but his eyes were focussed on a spot halfway up the back of the seat next to Caitlin. She interpreted this as him pondering deeply.

He pushed aside his plate and dabbed his mouth with his napkin. He put that on the plate. He sipped his wine. He thought. Then finally, just as she was seriously thinking about screaming at him, he said,

'God, what a mess!'

Caitlin deflated like a soufflé. She had hoped for something a little more helpful. But then she realised that he was preparing to expound.

'Very well, this is what we'll do. You will arrange for an expert to value the items you took from the cottage, and you will also immediately insure the lot for twice that value. That will be expensive, so if you find it's beyond your means, I will very happily arrange an advance for you from the estate whilst we're waiting for probate to go through, as that will take a while. You've already, very wisely, arranged for someone to house-sit the cottage and you'll be house-sitting Mr Mitcheson's property up here. And you've had all the locks changed.'

'Again,' she said.

'Again,' he acknowledged with a slight nod. 'Now,' he said, 'Show me this video footage.'

While he fished his tablet out of his briefcase and rummaged for some earbuds in a little leather case, she moved around to his side of the table and squashed herself in next to him. He moved up obligingly but left his arm draped across the back of the seat. She liked having it there behind her. It felt like a sneaky teenage clinch.

He held up the earbuds, 'I assume there's sound?'

'Absolutely.' She plugged a memory stick into his tablet.

He nodded, put in the earbuds and then watched the video through twice. After the third time, he pulled out one earbud and said to her, 'I know I saw them at your grandfather's funeral, but remind me who these people are.'

She pointed to each one in turn, named them and told him their relationship to her, and to one another. At least, the relationships they'd originally told her, because now she wasn't so sure. With what Brenda had told her, and what she'd overheard, and what Michael had said, it was now a bit of a grey area. She told him anything else she knew about them.

'So,' she said. 'I now think only Becka, or possibly Becka and Laura are genuinely my cousins. Michael is not Michael-my-cousin, because according to the neighbour, Gramps told her that he died some years ago. And Gareth is just Laura's partner.'

He nodded, his expression grave.

She put her phone away after sending the footage to Henry, they ordered dessert and coffee, and then Caitlin got out the old photos from Gramps' chest of drawers. She told Henry again what Gramps had said in the hospital the night he died.

He looked through the photos in turn. Caitlin told him the little she had learned from Kath.

'That is my grandfather, and that is my grandmother, Isobel. We think this young girl is Isobel's sister, my Aunt Pamela.'

'Isobel was very beautiful,' he said. 'You look just like her.'

Caitlin coloured at that but felt pleased. No one had ever called her beautiful before. At most she had been described as 'not bad' looking. She filed the compliment away for gloating over at a later, more leisured time. Possibly with her friends.

'This third woman Kath says looks like a lady called Barbara Kennett, and if it is, Kath thinks one of the young men could be Barbara's brother Stanley. But she says she might be wrong about that. And even if she's right, that still leaves one young chap and a young woman unnamed.'

And then Caitlin had a brief crisis of confidence, and quickly added, 'Of course, I don't know if any of this is relevant, or if it even matters. It might be nothing at all to do with the cousins and what they've been trying to do. It's just part of the huge puzzle that has become my life now.'

He nodded, looking through all the photos several times, as if trying to commit to memory all their faces. Then he handed them back. He made no further comment and Caitlin was deeply disappointed.

He said, 'I'll look through your grandfather's file again, to see if there is anything there that might be useful, and I'll let you know.'

'What about these papers my so-called cousins are looking for? Do you have any idea what they might? Did Gramps ever mention anything to you?'

'Presumably they are looking for receipts or bills of sale, but I'm not sure... Oh, actually there could be an inventory of some sort included in the older part of my files. If these antiques are worth a lot of money, there could be old provenances or insurance documents. With paperwork of that sort, the items will certainly attract far better prices.'

'But how much can they hope to get?' Caitlin asked, adding, 'I asked Kath this same question. I mean, even if the furniture brings them, what, say ten thousand pounds, divided between them, that's not really a lot of money by today's standards.'

'I know very little about antiques, I'm afraid. Clearly, they think it's worthwhile. Get an expert in to tell you for sure.'

He drank the last of his coffee. Pushing aside his cup, he tentatively took her hand.

'I'm so sorry about your grandfather, Caitlin. Your last relation in the world, apart from one of these shifty cousins. You must miss him terribly?'

'Miss my grandfather?' Caitlin asked.

Henry nodded. His huge grey eyes were deep enough to drown in. She was half in love already.

'I don't miss him at all,' she said with a sardonic laugh. 'I didn't love him. I hated the bastard, and I'm glad he's dead.'

Their conversation went along more ordinary, safer lines, she set herself to trying to make him laugh.

'*Bake Off* or *Come Dine With Me*?' she asked him with a smirk. Would he even know what she was talking about. He pretended to be offended.

'*Bake Off*, obviously. I'm slightly shocked you even had to ask.'

That made her laugh. '*Big Brother* or *I'm A Celeb Get Me Out of Here*?'

He shook his head. 'No, sorry, I don't do those.'

'You're not a soap opera fan, are you?' She made it sound as though it was an earnest enquiry. A bit like she was asking if he was an alcoholic. He laughed again.

'No, of course not. My mother keeps me up to date on those. I might watch the occasional *Marvel* universe type thing. Or cricket.'

'I knew you'd like cricket!' she laughed. It felt very warm in there suddenly, she thought. His eyes were very intense even if his smile was wide and relaxed. His arm was a little closer about her shoulders, and he kept looking at her lips.

But panicking a little once they got outside, by the door to the restaurant, she'd just grabbed his hand before he could touch her, given him a quick, rather impersonal hug.

'Well thanks for a lovely evening, I must get off.'

'Oh let me walk you back to your car, at least,' he'd said, and did so in silence.

He'd seemed surprised, and possibly a little

disappointed, or perhaps she just hoped she was. He'd said goodnight, briefly touching her arm as he said it and then she got in her car and drove away, feeling let down, yet it was her own fault.

*

Chapter Twelve

It was back-breaking, neck-aching work, going through every single bit of paper she could find in Gramps' house. But she forced herself to keep going, even through drawers and cupboards she knew she or Brenda from next door had already searched.

Just in case.

Because surely, *surely*, she kept telling herself, it had to be here somewhere. That one piece of paper or document that the cousins seemed to think justified breaking into her grandfather's property, and her own flat. It must be a will from an earlier generation, or an inventory of property, perhaps from Gramps' childhood home, or even an insurance document or a bill of sale. It had to be something that provided information about either the house in Sussex or an item of furniture, and was vital to securing a good price for it.

At last she was forced to sit back on her heels, looking at the paper mountains all around her, and admit there was nothing remotely useful amongst any of it. Most it she just looked at, shaking her head, and wondered why on earth he'd felt he wanted to keep it in the first place.

Her phone pinged. She felt a surge of excitement on seeing that it was a message from *Phwoargeous sort-of Boyfriend Emphatically Henry*. He said:
If you're at a loose end at all, would you be interested in meeting me for lunch?

Her text back was a simple one: *Hell yes! When and where?*

His reply was immediate: *In ten minutes. Same place as last night?*

As was hers: *Okies.*

'Okies?' he asked with a shy grin as he got to his feet to greet her. She leaned towards him, expecting a polite peck on the cheek, but was surprised when he kissed her firmly full on the mouth. He didn't let go of her hand as they sat down.

His business-like approach—and the fact that he had an hour for lunch, no more—meant they chose their food and he ordered it quickly, without wasting time on conversation. Once he came back from the bar and sat next to her, she explained *Okies* was short for okey dokey which was what she and her besties always said to one another.

He nodded. There was a pause, then he said, 'Was that the two ladies I met at your grandfather's funeral?'

'Yes. Jen and Sonia. We've been close for a long time now.'

He nodded again. 'So does that mean I'm one of your besties, too?' He grinned at her again, a broad grin that revealed a tiny dimple in his right cheek.

She leaned forward to kiss the dimple softly, and

with a slightly unsteady laugh said, 'You're definitely a bestie.'

'Good.' He smiled down at his hands. 'So, have you found what you were looking for at your grandfather's house?'

'Ugh, no!' She raked a hand through her hair. 'No, I've been through the entire place. I gone through so much old rubbish, bits and pieces and still found nothing whatsoever of sue. It's *so* frustrating!'

'I've spoken to my father. He said that the only things we have on file relates to the house purchases, both of them, but nothing out of the ordinary. I'm happy to pass them on to you if you want to take a look, but I honestly don't think they'll be of the slightest use.'

'Hmm,' she groaned, 'I was afraid you'd say that. I don't think there's any point in me looking over them.'

'No.'

Their food arrived and as they ate, the conversation revolved around more personal things.

'Did you always want to be a solicitor, right from when you were small?' she asked him.

He shook his head. 'No, I wanted to be an astronaut, but sadly that didn't work out.'

'There's still time,' she joked. 'You're only, what...?'

'Forty.'

'Ah. Well, maybe you could be one of the astronauts that test the spacecraft but don't go all the way to the moon.'

'That sounds like a good safe job, testing spacecraft that might not work properly. I think I'll stick with the law, thank you.'

He talked a little more about his childhood but turned it back to her, asking her about hers. Little by little, things came out, more than she'd expected, more than was perhaps appropriate for what was, in essence, a second date. But she felt safe with him, comfortable, it seemed okay to tell him things she normally would never speak of.

As they said goodbye outside the pub, he wrapped his arms around her and held her close. They kissed. Her heart singing, she said a reluctant goodbye, and he said he'd call her later.

When she walked back to her car, she looked back over her shoulder. He had done the same, and that made her smile even more. She waved to him. He waved back. She could see his smile from there.

'Lovely man,' she said to herself with another smile.

She went back to Gramps' house full of determination to get to the bottom of things. She needed to deal with it all and get it out of the way to concentrate on building a relationship with this good-looking, sexy but shy solicitor.

In less than five minutes of research on the internet that evening, Caitlin had the phone number of an auction house in the Brighton area. A scan of their 'About us' and 'Meet the team' sections showed no sign of anyone she recognised—hopefully she wouldn't have Gareth or any of the others turning up at her door. She decided to give them a call in the morning to arrange an appointment for someone to come and assess the items that had been 'liberated' from the cottage and were now in storage.

She was spending the night at her grandfather's London house. On her way there following her impromptu dinner with Henry she collected bedding and a few supplies from her flat, and on arriving at the house she first popped next door to let Brenda know she would be there.

The Cousins

The sitting-room had always given her the creeps for some reason she couldn't explain, maybe it was the vast number of ornaments or pictures or just the memory of all the stuff spilled out over the floor that morning, so she decided to sit at the kitchen table: she felt snug and secure there. The curtains were closed, the back door to the garden was locked and bolted, and the front door had not only been locked and bolted but there was also a new security chain in place. She sincerely hoped that would be enough to keep out even the most determined of 'cousins'.

Even more reassuring, she had received a text from Kath's grandson Ian in Southdean to say that two of his mates—strapping rugby players aged 19 and 22—were staying at the cottage and had been warned to take 'no nonsense' from anyone claiming to have been sent by Caitlin. It was strange to have so many kind people on her side. She wasn't used to that.

Next she had some research to do. Her specialty was family history, although for her job she also did research into local social and even industrial history. She had earned her living for the last fifteen years helping others to do what she now had to do for herself. She knew people thought it odd that she'd never looked into her own antecedents. Clients had often asked her, 'How far did you trace your own line back?' only to be told, 'Well actually, I haven't done much...' It had cost her several commissions from private clients who assumed it signified something lacking in her professional skills.

But she had never done any research into her own family tree apart from the small project that had been part of her professional qualification. At that time, she'd concentrated on her father's family and had managed to trace her father's paternal line through many generations of military or domestic service all the way back to the 1400s.

She had ignored her mother's side of the family completely. Her watchword had always been, you can't unknow what you find out. And quite simply, she just had not wanted to know.

Until now.

She still didn't *want* to know. Now though, she had to find out as much as she could, and as quickly as she could. She logged on to the family history research sites she subscribed to, and taking out a notebook and pen, she began to make some headings at the top of several pages.

It was fortunate that all her enquiries would be focused on the relatively recent past. That made it so much easier to find the information she was looking for. If she'd been looking into the really old stuff, that would have taken more time and definitely a lot more ingenuity. Plus she'd need to go to various other depositories of information. But generally speaking, the recent past, the last hundred years or so, was quite easy.

Ordinarily when she undertook research for a client, or if she was just giving someone a bit of guidance, she could get a quick overview of their tree from the internet, but she would not consider the information as proven until she had obtained or verified for herself the original sources of the information. Some sites had information that contained errors or gaps or had been uploaded by people who just hoped or assumed it was accurate. Caitlin had often found that even in family tree research, pride and a desire for importance meant that people grabbed at certain information or ignored information rather than admit that their ancestors weren't rich or famous or mentioned in chronicles. Sometimes people didn't want to be 'ordinary' even if it was four hundred years earlier.

For these reasons, she never took what she found at face value until she had proved it for herself, either by seeing an original source, cross-checking with other sources, or by ordering a copy of a certificate, in the case of relatively recent individuals, born in England or Wales after 1837.

This was the part of family history many amateur researchers didn't bother with, often lifting their research wholesale from a variety of different sites, some good, some less good, but doing nothing to verify for themselves that what they had found out was true or accurate. In the space of an evening, they could create for themselves an entire family tree and consider that they had 'done research'. But they had confirmed nothing, checked nothing, had no evidence to serve as proof.

Not so the professional genealogist. Every source had to be checked and if at all possible, cross-checked. So many times Caitlin had found data had been wrongly transcribed, misfiled, misread or misspelled. Or was just plain wishful thinking on the part of someone who had found a person with a similar name to their own ancestor and made an assumption that it was the same person.

Much of what many people took for granted was only one part of the story of a family tree. In Caitlin's view, it wasn't enough to learn that Person A married Person B and Person C was born. She wanted to know where they lived, how they lived, what they did for a living, how much they earned and the kind of life that wage bought them. She wanted to know what they thought, how they felt, what they believed in. She wanted to know if they were educated, readers, artists, if they liked the countryside or preferred the town. She wanted to know as far as possible everything there was to know about them. She wanted them to become real, fully fleshed human beings, alive in her imagination.

And for her, that was where 'proper' research came into the equation.

But for tonight, all she needed was an unconfirmed but viable overview of the last three or four generations of her mother's family, and she wanted it in the amateur's style—copied directly and unconfirmed from the internet. Proof could, if necessary, come later.

Just two hours later, she decided she had everything she needed.

Her phone rang. The screen showed the caller as *Emphatically boyfriend Henry*.

He sounded a bit unsure of himself.

'I-I know it's a bit late. Sorry about that. I was—erm—I was just ringing to say thank you for a lovely lunch,' he began, then lapsed into silence.

Smiling to herself, Caitlin assured him she had enjoyed it too, and she added that she hoped they could see each other again very soon.

'But,' she said, 'I'm going down to Sussex again tomorrow and might stay for a couple of days.'

'I see. Made any headway?'

She told him that she had got someone staying at the cottage for tonight, so she felt reasonably sure things would be all right on that front. And that she had the contact number for a Brighton-based auctioneer to get the valuations carried out and planned to call them in the morning.

'I've been doing some rough family tree research,' she added, 'and I've been able to more or less confirm my suspicions about my cousins.'

'What have you found out?' he asked.

She thought he sounded a bit tense and hastened to reassure him.

'Don't worry, it's nothing that would change my inheritance. Nothing that could reflect badly on your firm or your work, nothing like that. It's just that I searched for the birth of a cousin. First of all I found the marriage of my Great Aunt Isobel's sister Pamela, who married a chap named Donald Leafe. They had two children, Michael Leafe—he's the one Gramps' neighbour Brenda Cahill said died of a drug overdose or something like that, according to what Gramps told her. I've found the date of his death, but I need to order the actual certificate to find out the details. Then there was another child born a couple of years later. In fact, those are the only two births to that surname in Sussex for the whole of the period from 1950 to 1990, so it pretty well has to be them. The other baby was a little girl who was named Rebecca May Leafe, so I'm fairly confident that is Becka.'

She could picture his serious expression, his gorgeous eyes, as he pondered this. She would have liked to see that dimple again, but his phone was only on talk mode, not video. She'd just have to remember his face.

All he said was, 'And the others?'

'I don't know. But as I mentioned before, the one calling himself Michael Leafe is obviously not who he says he is. I suppose he could genuinely just be her boyfriend or partner. But it's the other two I can't get to grips with, Laura and Gareth. Who are they and how are they involved in this?'

'That will be the crucial bit,' he agreed. He was silent again. A bit too silent, she thought. Did he have something on his mind? Was he having second thoughts about getting involved with her? After a few moments he said in a very quiet, very solemn way,

'Caitlin, there's something I want to tell you. Need. I *need* to tell you something, before this goes any further...'

Caitlin, hearing this, felt a surge of panic. He's going to break up with me. After just two date. Not that either was a proper date as such, but... Because of what I told him. He's going to say that he likes me, but he doesn't think we're suited, and that it could never work, and... Oh God. She was vaguely aware of him asking her to listen to him, but all she could think was that she couldn't talk about this right now, she couldn't cope, didn't want to hear it, not right now. Please. She had to stop him. So she said in a quick, mad rush, 'Oh, sorry, someone's at the door, I've got to go, sorry, stay in touch, sorry, bye!'

And she ended the call.

A glance at the dark screen of her phone showed that it was now ten minutes after one o'clock in the morning. She thumped herself on the forehead. Moron! How many people come to the door at one o'clock in the morning? And who would even answer the door at that time?

Feeling ridiculous, she muted her phone and threw it back in her bag. She was exhausted but irritable. She turned off her laptop and packed it away ready for the trip to Sussex in the morning, and she went up to bed.

Tomorrow she'd be off to the cottage again. One or two days away would give her the chance to sort herself out before calling Henry back to apologise for being an idiot and to tell him how much she'd like to see him again.

It took her forever to fall asleep. Her dreams were unsettling, strange and vague, and she awoke feeling like she hadn't slept in years.

On her journey down to Sussex the next day, she was still feeling furious with herself.

'I acted like I was on speed, or drunk, or something. I was crazy! What the hell is wrong with me? Even if he wasn't going to break up with me, he will now! And I can't say I'd blame him if he never wants to see me again,' She ranted to Jen during a handsfree call as she drove.

Jen did her best to soothe her, and then Caitlin remembered to ask after not-too-sure-about-Rob. She heard way too much about what Rob thought, what Rob had said, and even more way too much about bedroom-related things. If she hadn't been driving, she'd have put her fingers in her ears and said, 'Not listening, not listening.' She ended by promising they'd have a girls' night in when she got back in a day or two.

In the relative silence of the car, she went back over the brief conversation with Henry in her head. Eventually after running over and over it, her thoughts began to quieten. He had wanted to tell her something. She had assumed he wanted to say something like, he felt they should keep their relationship professional. Instead of discussing it maturely she had freaked out and retreated. She was an idiot. And had pretty much proved his point for him. She heaved a great sigh as she signalled and turned left at a junction.

'I should have heard him out,' she told herself yet again as she joined the now-familiar queue for the motorway. 'I at least owe him that much. It might not have been anything bad. Because why would he phone me at one o'clock in the morning unless it was something really important to him? Something that he just had to tell me, or he'd never get to sleep. And I—I just acted like a child. Shit.'

She was glaring at the man in the car next to hers, completely unaware of what she was doing. When she became aware of him, he was looking at her with a 'What did I do?' face, his hands turning upwards. She waved her hand in apology and turned away to glower at something else.

Poor Henry, she thought. I must ring him later and explain.

He had been surprised, she remembered, when she had revealed how much she had hated her grandfather. And he had wanted to know why, of course, and because she was hoping to get to know him better, maybe be in a relationship with him, she wanted him to know the truth. Although she had felt uncomfortable talking about it there and then in the pub like that, on their first date, without thinking about it first.

The problem was, she thought, almost everyone these days seems to have been sexually abused by a trusted person, often a family member. The media was full of it, and it was beginning to be something of a cliché, people generally were becoming dismissive of it, even bored by it, they were so sick of hearing about it all the time, everywhere. Compassion fatigue. Like, oh so you were abused by your grandfather? Welcome to the club! We were all abused by someone, you're not special.

So she had only told Henry about it very briefly. He had been shocked, she could tell, but he had been concerned, sympathetic and even horrified that she had suffered such a thing.

'People always used to think he was a lovely man,' Caitlin had told him. 'He was so charming, so plausible, so correct in every way.'

'It's very difficult for me to equate what you've told me with the man I met on just a couple of occasions, but he was always so, yes, you're right, he did come across as charming. He *was* charming.'

Caitlin had nodded sadly and looked down at her coffee. He didn't believe her, she knew it. And now that she had told him everything, it would be uncomfortable between them, and he would probably make an excuse, 'Got to be up early for work!' or something like that, and the evening would end. And he'd never call her again. Or perhaps just once more, to tell her he didn't think they were suited, that he hoped she'd meet someone just right for her really, really soon, because she was *such a great gal*. She began to wish she'd continued to pretend to be grieved by the loss of her grandfather. Her relationship with Henry was over before it had even begun.

But then, he had said, 'It must have been very hard for you to make people listen to you.' Then he had just briefly touched her arm. 'You must have felt betrayed.'

She had looked up. He had been gazing at her, his eyes fixed on her.

'Yes,' she had said. 'But mostly I felt guilty. I changed. I became the badly behaved brat, the ungrateful child and teenager who didn't appreciate all that he did for me. I did everything I could do to avoid him. And I always felt bad for the way I acted, but I just couldn't help it. I just couldn't sit at the dinner table with him on a Sunday and pretend everything was lovely and normal and that we were one big happy family. So that meant I fell out with my parents too. And the problem was, I didn't want to hurt either my parents or him, even.'

'Did you ever tell them?'

She shook her head.

'No, there didn't seem any point. But we didn't see

that much of him anyway, my dad's job kept him busy, and as I got older I managed to avoid seeing Gramps for most of the year, apart from Christmastime. And I became something of a genius at avoiding difficult situations. And then they died, my parents, my grandmother. I just used to dash in to make sure he was okay, then dash out again. But I was at uni, then working, so that made it easier. And now—he has left everything to me, and I feel... just... terrible.'

There had been a long silence, awkward, tense. She drank the last drop of her coffee and tried to change the subject.

'What about you? What have you done with your life apart from longing to be an astronaut?'

They had talked a little on personal lines. It was all a bit depressing—his divorce, (no children), her failed relationships, but at least by the time they were ready to leave, they knew a lot more about each other.

And now, she thought, pulling the car off the motorway, I'm never going to see him again unless I want to sue someone or make out a will.

When Caitlin reached the cottage, she was surprised by a flood of emotion that filled her as she drew the car onto the drive, noting the same old trees, the same old ruts in the mud, the white walls and black beams, the thatch. She had a sense of homecoming that was entirely new to her.

She was growing to love this cottage.

*

Chapter Thirteen

Kath was there, with the kettle already boiling. She was in the process of serving slices of a large fruitcake onto dainty plates.

'I let the boys go, they had stuff to get on with,' Kath explained. 'But they said it was quiet here last night, not a dickey-bird. So maybe your cousins have given up?'

'Hmm. I wish I could believe that,' Caitlin said. She told Kath she was meeting the auctioneer at the storage facility later in the day. 'But first I thought I'd pop into the little parish church, on the off-chance they've still got any original church records. I've worked out that it's the woman called Becka who is, I think, genuinely my cousin, but I still don't know who the other three are. I need to check a few details at this end in case they shed any light.'

The vicar was kind enough to leave the registers with her. Of course, she was a qualified genealogist and knew how to handle source materials, and the registers in question weren't particularly old or fragile, so he didn't need to worry about them coming to any harm.

But even so, she pulled out a pair of thin cotton gloves from her bag, and had a pencil with her notebook, so that seemed to completely satisfy him. Pencil marks can—often, though not always—be erased. However, pens or any kind of ink-containing implement are forbidden from coming into contact with primary sources, in case carelessness or deliberate sabotage causes someone's great-granny to be expunged from the records permanently. And as for food or drinks being allowed within half a mile of a primary source—forget it!

She found her own baptism in 1988, and from there easily confirmed details of her parents' marriage in 1987, then went back to find that of her grandparents in 1963: Richard Reginald Mitcheson to Isobel Clay on Saturday, December 14th. Searching forward from there, she found her mother's baptism in the following December, on the 3rd of the month in 1964: Marian Susan Mitcheson.

Next, Caitlin searched for and found her great-aunt Pamela's wedding in 1978 to Donald Leafe followed by the baptisms of Michael Leafe and Rebecca May Leafe in 1980 and 1982 respectively. So far, so good.

It was as she was just idly browsing through the pages she began to notice the prevalence of the surname Jago.

At first she was quite excited, thinking it was a fun coincidence. Amongst the several Jagos baptised between 1970s and 1995, she found one single baptism of a Henry Jago: in March 1984. This was just the right time to be 'her' Henry Jago, and was the only Henry Jago she could find within ten years' worth of entries. Hmm.

Well, she told herself, it could just be a coincidence. But then she followed the records back and found that Henry's parents' marriage: another Henry Jago, occupation: solicitor, and his wife Sarah Kennett.

She sat stunned, just staring at the page.

This had to be 'her' Henry and his father, surely? Otherwise, it felt like a coincidence too far for Caitlin to be able to dismiss it as of no interest. She fished out her tablet from her bag and signed into her online genealogy accounts. She searched but found no other Henry Jago born in that year, or indeed, within two years either side of the estimated 1984 year of birth. He'd said he was forty, but that could be anything from 'forty today' to forty 364 days go, almost a variation of two years. She searched for the period 1970 to 1990. There was a Harold Jago born in Lancashire in 1977—but what had Henry said? Emphatically Henry. And Harold Jago would now be approximately 47, so...

She had to accept she had accidentally found the right Henry Jago.

But now, an unpleasant and highly unwelcome idea began to suggest itself in Caitlin's mind. She dismissed it though, reminding herself that the prevalence of the surname Kennett was purely regional and didn't necessarily link Henry or his mother to the Barbara Kennett who had been suggested by Kath Green as one of the girls in the old photographs. There were bound to be Kennetts everywhere in this part of Sussex, just as there were plenty of other local surnames such as Epps or Dunk.

And years ago every other female child had been called Pamela, Barbara, Brenda, Jean, Doris, all the kind of names that these days were no longer so much in vogue.

Caitlin began chasing back through the records. And with her cautions to potential clients echoing ironically in her own ears, she soon discovered much more than she had bargained for: in 1985, a marriage between Henry Jago, widower and Pamela Leafe, widow.

This was getting worse! Groaning to herself as she returned to the baptism pages, in less than another ten minutes she found the entry:

The 1986 baptism of Laura Jago, daughter of Henry Jago and Pamela Leafe nee Clay.

She sat back in the seat, stunned.

It had to be the same person. It had to be more than mere coincidence now, surely? Which meant... Laura—her 'cousin'—was Henry's younger half-sister. So now, probably, definitely, surely that meant...? It had to mean...? Surely?

She shook her head to try to clear her thoughts. They seemed to have got jammed somehow. She couldn't think. She couldn't reason. She just couldn't seem to work it all out.

She felt sick. Shoving aside the register, her notebook and pencil, everything, she forced herself to her feet and stumbled outside into the graveyard for some air. Outside the cold air hit her, and she found it was raining heavily. Doubling over with the rain pelting on her back, she gasped in great gulps of air, and the nausea subsided, replaced by deep abiding misery.

You can't unknow what you find out.

How many times had she said to her clients, 'Sometimes you may find out things you'd have preferred not to know'? And now she had done exactly that herself, in the most horrendous way she could imagine, sitting there, thinking to herself, ooh look, a Jago, how funny if Henry's family came from this area too.

Henry Jago was Laura's half-brother. He was therefore some kind of relation to Caitlin, a kind of step-cousin, because he was Becka's stepbrother too as well as Laura's half-brother.

Therefore. It had to be...

In the time they had spent together they hadn't so much as mentioned siblings.

Caitlin, there's something I want to tell you, he had said.

He knew. Obviously. He *had* to know. Everything. He had to know... How could he not know? He had to be involved...

He had known this whole time. Since before the funeral. Since forever. She had showed him the video! And what had he said?

Remind me who these people are...

She doubled up, retching, but mercifully wasn't sick. And with divine timing, the vicar hurried to her side, all concern.

'Whatever is the matter, my dear?'

She struggled to catch her breath. He supported her as she fell back against the church wall, gasping, scraping her fingers against the mortar, snapping off the tip of a nail.

'Sorry. I'm afraid I don't feel at all well. I came out for a bit of air. I'm so sorry. Oh, but don't worry, I haven't made any mess on the registers.'

He chivvied her into the manse, sat her down in the kitchen amongst the pumpkins and the cotton-wool cobwebs and bustled about making her a cup of sweet tea, strong enough to satisfy the most demanding of bricklayers or other manual labourers. He plied her with a good solid sultana scone, thickly buttered, and after a few minutes, physically at least, she began to feel better.

She repeated that she hadn't done any damage to the registers, and he smiled so broadly she knew he was genuinely relieved to hear that.

'Is it—er—anything you'd like to—er—share?' he enquired, rather nervously.

She gave him a big broad smile, acting again, and said so sincerely that he believed her, 'Oh no, Vicar, it's nothing. Just felt a bit funny for a moment. I think I'm just a bit tired, been overdoing things a bit lately.'

That wasn't her last shock of the day.

As soon as the auctioneer saw the furnishings, he went into raptures. He asked if she minded if he took a few photos. She told him to take as many as he wished. He asked if she had provenances. She said she didn't know, but it was a possibility. She asked him how much it was all worth. He asked her to pinch him because he thought he might be dreaming. She pinched him. Hard. He winced, fought back tears and got out his little calculator. He tapped in figures for several minutes before showing her the sum it totalled up to.

Caitlin needed fresh air for the second time that day. She dashed to the ladies' at the storage facility, and was violently sick. She returned ten minutes later, white-faced and wobbly with a vile taste in her mouth.

'Please tell me that's a joke. You just wanted to get back at me for pinching you,' she said.

He almost smiled. Almost. He shook his head, and commented, 'Of course that's only a conservative estimate. At auction, these items could go for considerably more with the right people in the room, or more likely, online. Erm, and then there would be my fees to deduct, of course.' He looked politely hopeful, like a dog after a juicy treat.

He turned back to survey the glories before him, adding, 'That is the finest Aubusson carpet to enter the market—if, of course, it *does* enter the market—for many, many years. And the Chippendale drinks cabinet—simply wonderful, words cannot express... Even if it was made by someone else, anyone else, it would be a nice piece, but by the master craftsman himself, and with such *vigorous* decoration inside—such artistry, so fine, so delicate, so *highly collectable*.' He paused to mop his brow with what she suspected was an actual silk handkerchief.

Caitlin came to realise that the term 'highly collectable' was auctioneer's code for 'name your price'. Two of the little paintings Caitlin had dismissed as 'dreary' proved to be almost priceless, and the rest of the furniture was also expected to make a decent amount of money.

'I don't suppose you have any provenance, do you? I mean, it doesn't matter if you don't, I'm confident that the items are just what I think they are, but it might possibly help the sales along a bit.'

'What sort of thing would you want? Invoices or receipts?'

He shrugged, 'Well, yes, or insurance quotes, or anything basically that historically mentions the items.'

'An old will?'

He nodded. 'Yes, if the items are specifically mentioned. As I say, it's not too much of a problem. The clients I already have in mind know their stuff, they will know far more about these things than I do, and will recognise their value.'

'My friend Kath said my grandfather told her the

carpet was worth as much as the house. It seems he wasn't far wrong,' Caitlin said.

The auctioneer smiled and nodded. 'Well, house prices have certainly come on in the last few years, haven't they? Though not quite that much,' he said. 'So, would you like me to—um?'

'Does anyone named Gareth work with your firm?'

He looked puzzled but immediately said, 'No, definitely no Gareths. We've got a Mrs Gordon?'

'No, it was definitely a Gareth I wanted to avoid.'

'I think I can promise you no Gareths at the sales office.'

Caitlin thought for a moment. She did love that carpet. And the sofas, and even the naughty little drinks cabinet. But if they were worth that amount of money, she would constantly be worrying about them getting either damaged or stolen. And then there would be the cost of the insurance. And you couldn't use the carpet for—well, actually walking on, it was too... too... She made up her mind.

'Sell the lot,' she said.

The auctioneer, pausing in the act of trying to hug Caitlin, instead stepped back, held out his hand to shake hers, and thanked her profusely. Then immediately got onto his phone and began barking orders at minions before she could change her mind.

'We'll get everything collected today or tomorrow at the latest, and transferred to our own secure, temperature-controlled facilities. I can assure you our security is extremely comprehensive; you need have no concerns. I'll email you an agreement outlining—um, everything—and if there are any further queries, please, phone me any time.' He presented a business-card with a flourish and with a last longing look over his shoulder at the carpet, he hurried back to his car, already getting out his phone again, no doubt to pass on the good news to rivals.

Caitlin went to settle up for the rental of the storage unit and to let the people know what was going on.

She was tired, she still felt nauseous, her head was pounding, and above all she felt deeply depressed. She thought back a few nights to Becka wittering on about her maladies. Maybe they had more in common than Caitlin had realised. All she wanted now was to get back to the peace and quiet of the cottage and lie down.

She planned to take a nap but, in the end, she slept too long and too deeply, and dreams plagued her. All about her was in darkness and she was lost, walking in a forest where the trees met above her head and blocked out all the light. She couldn't find her way.

When she awoke she felt, if possible, even worse than before. Her nerves were shredded, and she just knew that the slightest little thing would have her bursting into tears.

She didn't want to think about what she'd discovered, yet how could she think of anything else? And if she didn't face up to the truth, she could be making things even more difficult for herself than they already were. It was a horrible mess.

She recognised Kath's tentative tapping on the front door—she never used her key to let herself in if she thought Caitlin was at home—and as Caitlin went to open it for her, she again thought about how she had warmed to Kath and come to see her almost as a mother-figure. Or perhaps more like a favourite aunt or something.

As soon as Kath came in, she took one look at Caitlin and said, 'You look like you need an early night.'

Whereupon Caitlin did finally burst into tears.

Sitting in the dining-room once again, sniffing into a wadded-up bunch of toilet tissue, Caitlin poured out to Kath everything she had discovered. And she told Kath about her embryonic romance with Henry Jago, now clearly doomed, and of her fears that he was involved with the cousins in the scam, which had clearly been to ransack the property and divide the— as she now knew—very generous spoils between them.

'I just found out this afternoon,' said Caitlin. 'Remember you said my grandfather told you that carpet was worth almost as much as the house? Well, it turns out that's pretty close to the truth. Actually, the house is worth slightly less. Anyway, he wasn't kidding. And that lovely globe with the drinks inside? Those naughty pictures? And all the rest of the furniture he had down there? Altogether the cousins would have got a decent whack even if they had to divide the money four ways.' Or five, she mentally amended, adding Henry into the mix.

She looked down at the floor, desperate to get a grip on her emotions. Kath poured them both another cup of tea. She pushed a packet of biscuits close to Caitlin's elbow. Almost without thinking, Caitlin took one and ate it.

'So you think your Henry Jago knew all along what they had planned, and he did nothing to warn you?'

'Worse than that,' Caitlin said miserably. 'I think it may have been his idea in the first place. He said all he had at his office were the purchase details for both houses. But now...'

'Now?' Kath prompted. Her eyes were sad as she looked at Caitlin. 'Now what?'

Caitlin was searching for the words. 'I mean, he said, all very vaguely, that it was 'just possible', that

The Cousins

he 'thought he may just have seen something' a long time ago somewhere in the files. But then, like I say, he said no, it was only the purchase agreements for the houses. But that had to be a lie. To me it's as clear as day. Who is better placed to know what my grandfather had down in that cellar and how much it was all worth? He must have known for years. Ever since he took over the account from his father.' She shook her head. 'And he's a brainiac. The plan to carry out all this had to come from him.' She covered her face. It felt too enormous to take in, but it had to be the truth, surely?

'What are you going to do?' Kath asked.

Caitlin sighed. She looked at her hands. She worried at a hangnail until she pulled it away and made her finger bleed. 'I think I'm going to sell the house.' She waited for a moment, but Kath said nothing and gave no hint of what she was thinking.

'I've already told the auctioneer guy that I want to sell everything from the cellar. Having found out how valuable everything is—especially that carpet—I'd be terrified of something awful happening to it. I'd never be able to relax again. What if there was a flood or everything got damp or mouldy, or something? Or I spilt coffee on it? Or a bunch of cousins broke in and... No, it's got to be sold. I can't look after it the way it all needs to be looked after. It's too beautiful to risk the damage that could come to it all.'

Kath nodded. 'I know what you mean. I have to admit, I always thought as how nice everything was, but I never thought it was quite *that* nice, if you get me. Really now, it's *too* nice. Makes you feel a bit uncomfortable with it.'

'That's what I thought too.' Caitlin nodded then fell silent again. She was dimly aware of Kath pottering about, doing things around her, going backwards and forwards, but she was too absorbed in her thoughts and feelings to pay much attention.

After a while, Kath rejoined Caitlin at the table in the dining-room Caitlin had initially dismissed as gloomy and a bit small, but which she now rather liked.

Kath said, 'Of course you could refurnish this place. It could be really nice. Maybe redecorate? Make it all new and modern. It could do with a lick of paint anyhow, and get rid of all that old stuff. It'd be your place then. You could stamp your own personality onto the place. It seems a shame to let go of everything. That cellar would make a lovely office. You could work from home, doing your research and whatnot. Or have you changed your mind about Mr Mitcheson's house in Town?'

Caitlin shook her head. 'No, I'm still planning on selling that too, just not through my fake-cousin's estate-agency.' She had a brief memory of her lunch and her evening with Henry, and felt sorrowful all over again at what she now knew. 'And I probably won't be able to use the practise of my solicitor-also-my-fake-cousin for the conveyancing, either. Beyond that, I just don't know what to do.'

'You don't really need to make up your mind right now, though, do you?' Kath pointed out.

Caitlin had to admit that was true. She was still thinking about Henry Jago, mulling over the whole situation. She felt horribly undecided. She wondered if Kath could help her with that situation.

'So as I already said, it turns out Henry Jago is from round here.' She dug in her bag for the old photos, and her notebook and pen. She flipped through the notebook until she found the relevant information.

'His father married my great-aunt. They had both

been married before, been bereaved, and left with young children. They got married, and then they had Laura, she's the youngest. So Henry himself is a kind of step-cousin of mine, you could say.'

Something came back to her then, and she thought out loud. 'That's right, and he told me I didn't need to feel bad about inheriting everything from my grandfather at the expense of my cousins because, according to him, my cousins, which presumably includes Henry himself, had inherited something from their grandmother, my grandmother Isobel's sister Pamela. And he met them at the funeral, *and* at the lunch afterwards, so obviously a) he recognised them in the video Ian took but didn't admit it to me, and even asked me to tell him who they were again or b) he already knew them anyway, even though all of them stood there and waited for me to make the introductions like the fool I was, and c) he obviously knew they weren't who they claimed to be, which means d) he definitely had to be involved which means,' she said, as her eyes welled up with tears again, 'e) he is a scumbag through and through.' She hung her head and tried to choke back the sobs. '*And I really liked him!*'

'Girls always go for a wrong 'un,' Kath said soothingly, patting Caitlin's hand. 'Don't blame yourself. He—and they—deliberately set out to win you over. It's not your fault, any of it. How could you have known what they were up to?'

Caitlin blew her nose and wiped her face again and managed a weak smile for Kath.

Kath, looking at her watch, jumped up in dismay. 'Oh! My casserole!' she said, and she grabbed her coat and bag, stepped out of her neat little house-shoes and into a pair of sturdy old-lady short boots with the furry bit round the ankle. 'So sorry, my love,

I've got to dash. Do pop in for a bit of tea with us about six o'clock, there'll be plenty.'

'Thanks very much, you're so kind. But I think I'll just go to the pub. Sorry, but I don't feel very sociable. I won't be gone long, so I'm hoping the place won't be broken into while I'm out this time, which would make a nice change. I'll probably sleep here tonight and go back to Town tomorrow. Again. I must admit I'm getting a bit fed up with the commuting.' She kissed Kath on the cheek, thanked her, and waved her off, standing at the door to watch her go.

Over her shoulder Kath called out, 'If you change your mind, you know where we are. You're always welcome.'

Caitlin smiled at this and closed the door. She spent a few minutes getting ready then set off to the pub. She was driving but that didn't matter as she wasn't intending to drink any alcohol anyway. She checked and double-checked the front door was locked before she left. There were no vehicles within sight as she left the cottage.

At the pub, she was glad to find a tiny table next to the ladies' toilets. The pub was busy, and the conversation along with the music made a wall of sound against which she could really have a good think.

She ate her pie and drank her zero-sugar cola. She looked through her notes and she stared at the photos.

She had a strong conviction that the photos, her notes from the church registers, and all the recent events were tangled together and all part of the same story. It all had to be part of the same story. She had the bare bones, but something crucial was missing. What was it?

Six youngsters, if you counted the little sister Pamela, which Caitlin felt she had to do because Pamela had grown up to be the mother of Becka and the deceased Michael, then of Laura and stepmother to Henry.

Six youngsters, teenagers, possibly with hormones running riot, all hanging out together in the months of 1963. A boy, his girlfriend, her little sister, another girl and—if Kath was right—possibly *her* brother and another youngster or two.

And then many, many years later an old man dying, saying that he knew she never told anyone.

'...Like you promised. No one knows.'

Those were the words he'd said to her the night he died. Caitlin could remember it vividly—the hospital ward with the curtains drawn around the bed. The sheets that she had straightened just for something to do. She remembered he looked at her and smiled and called her Isobel.

And he had said, 'You didn't say anything about the boy?' Then later on, just a few minutes later, he had said, 'I know you didn't tell anyone, just like you promised. No one knows. No need to fret, it'll be all right.' And he had said something about, 'All of us, that spring'.

Who was 'the boy'? What had been so special about 'that spring'? Why was it important no one had been told about—whatever it was?

And why would he need to remind his own wife not to fret about it? That seemed quite sinister. Or perhaps he had simply been rambling, an old man literally on his deathbed, who didn't know who he was talking to or what he was saying. Just uttering nonsense, unaware of what he was saying or who he was saying it to? She could have dismissed the whole thing as her over-active imagination, except...

...when she had looked around Gramps' house in London, she had found the photos in just the place he had said, and on the backs, the date: 14th May 1963. May was in the spring, after all. Was it 'that spring'?

It all hanged together so far. In 1963 Gramps would have been twenty-two or twenty-three. Older than Caitlin had initially thought. But in the photos all the youngsters could have been practically any age between fourteen and forty, with the same hairstyles and the same clothes as their parents also wore in those days. And Isobel would have been a little younger than him, Caitlin thought. Checking her notes, she found that Isobel would have been almost nineteen, Pamela almost ten years younger than her sister at around eight or nine years of age that year.

A thought occurred to her. Could one of the young lads in the photos be Donald Leafe, Pamela's first husband? She had no way of knowing, but it was another possibility. She huffed out her cheeks for a moment as she mused on the little group in front of her.

It was so frustrating, not being able to add a name to each face in the photos. She needed either an elderly person who knew everyone in the photos and had an excellent memory, or she might be able to find out something in the local library the next morning. There may even be some old local newspapers available on microfilm if she was very lucky.

Her phone rang. She looked at the screen and felt a sinking in the pit of her stomach. *Horrid Henry* was trying to reach her. She swiped the 'ignore' button on the screen and went back to her thoughts. He called twice more, and she did the same, but her mood was spoiled, so she went back to the cottage.

All was well. No one had broken in, that she could see, and so she turned off her phone, checked the front and back doors were locked, then went to bed, glad to have plans for the next day to focus her energy and stop her thinking about Henry. And having thought that, she lay there in the dark and thought about him for another two hours.

*

Chapter Fourteen

She awoke from another terrible night's sleep but felt more positive and purposeful. She determined to push Henry out of her mind, ignoring her hurt pride and sense of disappointment. She was going to get on with her day, and that made her feel pretty pleased with herself. She was heading into her comfort zone today: research.

When she turned on her phone there was a flood of missed calls and pleading texts from Henry, all of which she deleted. She stopped short of actually blocking him, though common sense told her she should probably do that too.

There was also one from Becka, which intrigued her. For twenty minutes, as she got ready to go out, she managed to ignore it, but when she got into the car, throwing her bag onto the passenger seat beside her, the phone, nestling in the top of her bag, briefly came to life and seemed to lure her. So she grabbed the phone and opened the message from Becka. It read:

> *Caitlin, I know you probably hate us and I don't blame you. What we did was horrible, but please, please don't blame Henry, he wasn't involved and he is so angry and upset with us because he really, really,* really *likes you. Please don't block his calls. He needs to talk to you. He's been trying to tell you about it. And I know it won't make any difference now but I'm really sorry too. We shouldn't have done it, and I really wish we hadn't because you were so nice to me even though I was being a total bitch. Becka xx*

Like it was burning a hole in her hand, she threw her phone back into her bag, screen side down, slammed the door and in one smooth move starting the car and fastening her seatbelt. She pulled out into the lane and was halfway to Rottingdean before she realised she was holding her breath.

She didn't dare think about anything other than the task in hand. She couldn't allow herself even a second to reflect on what Becka (her *real* cousin!) had said, or to think about Henry and all his unsuccessful attempts to speak to her. She just couldn't risk opening the emotional floodgates when she had work to do.

So she was more than usually brisk with the poor librarian who was, after all, only there to help. It wasn't her fault some of the materials Caitlin wanted to view were not where they should have been. Left to her own devices at last, Caitlin positioned her notebook, pen and a pile of small change by the old-fashioned microfilm reader/copier, wishing it could all be done 'on the app' for greater convenience.

And so she began.

The earliest records available were only five years

older than the time-frame Caitlin had already worked out in her mind, so she thought she may as well begin at the beginning. She was surprised at how much she learned of what might be termed 'background'.

She saw the small column with the blurry picture of a rambling great mansion and the headline: *Farewell To The Hall For Troubled Mitchesons*. The story went on to explain in the most unashamedly emotive style the terrible losses and bereavements suffered and the grievous toll of death duties on the family's fortunes.

Caitlin pressed the 'print this' key and shoved a few coins in the slot. She folded the still warm paper and put it away in the back of her notebook and continued her search.

There were another couple of pieces in the same vein about the Mitchesons' misfortunes. She also found the birth announcement of her grandfather Richard Reginald Mitcheson, and although there were no pictures and no details she didn't already have, she printed it anyway.

After another hour and another microfilm, she had found nothing else of value, apart from the obituaries she'd been expecting. The people she was interested in seemed to have kept annoyingly low profiles. She stretched her stiff shoulders and neck, then sat back down again to get on with her research, with a sneaking doubt in her mind that she was going to find anything else that might be useful to her.

Decades later, just as she was thinking of giving up, she came across a picture with the caption *Local Scouts Help Out The Old Folks!* And there in the middle of the smiling troop of boy scouts was a young Henry Jago, looking annoyingly cute. And by his side, their arms across each other's shoulders, was Laura's husband, 'Michael'. He had changed so little that even in grainy black and white it was impossible to mistake him. Underneath the photo, as was usual for those days, all the youngsters were named.

And the name of the boy standing next to Henry Jago was given as Andrew Kennett.

Caitlin stifled a whoop of triumph, and with an excited sense of having found the key to the whole thing, she hit the button to print once again and gleefully added the copy to her notebook. Then she reread the legend under the photo.

Kennett.

That name again! She puzzled over it. Another one to add to her mental list of Kennetts: Sarah Kennett who had been Henry Jago senior's first wife and Henry Jago junior's mother, then Barbara Kennett and her possible brother Stanley in her grandfather's old photos. And now Andrew Kennett...

Hmm.

But she had been sitting there for two and a half hours, her back, neck and shoulders were stiff and aching. She needed a break. She packed up her things then stopped off at the librarian's desk.

'Would it be possible to use the microfilm reader again in a little while? Or is it booked up?'

The librarian grinned at her. 'Going to the pub for a break? I don't blame you. I don't think the reader's booked out at all this week, but just let me check in the book.'

She disappeared into the back office, reappearing after just a few minutes.

'No, it's fine. I've pencilled you in for the rest of the day. Just come back when you're ready. If you need any more films, just give me a shout.'

Caitlin thanked her, feeling doubly guilty about

being snippy with the poor woman earlier.

The pub was very quiet. It was slightly early for the lunch crowd but she thought she might as well eat now rather than come back in another hour, she was already peckish and hadn't bothered with breakfast. She ordered a Thai chicken baguette to go with her half pint of cider. She chose one of the much-coveted tables by the window, making the most of the fact that for the first time in the entirety of her visits it was quiet enough for there to be a choice of places to sit. She gazed into space, musing on what she had learned so far.

As she was deep in thought, the barman brought her food over. She thanked him, and reaching for a paper napkin, she glanced up. Through the window she noticed something that she had been staring at for ten minutes without even seeing.

The name of the convenience store across the road from the pub was Kennett's Kwikmart.

She ate her food and drank her cider at lightning speed and hastened to cross the busy road.

She pushed open the door and heard the bell tinkling to let the proprietor know she had a customer. Caitlin saw a large lady, about Kath's age, with greying, tightly permed hair. She was wearing a blue house-coat similar to that sported by Kath when cleaning. The woman looked up and smiled at Caitlin in a pleasant way.

'Yes, love, what can I do for you?'

Caitlin embarked on a complicated explanation but noticed how quickly the woman's pleasant and friendly face took on a grim expression, and she folded her arms across her ample bosom.

'Stanley Kennett? Why do you want to know?'

Caitlin, worried now that the woman would decline to help, was reluctant to continue, but she had come this far, she couldn't very well back out now. She explained about her grandfather dying and leaving her the cottage.

'The Mitcheson house, you mean? Your grandfather is Richard Mitcheson?' And the woman practically spat the name.

'Well, yes he was, though he'd dead now, but...'

'Get out.'

'Excuse me?'

'Get out of my shop now. This instant. I'm not having any of your lot in here. Get out!'

Caitlin put up her hands palm down in a 'calm down' gesture and still smiling, began to say, 'Please, I'd just like to...'

But Mrs Kennett, as Caitlin assumed she was, was having none of it. Bright red in the face now, she extended her arm to point in the direction of the door with a trembling finger.

'*Get out!*' she screamed, 'Or I'll have the police on you!'

Caitlin had no choice but to leave.

She sat on the wall outside the library for a few minutes, shaking with emotion. She was more upset than the situation had warranted, and she didn't know quite what to do. She saw Mrs Kennett come out of her shop with a man Caitlin assumed was Mr Kennett and together they stood looking up and down the street but mercifully they failed to notice her, half-hidden as she was by a large sign notifying library-goers of the opening hours.

An idea came to her, and she rummaged in her bag for her phone. In response to the text from Becka, she simply tapped in *Who was Stanley Kennett?* and pressed send. Knowing that Becka would be at work, she didn't expect an immediate answer, so she put her phone away and went back into the library with a heavy heart.

It took her an age to find what she was looking for. In the earlier session she had concentrated on searching for anything containing a reference to the names Mitcheson or Jago. This time she was looking for Kennett. She waded through literally hundreds of references to people she hoped were all the wrong Kennetts. When she found what she was looking for, unlike earlier findings, this discovery gave her no sense of achievement or triumph, no feeling of closure, only a cold knot of dread in the pit of her stomach as she started to see a picture slotting together in her mind like a jigsaw puzzle. All the little pieces she had found so far were tiny parts of the same, overall story, and now she was starting to see the emergence of a whole new set of ideas. She clicked print and put in her money.

Caitlin packed up her things and went back to the cottage. When she arrived, she sat in the car for a few minutes fighting back tears. This had been an emotional rollercoaster of a week, and it wasn't over yet. Her head was pounding again; it took everything she had in her to summon the energy to get out of the car.

But she had to. She clicked the button of her electronic car key then turned to see her cousins—all five of them, real and pretend—waiting for her by the front door, initially shielded from her sight by the spreading trees. And Kath was there too, biting her lip and looking worried, with her husband Eric beside her. Seeing Kath there gave Caitlin a double jolt.

She didn't say a word. They all silently fell back to make room for her to unlock the front door with shaking fingers, and she was forced to concede that no matter what was about to happen, at least they hadn't changed her locks again. She walked in, leaving the door open behind her. They could enter or not, whatever they wanted, she didn't care. She no longer had the energy for their mind games. She walked into the sitting-room, dropped her stuff on the floor, and stood there defeated, clueless as to what she should do next.

It was Henry who pushed a small tumbler of whisky into her hand. Wondering if it was from the tantalus, then remembering that had gone now, she tried to give it back to him.

'I don't like...'

He guided her over to the sofa, then pushed the glass back into her hand. 'Just a sip. You look like you need it.'

With a grimace she took one tiny sip, swallowed the liquor and shook her head in an automatic reflex to the taste, spluttering. She handed him back the tumbler and he disposed of the remaining contents with one gulp. She felt the small sip burn all the way down her throat and into her stomach.

He set the tumbler down on the coffee table and sat down beside her on the sofa. When he swung his arm round her shoulders and pulled her against him, she was too tired and depressed to push him away. She managed a grumble.

'You're not boyfriend material anymore, get away from me, you liar!'

'Caitlin, I'm so sorry.' He kissed her hair, letting out a huge sigh, then leaned his cheek briefly against the spot he had just kissed.

'So what do you know?' he asked. He sounded almost as tired as she was.

She pushed him away and sat upright. 'More importantly what do *you* know? Becka claims you weren't in on the 'let's-swindle-Caitlin-the-idiot-then-nick-all-the-expensive-antiques-and-flog-them' scam.'

'No, I wasn't.'

She glared at him. 'But you *were* in on the let's-make-Caitlin-look-like-an-idiot-by-pretending-we're-her-cousins scam!'

He sighed again, but said nothing, which she took as an admission of sorts.

Caitlin watched as the others took their seats, apart from Eric and Michael/Andrew who went to fetch extra chairs from the dining-room. At length they were all seated. Michael/Andrew got a hard nudge in the ribs from Becka and cleared his throat and said, with no hint of his previous bluster or salesman smoothness.

'W-we owe you an apology, of course. A full and comprehensive apology. Caitlin, I'm so sorry, we never should have...'

'But you did.' Caitlin gave him a withering look, unable to think of anything else sufficiently pointed to say. She turned away to stare into the fire, noticing for the first time that it was blazing in the grate. Then she remembered that Gareth had got the fire going as soon as they came in. It crackled merrily and the dancing flames seemed to revive and thaw her. After a few moments of staring at the fire, she felt able to think and speak again. Shifting to the edge of her seat, she turned to face them all.

'Look,' she said. 'You tried to frighten me out of this house. You tried to steal all the stuff in the cellar so you could sell it and split the money between you. You made a toast to me, wishing I would fuck off. You broke into Gramps' house in London, you broke into my flat. Michael or Andrew or whatever the hell his name is actually *threatened* me. What am I supposed to think? And what do you expect me to say to all that? 'Oh never mind, these things happen'? You conspired against me, all of you, in a really horrible, cynical way. You manipulated me. You set out to swindle me.' She caught Henry's expression and said again, with emphasis, '*All of you*. Henry, you lied to me. Or at the very least you pretended not to know this lot or the fact that they were up to something. 'Remind me who these are again', you said.' She imitated his voice in a somewhat unflattering way. 'How could you? I feel so stupid. You let me stand there and introduce them all to you when it was me who was the only one who didn't know them. Even after the information I shared with you, you could have told me... And I thought that you and I... I really liked you, I thought you liked me. I thought...' She broke off with a sigh. Shrugged her shoulders, and added in a low voice, 'I really thought we had something. I was so stupid.'

She had to stop there. There was no way she was going to risk bursting into tears in front of all these people, some of whom she had no problem with never seeing again. She bit her lip and turned back to stare at the fire.

Becka said, 'Caitlin, your grandfather killed Stanley Kennett.'

Caitlin closed her eyes for a second and took a long, slow breath in. She heard Gramps' words all over again. *You never told anyone, did you?* She was shaking her head, but his own words kept coming back to her. *All of us, that spring.* She saw again the news article on the microfilm, saw the black and white print and felt again the lurch in her stomach as she finally let the truth sink in, as she *knew*. But still she fought against it.

'If that's true, it's terrible. But what does it have to

do with me?'

It was Kath who took up the story. *Not Kath too?* Caitlin looked at her, trying to stay calm and concentrate on what she was saying, still trying to block out the sound of Gramps' voice. *You didn't say anything about the boy?*

'When it first got round that Stanley Kennett was missing, his friends—Richard Mitcheson, Isobel Clay, Henry Jago senior, Don Leafe, and even Stanley's own sister Barbara said that he had run off after they had a row because they caught him molesting Pamela. There was never any doubt it happened. Even his own sister said it was true. And young Pam, she had the marks on her to prove it.

'See, Stanley wasn't altogether the full shilling. He had what these days we call learning difficulties. In those days kids—and even adults, in fact especially adults—were a lot less understanding and much, much crueller. They used to taunt him and call him names, call him an idiot or a dunce. Hit him. Swear at him. Humiliate him. A lot of the boys—and some of the girls—would tease him and throw things at him, goading him and jeering at him. They made his life an absolute misery. He was a bit of a loner, probably because of that. He was simple in many ways, as we used to say back then, he couldn't do schoolwork and he would often be away in his own little world, talking to himself or singing a little song to himself.

'And he used to like to play with the little children, children much younger than himself, especially the little girls. That was his mental age, you see, but of course a lot of people put a nasty spin on that, because on the outside he looked like any other teenage boy nearly grown up, and people began to say things about him, say he liked to touch the little girls. And there were always people who were frightened of him because he was different. So of course, when the others said what had happened, and poor Pammie having obviously been attacked, no one had any difficulty believing he'd run away because he'd got caught and was scared of being punished.'

Caitlin shook her head. 'How do you know all this? You couldn't have been there, you're too young.'

'Well, I did used to be a Kennett before I got married. And I know that's something I should have told you before. I don't suppose it helps, but I am sorry for what's happened, I wasn't part of it, and I don't approve of how bad this lot treated you, that wasn't fair.' She turned to glare at the 'cousins'.

Caitlin wasn't ready to listen to that. After all, Kath clearly knew who they were, yet had kept quiet. When she said nothing and turned away, Kath went on with her story.

'My father was only a couple of years older than your grandfather, but already married, and he was the youngest of four. I was born later that same year, as I've already told you. My father and my mother had only been married a year, and they lived in the house next door but one to where I live now. And where I live now, that was my uncle and aunt's house, my father's older brother. They were Stanley's parents. And Barbara's, too, of course. When Stanley went missing, there was a search party got up to look for him. My father and uncle helped to look for him along with the local police and a lot of people from the village. But they never found a sign of him.'

Kath fell silent, thinking, lost in her memories. The only sound in the room was the odd crackle from the fire as it devoured the wood. Caitlin noticed that although it was still only mid-afternoon, the room was growing dark as outside a heavy rain fell like a curtain from the sky. She shivered. It felt like winter.

'As I say,' Kath continued a moment later, 'Stanley was never found. He has never been seen or heard from since. The shame made my aunt and uncle, Stanley's parents, turn in on themselves. They cut themselves off from everyone, even their own family hardly saw them. And when a week later Barbara killed herself—she walked into the sea, they found her body a day later, washed up on the beach in Brighton—well, it broke my aunt. She had never been strong and that finished her off. She took to her bed and never spoke again. She lived for another seventeen years but she never spoke, never got out of that bed. And my uncle, he was last seen walking down to the railway station and hasn't been heard of again. Not a word to this day, though I should think that by now he'd be dead too.'

There was silence. No one seemed to know what to say. The misery of such collective guilt puts an end to reasoning, to questions, Caitlin thought. It's too much to take in. And again she was reminded of her own words at her grandfather's funeral buffet.

You can't unknow things once you find them out.

*

Chapter Fifteen

Michael/Andrew went out for the takeaway, and to Caitlin's relief, he took Henry with him. Caitlin felt she could breathe a little easier without Henry beside her for a while, staring at her with his sad puppy-dog eyes. It was a relief, too, that there were no ghostly footsteps or banging windows from upstairs. At least that charade was over with.

Gareth and Kath went to set the dining-room table whilst Eric stood outside smoking a much yearned-for cigarette. Caitlin was left in the sitting-room staring at Laura and Becka.

She said, her voice a challenge, 'So, Becka, you really are called Becka, and you are genuinely a cousin of mine?'

Becka nodded. 'Yes, I am. I'm the oldest. Andy and I are genuinely married, so I'm Becka Kennett.'

'Still no children, or was that a lie too?' Caitlin couldn't resist the last little snipe.

Becka flushed and looked uncomfortable.

'Yes, we've got three as a matter of fact. All more or less grown-up. One's at medical school, he wants to be an anaesthetist, that's Sean, and then there are Sam and Gail at Uni. Sam is our middle one, a boy, and Gail, she's eighteen, the youngest and it's very quiet at home without her.'

Caitlin nodded as she absorbed the information and mentally filed it away for adding to the family tree later. She was still fuming, and she couldn't overcome her sense of betrayal, not to mention feeling humiliated by the way she had been duped so easily. But she was beginning to soften. She was beginning to wonder how much point there was in holding a grudge, no matter how well deserved. What was the point in developing any kind of feud with her own flesh and blood? A picture popped into her mind of Mrs Kennett at Kennett's Kwikmart, and her screaming rage. Caitlin turned to Laura. Laura seemed to be watching her rather warily as if she was trying to sum up the situation.

'What about you? Are you Laura or not?'

Laura nodded. 'Yes, my name is Laura. I'm Henry's half-sister, and Becka's stepsister, not that we differentiate between siblings and stepsiblings or halves. I used to be Laura Jago, now I'm Laura Preece. I'm married to Gareth, he's a complete outsider, I met him at work. He's only involved in this mess because of me.'

Caitlin didn't have a clue which part of this speech to pick at first. In the end she said nothing and turned back to stare into the fire again.

Suddenly Laura came over and flung herself down next to Caitlin on the sofa and grabbed Caitlin's hand, she said, 'Please forgive me! It's all my fault, I know it is! We just didn't think about what we were actually doing. It was all my idea. All we wanted was to find a way to hurt Richard Mitcheson's descendant and to get a bit of extra cash for ourselves as compensation.'

'But why? What on earth was the point? Why should I suffer for something that was done before my parents were even born, let alone me? I didn't do this!' She was almost on her feet, almost shouting. She made herself sit back and took a deep breath.

'I know! I'm sorry, we just didn't think... We saw an opportunity and we—just—took it.' Laura's hands were held out to Caitlin as if to plead her case. They fell back to her lap as she dropped her chin, continuing in a low tone: 'It was insane, and cruel, and wicked, I know that. But you see, we didn't think about what we were doing, didn't think about you as a person. We didn't think about the impact of any of this on you, and we just—we just had a crazy idea, and—we just went for it, and I am so, so sorry!'

She burst into tears on Caitlin's shoulder, sobs raking her body. Caitlin, alarmed by the force of emotion, found herself patting Laura's back in what she hoped was a soothing manner and over Laura's heaving body, she met Becka's look and raised her eyebrows in a query. Becka, balling up a tissue, dabbed at her own eyes, just smiled a crooked smile and shrugged her shoulders, and mimed the words,

'I'm so sorry too.'

It seemed an eternity before Andy and Henry arrived back with the curries, and they all went into the dining-room, Laura excusing herself to quickly go and wash her face and generally compose herself. Andy held out a chair for her, and Caitlin took a seat at the table, feeling oddly part of the family again. Though she was still half-tempted to send them all packing and have the food all to herself.

Henry kept his distance but smiled at her shyly

across the table, making an extra effort to pass her things she didn't particularly want and continually topping up her wine for her. He was trying too hard, and whilst she found it extremely irritating, at the same time she couldn't help feeling sorry for him, so the last time he topped up her wine she thanked him warmly and sent him a huge smile. He grinned back, only too clearly relieved.

Thank God, she thought, message *finally* received. Not that she really wanted to think about what that meant, but she was already tired of the misery and the stress of it all. No wonder, she thought, they say you can pick your friends, but you can't pick your family. A furtive glance about the room, and she thought, I'm stuck with this bunch of shysters, like a marriage, for better or for worse. And directly on the tail of that thought, I've been alone, or almost alone, for quite long enough.

As they finished eating and sat back, full and lazy, Caitlin looked down the table and said, 'So you all think that Richard killed Stanley? And because of the lies he told about Stanley attacking Pamela, that meant he was also to blame for Barbara killing herself? And for what happened to Barbara and Stanley's parents too?'

They all, including Kath and Eric, agreed.

'But why do you think it was Richard who did all that?' Caitlin asked.

There was an uncomfortable silence. Then Laura said,

'We think it was Richard who attacked Pamela. Barbara either saw or suspected something, or at least, she realised it wasn't true about Stanley being guilty, and yet she agreed to say it *was* him. I'm sure she didn't realise something bad was going to happen to Stanley.'

'Maybe she didn't actually see the attack on Pamela,' Becka said. 'But what if she saw Richard kill Stanley? He could have said he was trying to protect Pamela, or something like that.'

'We know what Richard was capable of,' Henry said softly, and Caitlin saw him watching her with sadness in his shadowed eyes.

She had to look away. She said nothing but couldn't deny what he'd said. She felt the weight of emotion in the room shift as everyone else turned to look at her, realisation hitting as Henry's words sinking in. But before it got maudlin and uncomfortable, Andy seized on this straightaway, leaning forward, his expression earnest.

'Caitlin, I'm...'

But she waved away whatever he was going to say, 'Don't!' And with a brisk, tight smile, added, 'I don't want to talk about that. It was a long time ago now. Water under the bridge. Let's go back to what we were talking about. In any case, my grandfather's dead now.'

'Good,' said Henry.

The others not only agreed, they even drank a toast to it, with Kath drowning out all of them with her comment, 'Good riddance to bad rubbish!'

That was a far cry from Kath's earlier praise of Gramps'. Caitlin wondered vaguely how many glasses of wine Kath had had.

'Thing is,' Kath went on, 'Everyone always used to go on about how odd and how wrong it was for Stanley to be playing with Pamela, who was so much younger than him. But if you think about it, what about Richard? He was what, twenty-two? Twenty-three? And Isobel, she was the oldest of the others at getting on for nineteen, the others was all about sixteen, seventeen, apart from Pamela of course. But did anyone stop to ask why a grown man just back from the war was wanting to hang about with a bunch of kids? No. Not for one minute, I bet! They just thought it was because he was mad about Isobel. But I'm not so sure. To me it seems just as odd, him hanging around with them, as people at the time said it was for Stanley to be hanging around with Pamela.'

'Richard was obviously a filthy pervert,' Gareth said, and again they all agreed.

'Basically we're all just guessing that based on...' She stopped, and saw they were all looking at her. 'Your guesswork. And yes, all right, based on my experiences too, now. But that can't be the only 'proof'. We can't be certain it had happened before, and to Pamela. In any case, what can we do about any of this now? Almost everyone connected with what happened then is dead now, so what's the point?' Caitlin asked. *The past is never as far away as we think*, she reminded herself yet again. She deflated with a huff, and a helpless lift of her hand. 'How can I ever go into Kennett's Kwikmart again if I can't—if *we* can't—do something?'

'They searched for Stanley's body for weeks,' Eric said. 'He disappeared one afternoon supposedly while they were all out together for a picnic. He didn't go home for a change of pants, a toothbrush, or the money from his piggybank or even a coat. He just... Left.'

'So something must have happened that afternoon during the picnic,' Henry said. 'Was that the same day as Pamela was attacked or had that already happened?'

'No,' Kath said. 'It was later that same afternoon.'

'Do we know where they went for this picnic?' Caitlin asked.

'There's a little stream at the bottom of the field

behind this cottage,' Kath told her.

'What this field? Where I park my car?' Jerking her thumb over her shoulder, Caitlin was surprised. But then, she hadn't crossed the field, just stayed on the side nearest the road, and the maize was tall and thick enough to obscure any indications of a stream. The others were watching her, also surprised. Caitlin grinned at their expressions.

'What? How else was I supposed to find out what you lot were up to if I didn't hide my car and generally sneak about? You were trying to screw me out of upwards of £800,000, don't forget!'

They all laughed in spite of an underlying hint of embarrassment, but it felt like a move in the right direction. Caitlin was a little bit glad. She knew it was going to take time to stop feeling furious with them, but hopefully all this would eventually be simply a hilarious story to tell their grandchildren. She couldn't help glancing at Henry as she thought that. He was looking down at his folded hands on the table, lost in his own thoughts. But a moment later, he said,

'I think Richard killed Stanley and threw his body down the well.'

Everyone turned to stare at him, Becka's hand flying to her mouth in dismay.

Thinking about that, Caitlin had to agree with him.

Henry continued. 'We know Richard was living here then, and living alone. So he had no one to work round or keep out of the way of, and with plenty of time and privacy, he could dispose of a body completely at his leisure.'

'The poor little bugger,' Gareth said.

Eric nodded. 'Crafty bloke, Mitcheson was, so they say.'

Caitlin went on, 'When I was a little girl, there was

a cover over the well, and I think it had been there a long time, I think I remember my mother telling me she used to do what I did and bang on the cover when she was little, and about playing noughts and crosses on the lid too, with a bit of chalk. It just became part of her childhood games, as it was mine. In plain sight, it was completely ignored. So it's entirely possible the cover dates back to Stanley's disappearance or maybe even earlier.'

'Right then,' Andy said decisively, a throw-back to his Michael persona. 'First thing tomorrow morning, that cover is coming off.' He halted abruptly, as if he had just remembered. He added, a little belatedly, 'Oh, er—that is, if it's okay with you, Caitlin?'

Caitlin said yes, it was okay with her.

They all began to move, to disperse for the evening. Andy, Becka, Laura and Gareth had booked into a budget hotel locally, and Henry was staying at Kath and Eric's place.

She waved them all off, and even managed to send Henry off to his bed happy by giving him a quick kiss.

She shut the door behind them all then went back to clear up the mess in the dining-room. She put the various cartons into a bin bag, and to minimise the fast-food smell, immediately carried the bag out into the garden to the rubbish bin, and the whole time she was thinking. About the Kennetts and their tragic histories. About Gramps. About the things he said as he lay in his hospital bed. About Henry. About the rest of the cousins. About Stanley Kennett. About the well.

Standing in the back garden, she paused for a moment. The ground was wet but the air was warmer than it had been for the last few days. There was a moon, half-hidden by racing clouds that promised more rain. She stood there for a few minutes and

with a heavy heart she looked in the direction of the well. Always a half-scary, half-exciting memory from her past. But now, it seemed even more ominous. She drew closer, putting out a hand to touch the rain-soaked lid. No longer just a strange, alluring feature from her past, it was all too real and solid.
Did that heavy wooden cover guard a terrible secret?

She made herself a cup of tea and carried it upstairs to the bedroom she was using. She didn't put the light on. The soft glow from the moon guided her. The window was much lower here than in modern buildings and the sill was deep. She took a pillow from the bed and placed it on the sill, then sat there cradling her cup of tea and gazing out into the darkness of the garden with the field beyond, her eyes gradually adjusting until she could discern dark shape against dark shape.
What a complex thing a human being is, she thought. In spite of the cool night she had the window open and even her city-dweller's ears caught the soft, almost confiding call of an owl. She thought she could make out the shape of the bird, darker, fleeting, against the darkness of the sky between the trees, but she couldn't be sure.
Take her grandfather for instance. He had abused her as a child. Now it also seemed entirely possible he had abused Pamela. From what Caitlin had found out over the years about sexual predators, it wasn't the kind of thing that tended to happen only once or to just one person. She wondered now if he had ever attacked her mother in the same way. Yet surely if he had, her mother would have said something? But then, perhaps that was the reason they had seen so little of her grandparents over the years? Or was she

simply reading too much into it? Caitlin had told Henry that she hated her grandfather, but ties of family and duty are altogether stronger and more complex than mere hatred, or love. And without evidence, it was all too easy to rewrite history on the back of supposition.

She had loved her grandfather with the wholehearted adoration of a child, until the day came when, even as an innocent young child, she had been aware that a border had been crossed and the balance of her life had fallen awry, never to completely recover. In making her keep secret what had happened, he had made her complicit in her own attack, and ever since that day she had struggled with an almost overwhelming weight of guilt.

Yet when she looked back, with all the detachment of an observer, she saw the complete trust of a guileless child, led like a lamb to the sacrifice, innocent of the impending disaster, but still she felt she should have known, should have found a reason, an excuse. That she should have refused to go with him, that she only had herself to blame.

But her adult mind told her repeatedly, she had not known, nor had she understood the adult mind. She could not have turned aside from what was to happen to her, because it had not been her fault. She had been a small child, no more capable of deciding where she went or what she did than she could have flown to the moon. The lamb cannot be blamed for its own destruction.

Years later, when as a teenager she began to really understand what had happened, she had talked to a teacher at school, and her teacher—wise and worldly for a woman who seemed so nice and safe and elderly—had given her advice that had helped her to understand the dual nature of her feelings for her grandfather: hatred and fear in direct opposition with a child's love and a sense of obedience. At university, Caitlin had able to attend counselling sessions and by taking one painful step after another over the years since then, she had to an extent freed herself from the hold her marred childhood had over her peace of mind. But the guilt never went away. And every dutiful contact with her grandfather renewed it.

When she had taken up her first post, with the Family Records Institute in her London borough she had learned at last to observe the past with detachment and create a new, albeit slightly distanced relationship with her grandfather. Because in the end, he was her family, he needed her, and strangely, she still loved him. In spite of everything.

Neither before nor after her parents and her grandmother had died, had anything relating to the abuse had ever been acknowledged or discussed between herself and her grandfather. She never demanded any apology from him, and he never gave it or even indicated an awareness of his actions. It was as if it had never happened. But she had wondered what he thought about it. Or even *if* he thought about it. Had he forgotten about it completely? Or did he just hope that *she* had forgotten?

She had read once that abusers often created such strong barriers in their minds between their actions and their conscience, that they could easily deceive themselves into thinking nothing ever happened. And, too, there were those who, convinced what they did was normal or understandable or explainable and not wrong, saw no need to remark upon or apologise for their behaviour.

Caitlin didn't know which of these her grandfather

was. She thought he was probably the former, but she had learned that it no longer mattered to her to try to explain it. It had happened, it had been wrong, it had damaged her young life, but it was over, and she would not permit it to have any more power over her future. Or at least, she would try not to let it. She had tortured herself enough to last a lifetime already. Gramps had her past. He would not have her future too.

And so, when Gramps had died, she felt guilt, she felt sorrow, she felt grief, was still grieving, but she also felt relief at his death.

That evening he had been standing at the top of the stairs. He had annoyed her with comments about how much more she should do for him, how much more time she should spend with him, if she had any *real* family feeling. If she were less selfish, less self-absorbed. No wonder she didn't have a husband, she was too wrapped up in herself, he said. He had turned at the top of the stairs, right on the edge, to say something spiteful, and she had been right behind him carrying his laundry hamper downstairs to the washing-machine. His foot had slipped, he had half-turned, his hand snatching at the rail to right himself but missing, and she had... she hadn't even thought about it, hadn't thought about what she was doing, she just... put out a hand to give him a little extra push. Just a tiny push, with almost no effort behind it, it had been enough.

He had yelped her name, panicked. And she stood there, frozen, and watched him fall, and as he fell, she felt a sense of triumph coupled with relief. She was aware of just two words in her mind.

At last.

Then she had carefully set the hamper back in its place, then calmly walked down the stairs to his side, but he lay there, crumpled and unresponsive on the dark hall carpet. She had felt for, but not found, a pulse. He hadn't seemed to be breathing. But she didn't check any further. She stood up in a daze, walked out of the front door, and went to her car. Her keys had been in her pocket. She had driven home. Then, sitting in her car outside the block of flats, she thought to herself, Where was I going? Or have I already been—somewhere?

There was a sense of something that needed doing but she couldn't remember what it was. She couldn't seem to think. She went indoors, made herself a hot drink and went to bed, confused about the tears running down her face.

The next day, the call had come. She had not needed to pretend shock, convinced as she was that it was all part of some strange dream. Then, at his house... Yes, then she had known. But she had wanted him to be dead. He had been falling, and she could have grabbed for him, helped him. But she didn't. She gave him an extra little push. She killed him. She thought she must have killed him. Then, instead of calling an ambulance, she had stepped over his body, left him there and gone home, half-hoping he was dead, half-dreading he might survive.

So complicated, us frail humans, Caitlin thought and scuffed away tears with her fingertips. I'll never be able to tell anyone—not even Henry—what I thought, what I did. Maybe, in the eyes of the law, I was just in shock, and I might not have been able to save him anyway, his hand could have slipped out of mine, or he could even have pulled me down with him. Now I know he wasn't dead, that he might have been helped. If I had called the ambulance immediately, had done CPR, there was a tiny chance he could have survived. We will never know, she thought. But I hardly knew what I was doing, but now, it feels wicked, leaving him there like that, even if I thought he was already dead. I stepped over his body like he was a bit of rubbish in the street.

The owl hooted again, louder this time and nearer, and distracted her. Peering into the darkness she wondered if the faint dark line she could see beyond the maize stalks was the line of the stream on the other side of the field.

Could it be true that Richard—Gramps—had killed poor Stanley Kennett? She felt it *was* a possibility. Of course, Stanley *could* have attacked Pamela, and he *could* have run away afterwards, afraid of the consequences. That too was a possibility, no matter how slight. But how likely was it that in that small group of youngsters, there would be two separate child molesters? It had been Richard, not Stanley, who had been the outsider.

In the darkness she shook her head. It had to be Richard. She just knew it had been him. Now they had to find Stanley's body, so they could bring it all out into the open and maybe even make it possible for Caitlin to show her face in Kennett's Kwikmart without Mrs Kennett screaming at her.

It would be nice, Caitlin thought, if poor Stanley could be laid to rest decently, respectfully in a proper grave with a proper headstone, a memorial service and everything. Maybe that would help those of later generations who wondered at the misery of that golden generation. It might even lay to rest the curse that seemed to hold the family in its grip.

She drank the rest of her tea. At last she was feeling drowsy, and in spite of what lay ahead in the morning, she felt surprisingly at peace. Strange how again she had united with her cousins. Their excuses had been lame, convenient, but they had been genuinely sorry, she thought, and even if they weren't, she didn't want to lose her small family now they had found her.

She would resign from her job before they fired her, quit her flat, sell Gramps' terraced house, and move down here. With the lump sum Gramps had left her, and the proceeds of the house sale and from the sale of all the furniture, she would have enough for a nest egg of her own, and still be able to cover the cost of interment and so on if they did find Stanley's body, then still have enough to live on comfortably until she was able to establish her own family tree research business in the new location.

The only thing she would regret leaving behind in London was Henry.

She got up and stretched. She carried her cup back downstairs to the kitchen sink, rinsed it and left it on the drainer, then checked her phone which was still in her bag on the dining-room table.

There was a message from *Henry the sneaky lying bastard*. It made her smile. It said simply: *Nice kiss, now I can't sleep*. She sent him a row of little text kisses back and changed his name to *My Phwoargeous Henry*, then put her phone away.

With the smile still on her face she went back upstairs and went to bed.

Maybe she could persuade him to move his business down to Sussex too?

*

Chapter Sixteen

In the morning, Caitlin wandered down to take a look at the stream. In daylight, on a mellow autumn day like this, after the light rain had ceased and the sun was peering between fluffy clouds, it seemed like such a lovely spot. She wasn't surprised that the youngsters had wanted to have their picnic there all those years ago.

On the opposite bank of the stream, a bare three or four feet away, a tree trunk leaned out, trapeze-like, over the water. From the size of the trunk Caitlin was convinced the tree had been there for decades, and if she had been a teenager she would have enjoyed jumping the few feet onto the trunk's seat—it wouldn't have been too demanding a leap, but the main thing would be the thrill of being in the air above the water. Like many youngsters, she knew she would have found that irresistible.

As she looked at the tree trunk looping out over the stream, Caitlin's imagination peopled the scene with images of the past. That afternoon in 1963. *All of us, that spring.*

She could imagine the kids—Isobel, at nineteen a young woman on the brink of marriage, but quite likely she'd been happy to set aside adulthood for an hour or two of fun messing about with her little sister and some friends. Barbara, for once not having to worry about her older, yet in many ways younger brother, Stanley. Her friends Isobel, Don Leafe and Henry Jago senior would all help her keep an eye on him, so that she could just be her age and join in the fun.

The picnic would no doubt have consisted of just a few sandwiches and biscuits or cakes made by their mothers—or by the girls themselves. There might be homemade lemonade, ginger beer or milky sweet tea in a thermos flask to drink with the food.

Caitlin glanced around her, picturing the scene: a blanket spread on the grass. It would probably be an old baby blanket or a shawl or something like that. Maybe they'd even sneaked one off their own beds, and their mothers would scold them later when they found out. The sandwiches would be put out on a tin plate or stay nestled in a cake box or tin. Maybe with some old cups and plates to use as picnicware. Jumpers and jackets would be thrown aside as they all played and chased about.

It would have been fun to jump across the stream from one bank to the other then back again. And probably even Pamela would have been able to manage it, as it wasn't a great distance. Obviously the boys would want to try and impress the girls and would show off and compete with one another, or at least, Don and Henry would, and perhaps Stanley would have a go too.

It would have made a lovely picture—a bunch of

happy kids all having fun, the laughter, the joking, the freedom of an hour or two outdoors on a warm spring day, away from school, or work or chores or parents.

But then, Caitlin thought, like the snake in the garden of Eden, a blight appeared to spoil their fun and their innocence: Richard Reginald Mitcheson. A full-grown man. A predator, smooth, charming, and with his own private agenda.

Caitlin had once seen a beautiful rose bush covered with some kind of fungal disease. Apparently in perfect health, from a distance it had seemed a glorious sight, but close to, it was riddled with galls and disfigurements, the flowers opening from the bud only for the petals to furl and die. The virus would not only ultimately destroy the entire rose bush but everything around it. The only way to stop it was to dig out and burn the affected plants. Richard Mitcheson had been just such a disease, she thought, in the lives of those youngsters.

What place did a twenty-two-or-three-year-old have in this picnic, with these innocent childish games? It was so true, what Kath had said. It was *Richard*, not Stanley who was the one in the wrong place. The one with perverse designs on the innocents who trusted him, who no doubt looked up to him, then paid dearly for doing so.

And that had not been the end of his evil, as Caitlin knew all too well. A different year, a different picnic, and another little girl left damaged and afraid by what had happened to her, perpetrated by the very man who had held out his hand to her in an apparent gesture of love. She had placed her hand in his, trusting him completely, as she skipped away with a smile on her face and a wave over her shoulder for her mother.

The Cousins

For the first time it occurred to Caitlin to wonder why.

Why had Isobel allowed it to happen? Surely she had known what he was like? After all the years they had been together, everything they had been through as a couple, she must have been able to guess, to anticipate what was on his mind? And hard on that thought came another, why didn't my grandmother protect me?

But it was wrong to blame her grandmother for what her grandfather had done, yet surely, *surely* she had known? How could she not have known?

Or had she too believed the lie, all those years ago?

Then, not for the first time, an old question came to her: how many other children had there been over the course of his long, active life? It seemed naïve to think, terrible though it was to admit the possibility, that his attacks had been limited to just two little girls: Pamela and herself. Research has taught us that this type of offender attacks often and over a sustained period, she reminded herself. They just can't stop themselves, their desires, urges, whatever you like to call them, became too hard to resist.

How many?

Caitlin gazed bleakly down into the water in front of her. The ripples caught the light and sparkled, dazzling her eyes and making them blur. She found a tissue in her pocket and dabbed at her cheeks.

Well, he couldn't hurt anyone now. She could only hope that someday, somewhere, he would pay for what he had done. She only prayed that she would never know the full extent of his abuse. It was hard enough for her to deal with the knowledge that besides herself there had been three other innocent victims in all this: Pamela, and as now seemed clear, Stanley, and Barbara the sister who had felt coerced,

Caitlin now believed, into accusing him. Then their parents too, they had also suffered. And from them, the ripples had spread out to engulf a whole family, to follow the pain down through the generations.

She stared at the water again, imagining them all there on the bank of the stream.

Had the boys, and even the girls, jostled and dared and nudged one another until all of them had attempted the jump across the water at least once? Had the stream swirled beneath their feet as they sat on the tree trunk? Did they sit there and let their legs dangle above the water, laughing at one another, feeling triumphant over small achievements?

Did she dare? She stole a quick look around. Her cousins were not yet in sight. Did she dare? Yes, she did! A quick leap, her right foot outstretched and she was there, a giggle of triumph breaking free as she clutched at the trunk to save herself from toppling backwards into the water.

From behind the tree there came the sound of clapping. Blushing to the roots of her hair she looked up to see Henry—younger and boyish-looking in jeans and a sweater instead of his usual formal suit—grinning at her. How long had he been there?

'Your turn!' She laughed as she executed a perfect dismount back onto the opposite bank of the stream. He laughed, a loud joyful sound, and to her delight, he made the jump easily and then jumped down again to join her on the other side of the stream.

And then, he swept her into his arms and kissed her with a very un-solicitorly passion. They were still smiling at each other when the others called to them as they came across the field.

The six of them congregated on the stream's edge. It was clear that here, these days at least, there was nowhere to hide a body. The ground was flat and hard all around with little in the way of undergrowth and hedges.

'Richard could simply have dumped the body in the stream?' Becka suggested. Clearly she had been thinking along the same lines as Caitlin. The moment of fun had passed.

'First place anyone would look.' Andy—who Caitlin still thought of as Michael—shook his head. 'He'd need to get the body out of sight into some place no one would think of searching. If he planned to put the body down the well all along, he wouldn't bother hiding it anywhere else first.'

'He couldn't carry or even drag the body of an adult male on his own across the field anyway, and there'd be the danger of someone seeing,' Becka pointed out.

'Like who?' Andy retorted, clearly reluctant to give up on his favourite idea.

'We don't know what it was like here then,' Laura reminded them. 'This field could have been full of crops. It was late spring, so there could have been anything growing here. Or there could have been a ton of farm workers.'

'Would he really take the risk of all the kids seeing what he did to Stanley? How could he keep, what, four or five teen and young adults quiet and trust they wouldn't tell their parents? Especially once Stanley was reported missing and people started asking the children when they'd last seen him,' Gareth said. He was looking around him, frowning. 'No, he must have made it into some kind of game, or found some way to make it all seem forgettable and normal.'

'Except for Pamela and Barbara,' Caitlin pointed out. 'They never forgot about it. I'm assuming your mum never mentioned anything to you, perhaps when you were older, Henry? Becka?'

Henry shook his head. 'I never knew a thing. Everything we now know, or think we know, has come through the Kennett side of the family. I spoke to my father last night. He said he didn't even remember a picnic, so it can't have been too memorable or it would have stuck in his mind. Barbara's suicide, and everything that occurred later, are the only clues we have to make us suspect that anything at all happened that day.'

'That and the fact that Pamela, like Caitlin, had definitely been abused, and that Stanley was never seen again,' Laura added.

They all stood there, gazing about them and shuffling their feet.

Finally Andy said, 'Let's get that cover off the well.' And he strode off in the direction of the cottage.

Everyone else looked at Caitlin questioningly. She nodded and shrugged.

'He's right, it *is* the only way to be sure.'

They turned to walk back to the cottage. Caitlin had a churning, nervous sensation in the pit of her stomach. Henry took her hand and clasped it tightly. It wasn't all innocent childlike fun now, but at least she had him by her side, all their recent problems set aside in the light of this joint quest.

When they reached the back garden of the cottage, Andy was already there heaving at the well cover, red in the face and puffing and panting. The lid wasn't budging an inch.

'Give me a hand!' he yelled at Gareth and Henry. Gareth ran to do exactly that. Henry simply stood there with his hands in his pockets watching them strain. Caitlin had to hide a smile when Henry commented calmly,

'I think you'll need to unscrew it first.'

Andy shot Henry a filthy look, said something unflattering, and stopped heaving to get out a gigantic handkerchief and mop his brow.

'And,' Laura said. 'I think we might need to get this out of the way first.' She stepped forward to grab one end of the flower planter, and Becka got the other end. Together they lifted it and carried it over to set it against the wall of the house out of everyone's way. Caitlin watched dreamily as a couple of woodlice, finding their home suddenly gone, ran down a crack between the boards of the cover.

Henry turned away, calling out, 'Caitlin, I'm going to Kath's for some tools. Do you want to come along?'

She did, and she ran after him to catch his hand.

'I might as well put the kettle on,' Becka said and disappeared into the kitchen, followed by Laura. When Caitlin looked back, Andy and Gareth, having found themselves abandoned and unable to do anything more at that moment, were pulling out a chair each and taking a seat at the table, for all the world like a couple of holidaymakers at some trendy pavement café.

'What else do you need?' Eric asked. He had given them a cordless screwdriver to unscrew the cover, and a small aluminium ladder. And he had kindly offered to drive them back in his beat-up Land Rover.

'A torch? A rope?' Henry asked hopefully.

'And a beanpole,' Caitlin added. They looked at her, puzzled. 'We will need to test how deep the water level is, if there is any water still in there after all this time. One of those six- or eight-foot bamboo beanpoles would be ideal, if you've got such a thing.'

Henry nodded, and she was ridiculously pleased to see he looked quite impressed by her suggestion. She felt a smirk of complacency spread across her face. Not wanting to miss the 'fun', Kath and Eric came back with them, Kath went with Caitlin in her little Renault, following Henry and Eric in what Kath termed the 'man car', Eric's beat-up and muddy Land Rover.

Back at the cottage, Becka was just coming out with the mugs of tea on a tray along with a plate of biscuits, and the others were all standing or sitting about in the little courtyard. Andy and Gareth grabbed the tools from Henry and Eric and immediately set to work getting the cover off.

Caitlin watched. She felt as though her heart was in her mouth. Kath looked as though she were having second thoughts about the whole idea of watching. But she said nothing, simply sinking into a chair. Eric put his hand out to pat Kath's shoulder, giving her a smile and squeeze of the hand in reassurance.

Slowly the old screws were forced to yield, and with more puffing and groaning from the men, the cover was prised free then lifted up and off the top of the well with only minor damage to the canopy.

Between them they had three torches pointed down the shaft but it was still too dark to see how far down the water was, if there was water in there still, and they certainly weren't able to tell how deep it was, or more importantly, whether there was a body hidden there in the darkness.

Of the men, Gareth was the smallest and thinnest, so presumably the lightest. It was he who was going to attempt to go down the well.

They positioned the ladder horizontally across the top of the well opening, and the rope was attached to it, then wrapped round the canopy supports, then lastly around Andy who was by far the heaviest of the men. They had tied large knobbly knots at one-yard intervals along the length of the rope and Gareth was confident that he could climb down.

Becka was almost weeping with worry. Laura was angry with him for agreeing to go down, and Caitlin, halfway between the two emotions, could hardly bear to watch as Gareth crawled along the ladder and lay hold of the rope, his hands covered by a pair of Laura's woolly mittens for protection. He had a torch in his back pocket, and once he got off the ladder and onto the rope, he carefully climbed down about six feet and then Eric passed him the eight-foot-long beanpole.

Gareth shone the torch down but still couldn't really gauge how far below him the surface of the water was. He climbed down another six or eight feet to Laura's and Caitlin's consternation, then he tried again.

'I think the water's about six feet or so below me,' he called up, his voice sounding oddly far-off. 'So I'm going down a bit further before I try to see how deep it is.' His voice sounded hollow and breathless to Caitlin. He may only be a few yards down, she thought, but he sounded as though he was deep, deep underground. The thought made her shiver.

They could all hear him puffing a bit with the effort of climbing down the rope. It had doubtless been twenty years since he'd done anything like this, when he was still at school, and the few rounds of golf he played each week hadn't really been sufficient to keep him in shape for this kind of activity.

'Okay,' he called up again a few minutes later, and his breath was really labouring now as he clung to the rope. 'I'm testing to see how deep it is...'

There was a long pause. Up above, on firm ground, they could hear and see nothing. Laura was wringing her hands with worry.

'I think it's about... Oh bugger!' he said, then there was an abrupt silence. They all craned forward even more to see, or hear, or catch any intimation whatsoever of what was happening down there in the darkness.

Henry called, 'What? What is it?'

Becka's sobs ceased as she held her breath, hands pressed to her mouth, as she leaned forward, trying to see or hear what was going on.

Laura was shining a torch down the well. 'Are you okay? Gareth?' She leaned right into the mouth of the well, causing Eric and Andy to grab hold of her to keep her steady. 'Gareth? Gareth!'

Finally, he grunted up to them, 'Yes, I'm fine, it's okay. I just dropped the bloody beanpole. But I'd already stuck it in twice, once on either side of me. I reckon the water is only about two feet or so deep. So, I'm going to get in.'

'What?' screamed Becka and Laura together. 'No!'

'There could be deep mud at the bottom,' Caitlin yelled.

But Eric looked at her with scorn. 'You wouldn't get mud at the bottom of a well,' he told her. 'Otherwise, the water wouldn't be clean enough to drink, would it?'

Feeling stupid, Caitlin had no answer for that.

'No, it'll be fine,' Gareth called up to them. 'Stop being such a bunch of bloody wimps.' There was a pause, then he called up, 'Okay, I'm in the water. It's bloody f-freezing. It's almost up to my arse. The floor is—it's solid, rocky. I'm fine, no need to panic.'

Another lengthy pause. Caitlin exchanged looks with the others. Everyone seemed less tense now they knew he was safe, but still, she thought, I hope he comes back up soon. And, she added silently, I hope he can get out all right and we don't have to phone the fire service.

'It's just water,' he called again. 'There's no body. There's nothing here. I've felt about with my feet and with my hands. There's nothing. He's not here, I'm absolutely certain. I'm coming back up.'

He battled to climb halfway up, his gasps painful to hear as he climbed, but he was wet to the skin and chilled now, and the weight of his wet jeans and shoes, coupled with the effort to climb made it a slow and difficult process. He abandoned Laura's mittens as they kept tangling on the rope and in the end, it was easier to grip without them. But the rope started to graze his hands and he was too tired and frozen to pull himself any higher. It took all three of the men at the top to hoist him up to ground level again, and he emerged into the sunlight to collapse panting and shivering onto the gravel.

'Where's my torch?' Eric demanded immediately, and Kath slapped him on the chest crossly for asking for that first.

'In my hood,' Gareth said, and sitting up, managed to dislodge it and give it back to Eric, who examined it carefully for damage, oblivious to his wife's annoyance.

They went into the house. Gareth went up to the bathroom to strip off his wet things and get into a hot bath. Kath and Eric went back home, Eric to watch football, and Kath to 'borrow' some of Eric's clothes for Gareth to change into, as he hadn't bothered to bring much with him.

Everyone was sick of endless cups of tea and coffee. They sat around the cottage despondently. They were all tense. No one knew quite what to do. Andy was driving Caitlin crazy by pacing up and down and saying alternately, 'Gareth must have missed something' and 'If it's not there, someone—

probably Richard himself must have moved it, but to where?'

Henry seemed distracted. He stood by the window looking out at the well, still uncovered like a gaping wound. When Kath returned with the dry clothes, Laura took them up to Gareth and a few minutes later he was back downstairs, comical in old-man corduroys and a sky-blue terry-towelling sweatshirt dating from about 1976.

As soon as Gareth came into the room, Andy began to badger him about how carefully he'd checked the water. In frustration Gareth shoved Andy away and Andy grabbed his arm. The tension in the room racked up another few defcons and for a few seconds the two men glared at each other, and Caitlin felt certain they were going to pound each other. Then Andy dropped his eyes and took a step back and the tension relaxed. He made a half-hearted apology.

Ignoring him, to everyone else Gareth said, 'The well's only six feet wide and I'd say the water is about two or so feet deep. Believe me I searched every inch of it. It's nowhere near as deep as I'd expected. There was nothing there apart from a drop of water. Nothing. No stones, no mud, no rotting clothes, no bones, just—nothing.'

He sank down on the sofa next to Laura, hugging her, and they all sank into silence, everyone avoiding each other's eye. No one knew what to do or say, they were all waiting for someone to think of something, anything.

Getting to her feet, Kath offered to take Gareth's wet things, wash and dry them then bring them back the next morning. At first he politely declined, but she pressed him, rather bravely, and so he finally accepted, if only to keep the peace. She bustled away, saying she'd see them in the morning.

It was still only approaching midday now. Caitlin didn't think she could cope with the prospect of a whole afternoon cooped up in the cottage with people who were as fed up and irritable as she was, and she quietly said as much to Henry. She felt as though she had cabin fever or was stir crazy or whatever the saying was. She had to get out for a while. Henry suggested going for a walk. She paused only to grab a jacket.

It was so good to be outside again. The rain had stayed away, and the yellows, reds and oranges of the trees gleamed in the soft autumn sunlight. She put her arm through his and it felt so right, so companionable. There was no pressure to talk, to entertain or fill the silence. They walked. Henry was taking them through the trees to a gentle grassy slope; he seemed to know where they were heading, and she was happy just to go along.

When she looked back once, she saw the other four were a little way behind them, also out for a walk, it seemed. They too were just ambling along, taking it easy, not talking, not trying to catch up, so Caitlin didn't feel any need to wait for them.

After about twenty minutes they reached the windmill.

For Caitlin it was like seeing something once familiar but now slightly odd, like walking past a childhood home or an old school. She had been there before, she thought, probably as a small child. But then she remembered Gramps' old photos, one or two of which had also included the windmill, and then she wasn't sure. Maybe she just remembered it from those photos?

As they came up close to it, she was surprised how big it was and how well preserved. Henry knew all about it, and to her great amusement he gave her a little impromptu lecture about it. She listened, watching his face, his animated expression, his hands moving as he spoke, emphasising his point, conveying his enthusiasm, his passion for history. That was when she really fell in love with him.

The other four caught them up now. Becka took a few photos with her phone. She held up her hand and gestured for them to get a bit closer to fit them into the frame, and it was as if someone had turned on a light in Caitlin's memory.

Gramps. Mummy and Daddy. And Grandma. The picnic. The blanket, pale blue with a thin yellow and green stripe through it, spread out on the grass. Daddy and Grandma lying down on the blanket for a nap in the sun that afternoon, while Mummy was packing away all the bits and pieces of the picnic, packing it all neatly away in the big basket from the back of the car.

Gramps, far above her little child's head, saying 'We're going for a walk down to the river,' and Mummy saying,

'All right but don't be too long, you two.'

Caitlin remembered looking down and smiling at the way her dress swirled out around her like a ballerina's. Mummy had made it for her earlier that week and this was the first time she'd been allowed to wear it. She showed Gramps, dancing along the narrow, winding path in front of him and making the skirt twirl out around her as she went. Then when the path dipped in amongst the dark trees, Gramps had called her to him and she had felt his hand heavy on her shoulder, on the back of her neck. And then, and then...

Later she had been sick, and some of it had got on the hem of her new swirly dress.

They got back to the place where they'd had the

picnic and Gramps was telling them she'd made herself sick by running about too much and Mummy was cross about the dress and Caitlin knew she'd done something very, very naughty.

And later, when Mummy put her in the bath before bed, she saw the bruises and the dried blood. Mummy had cried. Caitlin hated to see Mummy cry and it made her cry too and she felt very, very wicked and she wanted to tell Mummy that she was sorry, but Mummy brought her some warm milk and let her read in bed then Mummy went to talk to Daddy.

And when Caitlin drank her milk and put her book away and turned out her light and laid down to go to sleep, she could still hear Daddy angry and shouting and beneath all the words, loud although she couldn't hear what he said, she could hear the soft sound of Mummy crying and crying. And they never went to the cottage or the windmill again.

As Becka pressed the button to take another picture, Caitlin pushed her way out of the group and stumbled blindly into the longer grass then vomited.

She was shaking all over. She remembered it all now and it was too much. She didn't want to remember little Caitlin's picnic or the dress of pale yellow and white stripes with the full skirt that flew out around her as she pirouetted round and round and that had filled her with so much joy.

She threw up again and collapsed, sobbing, in the grass. She didn't want to remember but she couldn't make it go away. She was dimly aware of the others standing around helplessly, not knowing what to do, and she fervently hoped they wouldn't start asking her questions. She couldn't answer any questions right now.

But Henry—it was as if he understood. He sat

down beside her and scooped her onto his lap. He gave her his large, white handkerchief, laundered and smelling of lavender and neatly pressed into a neat, neat square of snowy linen, and he held her in his arms, tender as a mother's, wiping away the mess and the tears and rocking her.

He kissed her hair.

'It will be all right, my darling,' he said. And he sounded so sure, she believed him.

Later, very slowly, they walked back to the cottage. She drank a little cool water and went up to lie down for a while. As she went, she heard Andy say,

'We've got to sort all this out. We need closure. All of us.'

*

Chapter Seventeen

When she came downstairs again several hours later, it was to the wonderful smell of fish and chips.

She was ravenous and as soon as she came into the room, even as Laura was piling food on a plate for her, she stole a couple of chips from Henry's plate and greedily shoved them in her mouth.

'I'm starving!' she said. They all broke into smiles and nodded along, rather too obviously relieved that she seemed to be her normal self again.

Gratefully, she smiled at Henry. She wanted to tell him everything. But then it came to her that it wasn't just Henry, they all needed to know, they had all been affected by what happened in the past. It was a shock to suddenly realise she didn't need to keep secrets anymore. A little nervously she began to tell them everything, everything she remembered of what had happened in the past, triggered by Becka standing there taking her photos and telling them to smile and squash up a bit.

Then, following on from that, but fearful they wouldn't understand, she told them about the night Gramps fell down the stairs and how she had walked out of the house and left him lying there. She couldn't tell them about not grabbing him as he fell, or about that little extra push. She just couldn't tell them that... couldn't even explain how she had felt just stepping over his body to go to the door.

But even so, it was cathartic. She felt so light, so free. As if all the poison had been flushed out of her system. If she had been afraid how they would react, she was astonished by their sympathy and support when she finished unburdening herself. They were so completely on her side, furious on her behalf, hurt for her, and so glad Gramps was dead. Wiping away answering tears, Laura told Caitlin what she had kind of realised: that she had been in shock after his fall. *That* was why she had acted the way she had. It wasn't the whole truth, Caitlin knew, but it was a part of it. It probably wouldn't have made any difference to the outcome, but she knew she should have tried harder to help him. She wasn't ready to analyse how she felt about that. In the end, he was dead, and she was very happy about that.

A companionable silence settled over them. The six of them stayed there, lying back in their seats, the room dark apart from the dancing flames and shadows of the firelight. Caitlin didn't speak. She had said everything she could say, and now she just looked from one to the other and felt glad they were there. They had tried to cheat her, they had lied, they had cheered at her failure and cursed her triumph, but she no longer cared about any of that. It was good to have a family.

Thinking back over the last few days, her thoughts wandered back to the night when she had hidden behind the sofa in the cellar and listened to them planning to rob her.

She choked on a chip. Henry patted her on the back, and she gulped down half a glass of cola to shift it. When she could finally speak, she gasped out, 'The cellar!'

They all stared at her. There was no need to say anything more. Andy was already on his feet and racing to the kitchen door, sending his chair crashing backwards onto the floor. He called a hurried apology over his shoulder.

'Andy, wait!' she yelled.

He reappeared in the doorway to the sitting-room, shifting impatiently, obviously champing at the bit. She threw him the keys. He caught them one-handed, shot her a grin and then he was gone. They heard him running through to the back door and the sound of keys jangling.

They went after him in a rather more leisurely manner. By the time they reached the cellar door, it was open, the lights were on, and he was already standing in the middle of the room looking about him.

Caitlin had forgotten how vast and bare the space looked now with no furniture or the lovely carpet. They clustered together and just stared around the room.

Becka said, 'Well obviously the body's not going to be just lying about. The only place it could be is under the floor.'

Gareth said, 'We need a pick or something.'

Caitlin thought he still looked pretty funny in his borrowed clothes, but he was right.

'It'll take more than just a pick to get through this,' Andy said, tapping the ground with his foot, the knowledgeable estate agent back for a moment.

Gareth sighed, frustrated, and his shoulders sagged. Caitlin knew just how he felt. With the possibility right under their feet, it was hard to have to wait.

'We'll need to hire a jemmy or something to break all this up,' she said. 'I'll try to organise something in the morning.'

'It's Sunday tomorrow,' Henry pointed out. 'There's not likely to be anywhere in the area open for that kind of thing tomorrow.'

'Dammit, so it is, I'd lost track,' Caitlin said.

'And we don't even know if there's anything under here worth digging up. You can't just dig up the whole floor on the off chance, can you?' Laura asked.

She could be right, Caitlin thought. There was no absolute, irrefutable evidence, no real indications that this could be the right spot. But, Caitlin thought, it fits and it's plausible. She had a sneaking suspicion that Gramps would have enjoyed sitting down here in his butter-soft antique leather armchairs, with his feet resting on his almost priceless antique Aubusson carpet and thinking of that poor boy's body lying beneath the stone floor. He had that kind of personality.

'Stanley's here,' Caitlin said grimly. 'I just know it. It fits with everything I know about Gramps. And I don't care how much it costs or how much time and effort or trouble it is, I want all this floor up. Even if I have to do it myself with a fucking nail file.'

On Tuesday, half a dozen men arrived with a mini-digger and some heavy-duty power drills. They broke up all the surface of the floor and carefully packed it away into a couple of skips.

It was late in the day when they found a booted skeletal foot.

The police were informed, and on Wednesday afternoon the county forensic team arrived and began the weary task of removing the soil and debris then taking it away for analysis, whilst other staff continued to excavate and examine the entire floor area.

That evening, an older man arrived at the house. Becka answered the door, thn brought him through to the garden where Caitlin and Henry, Andy and Gareth were watching what was going on.

Even before introductions were made, Caitlin knew who the man was. His resemblance to his son was uncanny.

'Caitlin, it's such an honour to meet you. I've heard rather a lot about you,' said Henry Jago senior, and he actually kissed the back of her hand. 'I come bearing gifts.'

He held up a small attaché case, pulling out an envelope of documents. 'Two inventories, thirty years apart, as well as the insurance certificate from when Richard Mitchelson first inherited everything from his father.'

She smiled at him. 'Thank you. I really appreciate that. Nice to know that no one,' and here she directed a significant look at Andy, 'managed to get their hands on it, in spite of all their efforts. I'll tell the auctioneer I have these.'

'I see peace has broken out—very good of you under the circumstances.' He glared at his son who looked ashamed. 'I'm very sorry about everything that happened of late.'

'I just want to put it all behind me. What's the point of anything else?' she said with a shrug.

Henry senior nodded. 'Indeed.'

By Friday lunchtime, the entire skeleton of a young

male, presumed to be Stanley Kennett, was at last uncovered for the first time in a little over sixty years. A photographer from the local newspaper arrived to capture the moment for the East Sussex Echo, only to be told he couldn't enter the cellar or photograph the remains. He left, frustrated, with a few general local shots and a picture of Caitlin standing with her cousins outside the cottage.

He departed to file his story for the weekend edition of the paper.

Caitlin, Kath, Mrs Harriet Kennett from Kennett's Kwikmart, Laura, Becka, Andy, Gareth and Henry all stood beside the well and watched as the stretcher bearing the carefully covered remains of Stanley Kennett was carried up the cellar steps then through the house to be loaded into the back of the coroner's ambulance and taken away to the morgue for examination.

There was a sombre celebration at Kath and Eric's house that evening. Ern and his family were there. Sonia, Jen and Rob-the-more-than-okay had driven down from London, he was bringing everyone drinks and generally being surprisingly pleasant and helpful. Maybe Jen had chosen a good one after all.

Harriet Kennett, her husband, and her family also attended, and she made a point of thanking Caitlin for all that she had done, and she apologised profusely for her behaviour to Caitlin when she had gone into the Kwikmart that lunchtime the previous week. There were hugs and tears all round.

But through all this, Caitlin felt as though she was on the outside looking in. She sat back and watched the evening go by as an observer.

It seemed highly likely that the skeleton was that of Stanley, but formal identification would take weeks. They had all given statements to the police, telling all they knew, as well as donating DNA samples. Once identification was confirmed, the coroner could rule on the cause of death and determine whether or not the police could close their missing person's case. Only then could the remains finally be released for burial. There was, clearly, no possibility of bringing charges, but for the Kennett family in particular, just knowing was almost as good.

And so, finally, at some point in the near future, Caitlin thought, it would all be over.

Everyone would go back to their everyday lives.

Gramps' terraced house in London would be cleared and sold—by Andy, now that Caitlin had more or less forgiven him—and Caitlin had already given notice on her flat. And her job. That had been a very brief phone conversation, with relief on both sides, it seemed. Her manager wouldn't particularly miss her.

The police had given permission for a new floor to be laid in the cellar. Caitlin felt uncomfortable about the house now, knowing that it had harboured its secret for so long. But it was not likely to sell with its sad history in the current depressed housing market, and she had to live somewhere. She felt—she hoped—that in time she could make her peace with the house for what its former owner had done under its roof. So yes, she decided, she would stay. She would get her new floor put down, put down a nice, non-antique carpet, get new furniture. She would cover the well up again. And in time, she thought, it would all work out.

And...

To her astonishment, Henry was really keen on the idea of moving to Sussex. In fact, he had already decided to open up a second branch of the firm in

Brighton. His partner, the Mr Wilkes of the business title, was happy to remain in London, and Henry felt that it wouldn't be too much of a problem for him to go up to Town every so often for meetings and so on.

'Or Zoom,' said Henry, 'there's always Zoom.' He was looking forward to living on a day-to-day basis back in the rural idyll of his childhood.

Caitlin hoped that ultimately, she'd persuade him to move into the cottage with her, but she hadn't yet broached the subject with him, after all they had still only been on two official dates so far. You can't move in together after only two dates, she thought.

But maybe after three?

*

Epilogue

It was a beautiful sunny morning in late Spring when Stanley Kennett's remains were laid to rest in the graveyard behind the little parish church.

Eventually, his identity had been confirmed and a death certificate issued. He was found to have died as a result of a severe blow to the back of the head. There was not enough evidence to prove that the victim had died as a result of foul play, although the injuries to the body and the manner of disposal were suggestive of this.

If the coroner's open verdict didn't completely satisfy the Kennett family as a whole, at least they now knew a little of what had happened and his remains had been returned to them, which was something.

Several hundred people turned out on that Wednesday morning to witness the burial. The vicar said a prayer and the total silence that fell over the large crowd was like a blanket about her shoulders,

Caitlin thought. Apart from the birdsong and the vicar's solemn words, there was nothing but peace.

There was a nasty moment when one of the straps guiding the coffin down into the ground got stuck and the opposite end dipped suddenly. As one, the congregation gasped a collective, 'Ooh!' but the pallbearers quickly stepped forward to free the strap and the process continued without any further hitches.

Caitlin felt only relief that it was all over. She had been afraid that more bodies might be found there under the floor—if that had happened she would have left and never come back—but that hadn't happened, that was just her fear peeking over her shoulder.

The crowd began to disperse. A couple of men stepped forward to bring the floral tributes and place them on top of the coffin and around the gaping grave.

She turned away, looking for Henry. He was her partner now, had been since that day when they had searched the well. He knew, too, what had really happened that day at Gramps' house in London, and had said he would have done the same. It was so good to have no more secrets. To feel free of the past and be looking to the future.

He was talking to someone he knew. He shook their hand then came away with a smile, drawing her arm through his.

Andy and Becka were chatting with Laura and Gareth. They had their children with them, and it was the first time Caitlin had seen them all in their family groups. As she and Henry joined them, they exchanged kisses and handshakes.

Indicating over her shoulder, Caitlin said, 'That all seemed to go off okay.'

'More than okay,' said Becka, adding, 'I bet you're glad it's all over, aren't you?'

'Very.' She looked at them, feeling a little shy. 'It's been a while...'

'Things have been a bit hectic lately,' said Gareth. 'But it would be great if you could come over some time soon.'

'And congratulations, both of you,' Andy said, grinning.

Caitlin looked down at her gently expanding waistline and gave her belly an affectionate pat.

'Thank you,' she said with a big smile.

'So, when's it due?' Laura asked.

Henry, the proud father-to-be, told her the second week in September.

'Planning on getting married?' Laura asked.

Henry and Caitlin looked at each other and shrugged, laughing. 'We've only had two dates so far,' Caitlin said with a laugh. 'You can't get married after just two dates, can you?'

'You got knocked up after two, so surely getting married would be okay?' Jen quipped and got a high-five from Sonia and a laugh from everyone around.

'Well if you do, make sure you invite your cousins and your 'cousins' to the wedding,' Laura said, doing air-quotes. 'We don't want to miss a thing.'

'How are things at the cottage now?' Becka asked. 'Is the cellar finished?'

'Yes, the floor's been replaced, and we've got a new carpet down, and new furniture, it looks really good actually. We weren't quite sure what to do with it at first, but it does make a snug den, and we've even made one corner into a little office for both of us, so we can work from home. Which will obviously be important over the next few years.'

'Oh, and we've had the well filled in,' Henry said.

'It began to feel a bit creepy, and was just a worry, so in the end we decided it would be best to just get rid of it, so that's what we've done. It's been filled in and all the top bit above ground has been dismantled. Now, it's level with the rest of the patio, and we've got the table and chairs standing on it. Makes the garden seem a lot bigger. Also important for the next few years.' He beamed at them all, so obviously happy.

Kath and Eric joined them. 'We're doing lunch, sandwiches and so on, at our place now if you'd like to come? You'd all be very welcome.'

They accepted with pleasure. They turned back towards the car park, ready to join the exodus from the funeral.

Later that afternoon the cousins, friends, and children all came back to the cottage. Henry and Caitlin showed them around the now refurbished house, garden and cellar. The response was favourable.

'Wow!' said Becka, glancing round her at the cellar.

'It's completely transformed,' Andy said. 'I can't believe it's the same place.' He began to tell the younger ones what it had been like only eight or so months earlier.

'It looks better, doesn't it?' Caitlin said. She was making everyone tea at a side-table in the corner. 'We've even got a little bathroom through there, very handy. And obviously we can make drinks here, we've got a fridge for milk etc. We're really pleased with it. Because at first, I don't mind telling you, I didn't know if I could ever come down here again.'

'It's gorgeous,' Laura agreed. They took their drinks and found places to sit.

After a moment, Caitlin said, 'Do you remember those samplers that were above the doorway to the steps?'

Some did, some didn't, it seemed.

'I don't suppose we will ever know whether he inherited them, had them made specially or even did the needlework himself,' Caitlin said. 'But I'm certain now he kept them because of the sentiments. I hadn't remembered, but when I went to see everything being sold in the auction, I saw them again, and I was struck by how awful they were. One of them said, 'Let the little children come unto me'. Well for me that was self-explanatory. I know from my own experience that Gramps had a weakness for little children.'

Caitlin glanced round. They were all listening to her.

'Go on,' said Andy.

'Well, the other one said, 'You have armed me for battle, you have subdued my enemies under my feet'. It's another Bible verse,' Caitlin said. She could tell from the looks on their faces that they understood what she was saying.

'Oh my God!' said Becka, 'Was he boasting?'

'Maybe,' Caitlin said.

'Or do you think it was a clue and he wanted to be found out?' Gareth asked.

Laura shook her head. 'No. I really think he was boasting.'

'Definitely,' Caitlin said. 'I don't think he wanted to be found out. I think he thought he was too clever for that. And I think he wanted to sit here in that recreated version of his father's study, and he wanted to sip his fine old brandy from his fancy globe tantalus thingy, and to smoke his fine cigars from his nice little collectable cigar box, and he wanted to push his shoes off his feet and dig his toes into his eight-hundred thousand pound carpet and he wanted to think about poor Stanley's body lying beneath his feet for him to trample all over, and he wanted to feel powerful and successful and enjoy all of this in a very private pleasure no one else could share.'

'I know he was your grandfather, Caitlin,' Laura said. 'But really I think he must have been a monster.'

'He was,' Caitlin said. 'A monster who smiled and won everyone over with his charm.'

There was a chilled, tense moment, then Caitlin reached down into her bag and took out some photos.

'These were given to me this morning, by Harriet Kennett. Today is Stanley's day, his time to finally be recognised as one of the innocent victims in all this. These are pictures of him playing dollies with his sister Barbara, his cousin Sarah Kennett, who was Henry's mother, and my grandmother Isobel. The girls would have all been about eight or ten then.'

She handed the two photos round. They were black and white, of course, and slightly out of focus but they showed the three little girls with their hair done up in huge bunches on either side of their heads with big, floppy ribbons. They were all smiling at the camera. Next to them sat a little boy in dark shorts and a jumper, also smiling. He had obviously been in the middle of brushing a doll's hair and he was holding up a ribbon.

To Caitlin it looked as though someone had called his name, and he had just glanced up to give the camera a shy smile.

The other photo was similar, but none of the children was looking at the camera. Instead, they all had their heads together, with looks of fierce concentration on their faces as they struggled to get a lacy dress onto one of the dolls.

'Just a bunch of kids playing dollies,' Becka said, and wiped away a tear.

THE END

***

About the author

Caron Allan (usually) writes cosy murder mysteries, both contemporary and also set in the 1930s. Caron lives in Derby, England with her husband and an endlessly varying quantity of cats and sparrows.

Caron Allan can be found on these social media channels and would love to hear from you:

Pinterest: caronallan

Instagram: caronsbooks

Twitter: caron_allan

Mastodon social: caron_allan

Facebook: CaronAllanFiction

Bluesky: caronallanfiction.bsky.social

Also, if you're interested in news, snippets, Caron's 'quirky' take on life or just want some sneak previews, please sign up to Caron's blog shown below:

caronallanfiction.com/

Also by Caron Allan:

The Friendship Can Be Murder books:

Criss Cross: book 1
Cross Check: book 2
Check Mate: book 3

The Dottie Manderson mysteries:

Night and Day: book 1
The Mantle of God: book 2
Scotch Mist: book 3 a novella
The Last Perfect Summer of Richard Dawlish: book 4
The Thief of St Martins: book 5
The Spy Within: book 6
Rose Petals and White Lace: book 7
Midnight, the Stars, and You: book 8

The Miss Gascoigne mysteries:

A Meeting With Murder: book 1
A Wreath of Lilies: book 2

Others:

Easy Living: a story about life after death, after death, after death

Printed in Dunstable, United Kingdom